PRAISE FOR
NOT EVEN BONES

★ "[A] morally complex, edgy debut. . . .
Schaeffer's antiheroes show empathy and insight as they
struggle to define the line between human and monster.
It's a testament to Schaeffer's excellent writing that these
themes never overtake the characters' stories."
—*BOOKLIST,* starred review

"Deliciously dark and devious, with morally gray characters
that make you question what is good and what is truly evil.
Warning: don't read in the dark."
—**REBECCA SKY,** author of *Arrowheart*

"The thrilling plot proves thought-provoking."
—*PUBLISHERS WEEKLY*

"A slasher flick spliced with *Crime and Punishment,*
this engrossing debut novel asks complex philosophical
questions in a pleasingly hard-to-stomach way."
—*KIRKUS REVIEWS*

"Readers who are tired of the same recycled story lines will
find something original here. . . . The story is so compelling
that readers have to keep going to find out how,
or if, Nita gets out of this mess."
—*SCHOOL LIBRARY JOURNAL*

NOVELS BY
REBECCA SCHAEFFER

Not Even Bones
Only Ashes Remain

NOT • EVEN BONES

REBECCA SCHAEFFER

HOUGHTON MIFFLIN HARCOURT
Boston   New York

hmhbooks.com

The text was set in ITC Legacy Serif Std.

The Library of Congress has cataloged the hardcover edition as follows:
Names: Schaeffer, Rebecca.
Title: Not even bones / Rebecca Schaeffer.
Description: Boston ; New York : Houghton Mifflin Harcourt, [2018]
Summary: Nita's mother hunts monsters and, after Nita dissects and packages
them, sells them online, but when Nita follows her conscience to help
a live monster escape, she is sold on the black market in his place.
Identifiers: LCCN 2018007163
Subjects: | CYAC: Monsters—Fiction. | Dissection—Fiction. | Mothers and
daughters—Fiction. | Black market—Fiction. | Horror stories.
Classification: LCC PZ7.1.S33557 Not 2018 | DDC [Fic]—dc23
LC record available at https://lccn.loc.gov/2018007163

ISBN: 978-1-328-86354-6 hardcover
ISBN: 978-0-358-10825-2 paperback

Printed in the United States of America
DOC 10 9 8 7 6 5
4500798991

To all those who know the line between good and evil
is blurrier than people want to admit

ONE

NITA STARED AT the dead body lying on the kitchen table. Middle-aged, and in the place between pudgy and overweight, he wore a casual business suit and a pair of wire-rimmed glasses with silver handles that blended into the gray at his temples. He was indistinguishable on the outside from any other human — the inside, of course, was a different matter.

"Another zannie?" Nita scowled at her mother and crossed her arms as she examined the body. "That's not even Latin American. I thought we moved to Peru to hunt South and Central American unnaturals? Chupacabras and pishtacos and whatever."

It wasn't that zannies were common, but Nita had dissected plenty during the months she and her mother spent in Southeast Asia last year. She'd been looking forward to dissecting something new. If she'd wanted to cut up the same unnaturals as usual, she would have asked to stay with her dad in the States and work on unicorns.

Her mother shrugged, draping her jacket over a chair. "I

1

saw a zannie, so I killed it. I mean, it was right in front of me. How could I resist?" Her black-and-red-striped bangs fell forward as she dipped her head and half smiled.

Nita shifted her feet, looking at the corpse again. She sighed. "I suppose you'll want me to dissect and package it for sale?"

"Good girl." Her mother grinned.

Nita went around to the other side of the dead body. "Care to help me move it to the workroom?"

Her mother rolled up her sleeves, and together they heaved the round, deceptively heavy body down the hall and onto a smooth metal table in the other room. White walls and fluorescent lights made it look like a hospital surgery room. Scalpels and bone saws lay in neat lines on the shelves, and a scale for weighing organs rested in front of a box of jars. In the corner, a tub of formaldehyde caused everything to reek of death. The smell kept sneaking out of the room and making its way into Nita's clothes. She found it strangely comforting. That was probably a bad sign.

But, if Nita was being honest with herself, most of her habits and life choices were bad signs.

Her mother winked at Nita. "All ready for you."

Nita looked down at her watch. "It's nearly midnight."

"And?"

"And I want to sleep sometime."

"So do it later." Her mother waved it aside. "It's not like you have anything to get up for."

Nita paused, then bowed her head in acceptance. Even though it had been years since her mother had decided to illegally take Nita out of school, she still had some leftover instinct telling her not to go to bed too late. Which was silly, because even if she'd had school, she'd gladly have skipped it for a dissection. Dissections were *fun*.

Nita pulled on a white lab coat. She always liked wearing it — it made her feel like a real scientist at a prestigious university or laboratory somewhere. Sometimes she put the goggles on even when she didn't need to just so she could complete the look.

"When are you heading out again?"

Her mother washed her hands in the sink. "Tonight. I got a tip when I was bringing this beauty back. I'm flying to Buenos Aires."

"Pishtacos?" asked Nita, trying to hold in her excitement. She'd never had a chance to dissect a pishtaco. How would their bodies be modified for a diet made completely of human body fat? The promise of a pishtaco dissection was the only thing that had convinced Nita moving to Peru was a good idea. Her mother always knew how to tempt her.

Nita frowned. "Wait, there are no pishtacos in Argentina."

Her mother laughed. "Don't worry. It's something even better."

"Not another zannie."

"No."

Her mother dried her hands and headed back toward the kitchen, calling out as she went, "I'm going to head to the airport now. If all goes well, I should be back in two days."

Nita followed and found her sitting, booted feet on the kitchen table as she unscrewed the top of the pisco bottle from the fridge and took a swig. Not cocktail-drink pisco, or mixed-with-soda pisco, just straight. Nita had tried it once when she was home alone, thinking it would be a good celebration drink to ring in her seventeenth birthday. It didn't burn as much as whisky or vodka, or even sake, but it kicked in fast, and it kicked in *hard*. Her mother had found her with her face squished against the wall, crying because it wouldn't move for her. Then Mom had laughed and left her there to suffer. She showed Nita the pictures afterward — there was an awful lot of drool on that wall.

Nita hadn't sampled anything in the liquor cabinet since.

"Oh, and Nita?" Her mother put the pisco on the table.

"Yeah?"

"Don't touch the head. It has a million-dollar bounty. I plan to claim it."

Nita looked down the hall, toward the room with the dead body. "I'm pretty sure the whole wanted-dead-or-alive thing ended in the Old West. If you just turn this guy's head over, you'll be arrested for murder."

Her mother rolled her eyes. "Why, thank you, Nita, for teaching me such an important lesson. Whatever would I do without you?"

Nita winced. "Um."

"The zannie is wanted for war crimes by the Peruvian government. He was a member of the secret police under the Fujimori administration."

No surprise there. Pretty much every zannie in the world was wanted for some type of war crime. When your biological imperative was to torture people and eat their pain, there were only so many career paths open to you.

That reminded Nita—there was an article in the latest issue of *Nature* on zannies that she wanted to read. Someone who had clearly dissected fewer zannies than Nita, but with access to better equipment, had written a detailed analysis of how zannies consumed pain. There were all sorts of theories about how pain was relative, and the same injury on two people could be perceived completely differently. The scientists had been researching zannies—was it the severity of the injury that fed them, or the person's perception of how much it hurt?

They'd also managed to prove that while zannies *could* consume emotional pain, as well as physical, the effect was significantly less. Emotional and physical pain receptors overlapped in the brain center, so the big question was, why did causing other people severe physical pain feed zannies, while causing severe emotional pain had less effect? Nita privately thought it was because physical pain had the added signals from nociceptors, but she was curious to see what others thought.

Her mother continued, oblivious to Nita's wandering mind. "A number of interested parties have offered very large bounties for his head. They, unlike the government, don't care if he's alive to face trial." There was a sharp flash of teeth. "And I'm happy to oblige them."

She rose, put the pisco away, and pulled on her burgundy leather jacket. "Can you have him all packed up by the time I get back?"

Nita nodded. "Yeah, I think so."

Her mother came over and kissed the top of her head. "What would I ever do without you, Anita?"

Before Nita could formulate a response, her mother was out the door. There was a creak and then a bang, and the house was silent. When her mother departed, sometimes Nita felt like she took more than just noise. She had a presence, a tangible energy to her that filled the house. Without her, it felt hollow. Like the life had left, and there was only a dead zannie in its place.

Which, really, there was. Nita turned back to her newest project and allowed herself a small smile. A pishtaco or a chupacabra would have been better, but she'd still enjoy a zannie.

The first thing she did was empty its pockets. An old-fashioned timepiece, some Brazilian reais (no Peruvian soles though, which was odd), and a wallet. Nita gazed at it a long time before putting it on the tray, unopened. Her mother would have already taken the credit cards and used them to get as much cash as possible before ditching them. The only other things left in the wallet would be identity cards, club memberships—things that would tell her about the person she was dissecting.

Nita had learned a long time ago—you don't want to know anything about the person whose body you're taking apart.

Better to think that it wasn't a person at all. And really—it wasn't. This was a zannie.

Nita took an elastic and tied her hair back in a puffy attempt at a ponytail. Her hair tended to grow sideways in frizzy kinks instead of down. In the glow of the fluorescent lights, its normally medium-brown color took on an orange tint. No one else thought it looked orange, but Nita insisted — she liked orange.

She put a surgical mask over her mouth, just below her freckle-spattered cheekbones, before putting the goggles on. After snapping on a pair of latex gloves, she rolled her tool set over to the metal slab where the body rested. She slipped her earbuds in and flicked on her Disney playlist.

It was time to begin.

Nita couldn't remember a time when she hadn't been fascinated by dead things — perhaps because her home was always full of them. As far back as she could remember, her parents had acquired the bodies of unnaturals and sold the pieces on the internet. The darknet, to be specific. Black market body part sellers didn't just post their items on eBay. That was how you ended up with a short visit from the International Non-Human Police — INHUP — and a long stint in jail.

When Nita was younger, she used to run around the room, bringing her parents empty jars. Big glass ones for the heart, small vials and bags for the blood. Afterward, she'd label them and line them up on the shelf. Sometimes she'd stare at them, pieces of people she'd never met. There was something calming about the still hearts, floating in formaldehyde. Something peaceful. No more beating, no more thumping rhythm and noise. Just silence.

Sometimes, she would look at the eyes, and they would stare back. Direct, open gazes. Not like living people, who flicked their eyes here and there while they lied, who could cram an entire conversation into a single gaze. The problem was, Nita could never understand what they were saying. It was better after people were dead. The eyes weren't so tricky anymore.

It took Nita all night and the better part of the next day to finish with the zannie, put everything in jars of formaldehyde or freezer containers, and clean the dissection room until it sparkled.

The sun was up, and she didn't feel tired, so she went to her favorite park on the cliffs overlooking the ocean. Tropical trees with large, bell-shaped flowers covered the benches like a canopy, and blue and white mosaics patterned the wall that prevented people from tumbling over the side of the cliff and into the sparkling waters below. Newspapers sat abandoned on the benches, from tabloids announcing *Penelope Alvarez looks twenty at age forty-five. Good skin care or something more.'"unnatural"?* to official news sources with headlines like *Should Peru sign into INHUP? The advantages and disadvantages to an extraterritorial police force for unnatural-related incidents.*

Peru was one of the only South American countries left that wasn't a part of INHUP. There were always a few countries on every continent that stayed out so that black market dealers had somewhere to flee when INHUP finally nailed them. Certain people paid politicians handsomely to ensure it stayed that way.

Nita took a seat far away from the other people in the park. Under the shade of a floripondio tree, she cracked open her medical journals on unnaturals.

Sometimes it was frustrating reading them and knowing they were wrong about certain things. While lots of unnaturals were "out" and recognized by the world, most still hid, afraid of public backlash. So when the journals talked about zannies being the only species of unnatural that consumed nontangible things, like pain, Nita wished she could point out that there were creatures who consumed memories, strong emotions, and even dreams. INHUP just hadn't officially recognized them yet. INHUP was big on doing damage control, and part of trying to decrease racism and discrimination against unnaturals was not telling people just how many types there were.

It also kept people like Nita's mother from finding out about them. Sometimes.

Nita whiled the afternoon away in the shade of the tree, devouring medical research like candy, until the sun dipped so low there wasn't enough light to read by.

When Nita got home, she was greeted by a string of expletives.

She crept into the hall, shoulders tight with tension. Her mother could be unpredictable when angry. Nita had been on the receiving end before and wasn't eager to repeat the experience.

But ignoring her mother was more dangerous, so Nita padded into the kitchen.

"What are you *doing*?" Nita gaped, staring at the mess.

Her mother tucked a strand of hair behind her ear and gave Nita a wry smile. Around her, empty shipping crates littered the floor, along with packing materials like bubble wrap and Styrofoam worms. A gun sat on the kitchen table, and Nita briefly wondered what it was doing out.

"I want to have the zannie parts shipped out tomorrow.

We've got something new, and to be frank, this apartment isn't big enough to hold all the parts." Her mother flashed her another smile.

Nita was inclined to agree. Her dissection room was already at capacity, and they'd only dissected one zannie. There really wasn't room for a second body.

"Something new, huh? I take it everything went well, then?"

Nita's mother laughed. "Do things ever go well with unnaturals that aren't on the list?"

Among the unnaturals that were public knowledge, there was a list of "dangerous unnaturals" — unnaturals whose continued existence depended on them murdering other people. It wasn't a crime to kill them in INHUP member countries, it was "preemptive self-defense." But anything not on the list, the harmless unnaturals (which was most of them, in Nita's experience), it was very much a crime to kill.

Her mom mostly brought Nita unnaturals on the list. Mostly.

Nita knew her mother had probably killed a lot of not-evil, not-dangerous people and sold them. She tried not to think about it too much, because really, there wasn't much she could do about it, was there?

Besides, they were always dead by the time they got to Nita. And if they were already dead, it would be a shame to let their bodies go undissected.

Speaking of . . .

"What did you bring back?" Nita asked, weaving through the crates to the fridge, where she took out last night's leftovers and shoved them into the microwave.

"Something special. I put it in the dissection room."

Nita felt her fingers twitch, the imaginary scalpel in her hand making a sliding cut through the air, like a Y incision. She couldn't wait for the slow, relaxing evening, just her and the body. The straight autopsy lines, the jars full of organs watching over her, like her own weird guardian angel.

She shivered with anticipation. Sometimes she scared herself.

Her mother looked at Nita out of the corner of her eyes. "I have to say, this one was tricky to get."

Nita removed her food from the microwave and sat down at the kitchen table. "Oh, do tell?"

Her mother smiled, and Nita settled in for a good story. "Well, it wasn't hard at the beginning. Buenos Aires was lovely, and hunting down my tip was easy. Even acquiring our new . . . I don't even know what to call him."

Nita raised her eyebrows. Her mother knew every unnatural. It was her job. This one must be something really rare.

"Well, anyway." Her mother sat down beside her. "It wasn't even so bad getting him. Security wasn't too much of an issue, easily dealt with. The problem was getting him back."

Nita nodded. Airlines usually frowned on stuffing dead bodies into overhead bins.

Her mother gave her a conspiratorial wink. "But then I thought, well, why don't I just pretend he's a traveler? So I put him in a wheelchair, and the airline never even guessed."

"Wait, a wheelchair?" Nita scowled. "But wouldn't they notice that he didn't, well, move or breathe or anything when they were helping him to his seat?"

She laughed. "Oh, he's not dead. I just drugged the hell out of him."

Nita's fingers twitched, then froze. Not dead.

She gave her mother a sickly smile. "You said you put him in my room?"

"Yes, I spent the morning installing the cage. Bugger of a thing. You know they don't make human-size cages anymore? And I had to get the handcuffs at a sex shop."

Nita sat there for a long moment, smile frozen like a rictus on her face. Then she rose and began making her way through the crates to her dissection room.

Her mother followed. "This one's a little different. He's quite valuable, so I'd really like to milk him a bit for blood and such before we harvest the organs."

But Nita wasn't listening. She had opened the door to see with her own eyes.

Part of her beautiful, sterile white room was now taken up by a large cage, which had been bolted to the wall. Her mother had put a padlock and chain around the door. Inside the cage, a boy with dark brown hair lay unconscious in the fetal position. Given the size of the cage, it was probably the only way he could lie down.

"What is he?" Nita waited for her mother to list off the heinous things he did to survive. Maybe he ate newborn babies and was actually five hundred years old instead of the eighteen or nineteen he looked.

Her mother shrugged. "I don't know if there's a name for what he is."

"But what kind of unnatural is he? Explain it." Nita felt her voice rising and forced it to calm down. "I mean, you know what he does, right?"

Her mother laughed. "He doesn't do much of anything. He's an unnatural, that much I'm sure of, but I don't think you'll find any external signs of it. He was being kept by a collector in Buenos Aires."

"So . . . why do we want him?" Nita pushed, surprised at how much she needed an answer, a reason to justify the cage in her room and the small, curled-up form of the boy. His jeans and T-shirt looked like they were spattered with something, and Nita wondered if it was blood.

"Ah. Well, he's supposedly quite delicious, you know. Something about him. That collector had been selling vials of his blood—vials, not bags, mind you—for nearly ten thousand each. US dollars, not soles or pesos. Dollars. One of his toes went up for auction online last year, and the price was six digits. For a toe."

Her mother had a wide, toothy grin, and her eyes were alight at the prospect of how much money an entire body could make. Nita wondered how soon the boy's time would be up. Her mother preferred cash in hand to cash in the future, so Nita doubted the boy would be prisoner for long.

"I already put him up online, and we have a buyer for another toe. So I took the liberty of cutting it off and mailing it while we were in Argentina."

It took a few moments for Nita to register her mother's words. Then she looked down, and sure enough, the boy's feet were bare and bloody. One foot had been hastily wrapped in bandages, but they'd turned red as the blood soaked through.

Her mother tapped her finger to her chin. "The only problem is, his pieces need to be fresh—well, as fresh as we can get them. So we'll sell all the extremities first, as they're ordered. He should be able to survive without those, and we can bottle the blood when we remove them and sell it as well. We'll do the internal organs and such later, once we've spread the word. Shouldn't take too long."

Nita's mind spun in circles, not quite processing what her mother was saying. "You want to keep him here and cut pieces off him while he's still alive?"

"Exactly."

Nita didn't even know what to say to that. She didn't deal with live people. Her subjects were dead.

"He's not . . . dangerous?" Nita asked, unable to tear her eyes off the bandages around the missing toes.

Her mother snorted. "Hardly. He got unlucky in the genetic draw. As far as I can tell, everyone wants to eat him, and he has no more defenses than an ordinary human."

The boy stirred in the cage and tried to twist himself around to look at them. Nita's heart clenched. It was pathetic.

Her mother clapped her on the shoulder before turning around. "We're going to make good money off him."

Nita nodded, eyes never straying from the cage. Her mother left the room, calling for Nita to help her organize the crates in the kitchen so they could start packing the zannie parts.

The boy lifted his head and met Nita's eyes. His eyes were

gray-blue and wide with fear. He reached a hand up, but it stopped short, the handcuffs pulling it back down toward the bottom of the cage.

He swallowed, eyes never leaving Nita's.

"*Ayúdame,*" he whispered.

Help me.

TWO

NITA WAS NOT a heartless, murdering, body-part thief. That was her mother.

Nita had never killed anyone. Her plan was to keep it that way.

Why couldn't Mom have killed him before she came back? If she'd killed him before coming home, Nita wouldn't have had to see him like this. She could have just pretended he died naturally. Or blamed her mother and chalked it up to another of those *well, too late to do anything now* cases. But now he was alive, and in her apartment, and she actually had to think about this.

About the living, breathing person her mother planned to kill.

And have Nita dissect. *Alive.*

What would it be like to cut someone up while they were screaming at you to stop?

"Nita?" Mom came around the corner from the kitchen, and Nita realized she'd been standing in the hall staring off into space for the past few minutes. "Something wrong?"

Nita hesitated. "He's alive."

"Yes. And?" Mom's eyes were as tight as her voice. Nita had a sudden feeling she was treading on very dangerous ground.

"He talks." She shifted her shoulders in unease, more so from her mother's look than anything else.

Her mother's face relaxed. "Oh, don't worry about that, sweetheart. He won't be around for long. He'll be on your table shortly, and no one talks back to you there, do they?"

Nita nodded, appreciating her mother's efforts to quell her anxiety even as her nausea rose. "Yeah."

Her mother gave her an appraising look. "You know, if you want, I can go cut his tongue out now. I have some pliers—I can pull it right out. Then you won't have to worry about him talking."

"That's okay, Mom." Nita forced a smile. "I'm fine."

"If you're sure . . ." Her mother gave her another searching look before sighing. "All right. Shall we start packing some of those zannie parts?"

Nita nodded, glad for the change in subject.

They spent the rest of the afternoon filling up crates. Her mother had arranged the bribes to get them back to the family warehouse in the States. Her father would handle them from there. He dealt with the online sales, storage, and shipping of the body parts, while her mother dealt with the retrieval. Her father was also their major cover, if INHUP ever came sniffing. Nita was sure her mother had a record a mile long—her stack of foreign passports, driver's licenses, and credit cards was probably two feet high. That sort of thing usually came with a record, in Nita's opinion.

Her father, though, was squeaky clean as far as Nita knew.

By day, he worked as a legal consultant in Chicago, and by night, he sold body parts on the internet. Nita missed him, and their home, and their shitty Chicago suburb that was actually a two-hour drive from Chicago. She hadn't been home since she was fourteen.

She wondered what her father would say about this situation. Would he be unhappy her mother had brought a live unnatural home? And moreover, a harmless one?

It was one thing when her mother dumped a zannie or a unicorn on Nita's table. For one, they were monsters who couldn't continue to live without killing other people. And the world agreed—that was why there was a Dangerous Unnaturals List. It wasn't even a crime to kill them. You were saving lives.

But someone like the boy in the other room? How could she justify *that*?

Sighing, Nita wiped the sweat off her forehead as they closed another crate. No matter how she thought about it, she couldn't find a way to justify murdering that boy.

Well, except money.

"It looks like we're going to need a few more shipping crates." Her mother ran a hand through her hair. Her manicure caught the light, black and red and yellow, like someone had tried to cover a fire with a blackout curtain.

Nita poured a glass of juice. "Probably."

"I think we deserve pizza now. How about you?"

Nita heartily agreed.

After dinner, they realized they were low on bottled water.

Tap water wasn't drinkable unless boiled, and Nita's mother didn't like the taste. She'd been promising they were going to get a UV light for purifying water since they arrived a few weeks ago, but it hadn't happened yet.

Her mother sighed and got up, dusting pizza crumbs off her lap. "I'll go down to the store and get a seven-liter bottle. I'll start on the boy when I come back."

"Start what?"

Her mother grinned. "I sold his ear an hour ago."

Nita stiffened. "You're going to cut it off tonight?"

"Of course."

Nita swallowed, looking away. "But you can't mail it until tomorrow morning. It makes more sense to cut it off tomorrow. If freshness is important, like you said."

Her mother's eyes narrowed. Nita tried to resist the urge to shift in place, but failed.

Finally, in a small voice, Nita whispered, "I don't want to hear him screaming all night. I won't get any sleep."

Her mother laughed, throwing her head back, then came over and clapped Nita on the back. It was just a little harder than it should have been, and Nita stumbled forward a step.

"You're absolutely right, Anita." Her mother grinned as she walked back to the door. "We'll do it tomorrow morning."

Nita stood there, trembling, as the door closed with a thud and a click. She remained in place for a few minutes, calming her breathing before picking up a slice of pizza and walking back to the dissection room.

When she opened the door, she found the boy sitting

cross-legged in the cage, watching her. She approached with caution, and as she got closer, she was able to discern that yes, those stains on his clothes were definitely dried blood.

She put the pizza close enough to the bars that he could wiggle his fingers through and pull pieces off. She skittered back, afraid if she got too close he would leap at her. Not that he could do much, chained to the cage, which was chained to the wall. But she was careful anyway.

He looked down at the pizza and licked his lips. "*Gracias.*"

"*De nada.*" Nita was surprised at how hoarse her voice was.

She stood there for a long moment, awkward, not sure what to do next. Logically, she knew better than to talk to him. She didn't want to know anything about him if—when—she had to dissect him. But she also felt weird just giving him food and leaving.

This was the part where she could really have used more social skills practice. Was there etiquette for this kind of situation?

Probably not.

He wormed his fingers through the bars and ripped off the tip of the pizza. His hands wouldn't reach to his mouth because of the handcuffs, so he had to bend his head over to eat. He chewed slowly, and after one bite, just sat, looking at the pizza but not eating. She wondered if he didn't like pepperoni.

"*Cómo te llamas?*" he asked, still not looking up. His accent was clearly Argentinian, his *y* sounds blurring into *sh*, so it sounded like "*cómo te shamas?*"

His accent wasn't too hard to understand, unlike Nita's.

20

Her father was from Chile, and she'd lived in Madrid until she was six, so Nita's Spanish was a hopeless tangle of the two accents. Sometimes the Peruvians in the grocery store couldn't understand her at all.

"Nita." She hesitated. "*Y tu?*"

"Fabricio." His voice was soft. "Fabricio Tácunan."

"Fabricio?" Nita couldn't keep the incredulity out of her voice. "Is that from Shakespeare or something?"

He looked up at her then, and frowned. "Pardon?"

Nita repeated slowly, trying to make her accent less pronounced.

This time he understood. He raised his eyebrows, voice pitched slightly differently. More curious, less sad, his Spanish soft and barely audible. "Who is Shakespeare?"

"Umm." Nita paused. Did they teach Shakespeare in Latin American schools? If the boy—*don't think of him by name, you'll get too attached and then where will you be?*—had been a captive of a collector, had he even gone to school? "He's an English writer from the fifteen hundreds. One of his characters was named Fabrizio, I think. It's . . . I guess I thought it was kinda an old name."

He shrugged. "I don't know. I think it's fairly common where I'm from. One of my father's employees has the same name. But he spells it with a *z*, Fabrizio. The Italian way."

Fabricio looked down at his shirt, crusted with dried blood and swallowed. "He spell*ed* it with a *z*."

Oh.

Nope, too much information. Nita didn't want to hear about this.

Why did you even talk to him, then? she scolded herself. This was going to make everything worse later.

Nita turned to leave, but he called her back. "Nita."

She paused, wavering, before glancing over her shoulder at him. "Yes?"

"What's going to happen to me?"

She watched how he strained against the handcuffs, leaning forward in the cage. His face was tense, fear shining through in the angle of his head, the crease on his forehead, and the wide blue eyes.

She turned away. "I don't know."

But that was a lie. She just didn't want to admit it to him.

THREE

HEADING BACK INTO the kitchen, Nita found her mother waiting for her.

There was no water.

Nita paused when she entered the room, uncomfortable. Her mother was watching her with cold eyes, hand resting near her gun. Casually, not on purpose. Not that her mother had ever needed a gun. She preferred poison.

"You weren't talking with him, were you, Nita?"

Nita shook her head, looking at the floor. Her shoulders hunched as her body instinctively tried to curl into itself. Nita's mother had an aura around her, an unspoken sense of coiled menace when she was angry. Nita would never admit it to either of her parents, but she was secretly terrified of her mother. She'd only stood up to her once in her life.

When Nita was twelve and they'd been living and operating near Chicago, her mother had tried to get into the dact fur business. Dacts, small fluffy balls of adorableness people kept as pets, were totally harmless. Her mother would come home with groups of them in cages, never saying where they were from. And every night, after her parents went to bed, Nita would sneak down to the basement and take the cages to the twenty-four-hour emergency vet clinic and ask them to give the dacts to the SPCA or shelter. A few times they'd scanned the dacts for microchips and found they'd been stolen from someone's backyard.

Nita's mother had *not* been impressed. She'd come home one day with a cage of dead dacts instead of live ones, and Nita had responded by flushing five pounds of pure powdered unicorn bone down the toilet (that stuff sold better than cocaine and was more addictive by far). She took the dead dacts' bodies to the emergency vet clinic anyway.

Nita's mother hadn't appreciated Nita's discovery of morals. After her father calmed everyone down and ended the plan to sell dact fur, Nita's mother still hadn't been satisfied. So she'd poisoned the dact food in the pet store, and every single dact in their suburb had died. Her mother, knowing Nita's propensity for ignoring things that weren't right in front of her nose, took to putting the corpses in Nita's bed for a week.

It had only ended when Nita broke down crying on the front step, begging her mother to stop. Her father had agreed and told her mother it was affecting their profit margin — by that time Nita was dissecting most of the bodies coming through, and she was such an emotional wreck she hadn't worked in a week. Money convinced her mother to stop when nothing else had.

But there was an unspoken promise: if Nita ever disobeyed her mother again, the punishment would be far, far worse.

Nita swallowed and tried to push away the memories. "Why would I talk to him? What would I even talk about?"

"Of course you weren't talking to him, you're socially incompetent." Her mother took a step forward, and Nita nearly flinched. She kept herself in check. Barely. "Because, if you were trying to talk to the boy, you might develop sympathy. I don't need that. And I can promise you" — a sharp, mean smile — "you don't want that."

Nita shrugged, trying to play it nonchalant when every nerve screamed at her to run, run far and fast and never ever look back. "I gave him his food. He said thanks. I said you're welcome. Then I left."

Her mother gave Nita a long, searching look before bestowing a condescending smile on her. "That's good. It's always appropriate to be polite."

Nita tried to force a smile, but it wouldn't come. "I'm tired. I kinda want to go to bed. If you don't mind?"

Her mother waved her away. "After you pick up some water. I decided I didn't want to go myself after all."

So her mother didn't trust her. She'd just sat there, eavesdropping, and knew Nita had lied to her.

Great.

"Okay."

It was always best to obey her mother.

Nita grabbed her sweater and a bag on her way out, making sure to lock the door behind her. She took a deep breath, leaning her head on the door and closing her eyes. She felt like she was walking a tightrope. One wrong step, and she could fall to either side. The problem was, she wasn't sure what exactly she'd be falling into, except that it would be bad.

Would her mother kill Fabricio while she was out so Nita couldn't interfere?

No. Of course not. But she might start cutting off pieces.

Nita swallowed, hands clenched at her side. Would that be so terrible? It wouldn't be Nita's fault then—she wouldn't be here; she couldn't do anything about it. She could just brush it aside.

But she'd still have to dissect him when it was all over. Scoop out those scared blue eyes and put them in a jar.

Nita let out the breath she'd been holding. It would be a waste to start cutting pieces off Fabricio now.

She walked down the hall and to the stairwell, heading for the store.

Outside, it was dark and hazy, but the streetlights kept things moderately well lit. Nita lived in a nice part of Lima, right in the heart of Miraflores district, and she wasn't too concerned about safety at night.

The heat of the evening settled comfortably on her skin, and a gentle breeze brought her the scent of something spicy in a nearby restaurant. She'd only been in Lima a month, but she liked it a lot so far. It was one of the nicer places they'd set up shop.

Nita and her mother moved around a lot. They would move to a central location on a continent, and her mother would target all the nearby countries, hunting for unnaturals she could kill and sell. They'd spent years doing this in the US before they'd moved on to Vietnam, Germany, and now Peru.

She passed by the open door of a restaurant and saw a pair of American tourists snapping at a waiter. The woman was snarling something in English, and the waiter just stared at her, smile frozen on his face while shaking his head and trying to tell her, in a mix of broken English and Spanish, that he didn't understand.

"Well, find me someone who does!" snapped the woman, and then she turned to her husband. "You'd think they could hire people that speak English."

Nita rolled her eyes as she passed. Why was there this obsession Americans had that others should learn their language to accommodate them? They were in Peru. Why didn't those American people learn Spanish?

She saw it everywhere, the weird entitlement. Tourists who stole pieces of pottery and coins from German castles because they could. Rich men who flew in to Ho Chi Minh thinking they could buy anyone they wanted for a night and do anything they wanted to them, laws of the country be damned.

Nita kept walking past the restaurant and down the street.

Her footsteps slowed just beneath a plaque commemorating a battle against the Spanish. She thought about the Spanish conquistadores five hundred years before, who'd swept through South America and painted the whole continent red in their hunt for gold.

Something uncomfortable and squiggly shifted in her chest. The plaque was talking about Pizarro, the man who'd carved a bloody swathe through Peru. He'd taken the Inca— the ruler of the Incan people—hostage, and then ransomed him for a room full of gold. When the Incan people gave him the gold, he killed the Inca anyway.

Pizarro wasn't even the worst of the conquistadores. Christopher Columbus used to cut the hands off indigenous people who didn't dig enough gold for him each month.

Like her mother cut off Fabricio's toes.

Nope.

Nita really didn't want to think about that.

So she ignored the niggling little voice that told her she had no right to claim the tourists were being entitled jerks when her mother felt entitled to take these people's lives and sell their body parts for profit.

She went to the local bodega instead of the giant grocery store. She didn't like how crowded the grocery store was. People were always talking to her and breathing near her, and sometimes they brushed by her, and she found it uncomfortable.

The bodega was smaller, and she actually had to talk to the person at the cashier sometimes, but it was worth it to not feel the press of so many bodies around her. Also, the bodega never had a line.

As she was paying, Nita's eyes were drawn to the television sitting on a chair on the other side of the room, a stack of toilet paper and Kleenex packages on top. It was an old, boxy unit, and someone had put on the news.

"The debate over whether to add unicorns to the Dangerous Unnaturals List continues, as INHUP starts its third day of discussions over the proposal."

Nita smiled as a memory surfaced, one of the few she had where she really felt her mother cared. A man with blond hair and swirly black thorn tattoos had reached to ruffle her hair at a store, and her mother had nearly shot him right then and there. Nita had been swept away before the man could get too close, and while her mother never said, Nita knew that particular soul-eating unicorn was dead now. He would never again target virgins. She'd seen the new powdered unicorn bone stock.

Letting out a breath, Nita shook her head. Her mother might be many things, but she loved Nita. It was a scary kind of love, but it was there. That was important. Sometimes it was easy to forget, given her mother's suspicious nature and obsession with money.

A reporter was interviewing a scientist about unnatural genetics.

"Unicorns are another type of unnatural linked to recessive genes. This means these creatures can reproduce with humans, and the genetic makeup can lie dormant for generations before the right circumstances combine and two perfectly normal parents give birth to a monster.

"It's not only unicornism that's hereditary," the man on the screen ranted. "But other creatures. Zannies. Kappa. Ghouls. Even vampires, to some extent."

Nita thought of the pieces of zannie in her apartment. She wondered how many people it had tortured in its life to feed its hunger for pain. It was a good thought, because she had no guilt about cutting up a monster like that, and even admired her mother for killing it.

"Could you describe the proposal you've submitted to INHUP, Dr. Rodón?"

"Genetic manipulation. It's a very select series of genes unique to each species, so once fully mapped, it should be easy to screen for and eliminate them. If we catch it before they're born, we can eradicate all dangerous human-born unnaturals."

The clerk gave Nita her water with a smile, and she nearly ripped it out of his hand as she stormed out of the shop, unable to listen to another minute of that drivel.

Nita hated people.

While Nita agreed it might be an effective, even humane way to reduce the monster population, she *knew* people would take it too far. People *always* took it too far. How long before people started isolating genes from harmless unnaturals and eliminating them too? Aurs, who were just bioluminescent people? Or mermaids? Or whatever Fabricio was?

Or even Nita and her mother?

FOUR

THE NEXT MORNING, Nita woke to screaming.

She yanked the covers off and reached for the scalpel she kept on her nightstand. Her feet tangled in the sheets as she stumbled out of bed and fell on her knees with a thud.

The screaming rose in pitch, sharpening into a long, horrible shriek.

Breathing fast, Nita freed herself and climbed to her feet. She crept out of her room, scalpel first, toward the source of the noise. The screams were punctuated by the rattle of metal against metal, the scraping squeak of something heavy on the linoleum floor, and her mother's vicious swearing. Nita's heartbeat stuttered.

Her mother hadn't been testing her when she mentioned cutting off Fabricio's ear. She was actually doing it. Right now.

Nita opened the door to the dissection room and saw blood. It had spattered her clean white walls and floor. Droplets clung to her mother's angry face, and streaks of red tears patterned Fabricio's cheeks. He'd scooted his head as far into the cage as he could and had bunched his legs so his feet were pressed to the front of the cage. He rocked it from side to side, trying to prevent her mother from getting a grip. The padlock was on the floor, but the cage door had swung shut, and Fabricio was holding it closed by wrapping his remaining toes around the door and tugging.

Her mother was holding a syringe, probably something to sedate Fabricio. He knocked it out of her hand with his shoulder, and it clattered to the bottom of the cage. He used an elbow to smash it, spilling the contents and chunks of broken glass across the ground.

Both of them turned as Nita entered, and Nita flinched when she saw Fabricio's face straight on. Her mother had clearly tried to cut off his ear while he slept, and he'd woken up mid cut. His ear had been partly severed, and then the knife had slipped, slicing a deep red line across his cheek.

Nita took an involuntary step forward to stop this, to do something. Her mouth opened to protest. Then it closed.

You can't stop this, Nita. You can't save him.

If you show sympathy, your mother will make sure you regret it.

She wouldn't hurt me, Nita protested. But that didn't mean there weren't worse things her mother could do. The memory of small broken bodies stuffed between her sheets surfaced, but she shoved it away.

She let her hands fall to her sides as she talked herself out of action and looked away. She was no stranger to blood and carnage, but she hated that shard of hope shining from Fabricio's eyes. She didn't want to see it replaced by betrayal.

"Nita." Her mother rose, flicking blood off her fingers. "Good morning."

"Good morning." Nita paused. "Are you trying to get the ear?"

"Yes. He's not cooperating." Her mother beckoned her. "Give me a hand."

Nita hesitated only a split second before approaching. "How can I help?"

The hope in Fabricio's eyes cracked, and then melted into terror and anger. Nita tried not to look.

Her mother took out another syringe, presumably full of sedatives. "I'm going to try and hold him still. I want you to sedate him."

Nita took the syringe with trembling fingers, not letting herself look at Fabricio. It was better this way, wasn't it? This way he wouldn't feel the pain when his ear came off.

Nita wouldn't have to hear him scream.

"Why didn't you sedate him before you started?" Nita asked, hiding her shaking hand from her mother.

Her mother shrugged, nonchalant. "I thought I could cut it off fast enough."

No, Nita realized, looking at the half smile twitching across her mother's face. *You thought no such thing. You wanted this to happen, so I would wake up and be forced to help you.*

Nita was being tested. She didn't know what the consequences of failure were, but she knew they weren't good.

You shouldn't have talked to Fabricio and then lied about it to her.

Nita had been stupid. She should have known better.

Clenching her jaw, she put the syringe down. "I don't see how it'll be any easier to sedate him than it would be to just get the rest of the ear off." She showed her mother her scalpel.

33

"There's only a strip of flesh left. It won't take much to finish the job."

Her mother's smile widened until it seemed to consume her face. "If you think so, I'm happy to try."

"Nita." Fabricio spoke for the first time. "Nita, *por favor*."

Nita's mother laughed. "Oh, it figured out your name."

Nita clenched the scalpel in her sweaty palm and focused on the ear, ignoring Fabricio's crying and continued whispers of her name like a prayer.

Just get this over with. Then she could figure out where to go from there. But if she failed this, bad things would happen. She didn't want a repeat of the dact incident with parts of Fabricio in her bed each morning.

She tried not to look at his face as she pushed the scalpel through the cage bars, but she couldn't escape his sobs and cries. Her hand was shaking, and her palm was so sweaty that when Fabricio shook the cage again, the scalpel was knocked right out of Nita's fingers, leaving a deep, bloody gash across her palm along the way.

Nita yanked her hand back, swearing as the blood dripped down her arm.

Her mother gave her a tired look. "Well, heal it already, and we'll try again."

Nita turned away so her mother wouldn't see the flash of anger in her expression. Then she let out a breath and focused her body. She increased blood clotting factor in the affected area to speed up the scabbing process. She didn't want to do too much repairing until she had some disinfectant, though

—while she could stimulate her body's natural defenses against the microbes, it was just easier to wash the wound in soap.

Nita wasn't sure how old she'd been when she discovered that other people couldn't control their bodies the same way she could. Her mother did it all the time—enhanced her own muscles so she could run faster, hit harder, heal quicker.

The more Nita understood about her body, the more she could control it. But it was dangerous—there was a reason for swelling, and if you took away the symptom without dealing with the underlying cause, it could make things worse. She'd discovered that the hard way when she was seven and her father had to take her to a hospital because she'd accidentally paralyzed herself trying to make her bicycle-butt bruise go away. Only after the x-rays and scans, and the doctor's detailed explanation of the precise issue, had Nita been able to fix it.

After that, she'd been very cautious about how she altered herself.

"Are you done yet?" Her mother's voice was cold.

Nita nodded and turned back to her mother. "For now. But it'll take time to fully heal. I severed a tendon—I don't think I'll be able to hold a scalpel for a day or so."

Her mother scowled, clearly displeased. Nita made no comment and kept her face blank. It wouldn't do for her mother to see how relieved this injury made Nita feel, or for her mother to realize she was stalling and could, if she wanted, finish healing the wound much sooner than tomorrow. Now she had at least a day where she didn't personally have to do the slicing. That was something.

"Fine." Her mother picked up the bloody scalpel, gave it a quick rinse in the sink, and then, before either Nita or Fabricio had a chance to react, spun with near superhuman speed and threw it. It neatly sliced through the last piece of cartilage connecting Fabricio's ear to his body, and he screamed as the severed piece of flesh tumbled to the ground. He tried to clap his hands over his ear, but they were still chained to the bottom of the cage, and he couldn't reach. Instead, he wept as blood coated the side of his face.

Her mother scooped up the scalpel and speared the ear like a piece of steak. She showed it to Nita with a grin. "You know, I think my aim could have been better."

Nita resisted the urge to throw up.

FIVE

THERE WERE STILL zannie parts to be boxed, but Nita couldn't stand the idea of working with Fabricio's sobs punctuating her every move.

Nita turned to her mother. "I'm going for a walk, to get some fresh air."

"You do realize how polluted this city is?" Her mother was getting the packaging out for the ear.

Nita shrugged, averting her eyes. "Whatever, all cities are polluted. Besides, it's a mental thing. And the walk along the ocean isn't so bad."

Mostly, she didn't want Fabricio's eyes boring into her, judging and begging at the same time. She needed time to sort out her thoughts, away from her mother, away from Fabricio.

Her mother waved her off. "Pick up something for dinner on your way back."

Nita could hardly believe her mother had agreed. Maybe she understood that Nita needed time to not think about Fabricio. Time to settle her thoughts, to figure out what to do.

Or maybe she just wanted Nita out of the way so she could cut more pieces off Fabricio.

Nita didn't want to think about that. She'd never been confronted with this level of violence before. When dead unnaturals were brought to her, everything was calm and structured. Her smooth white walls comforted her as she worked. They didn't get spattered with blood and gore. That wasn't what Nita had signed up for.

Not that Nita had ever had a chance to sign up for anything.

But she liked it. Had liked it. Nita had always had a scientific mind, and there was something fascinating about dissecting and learning about different unnaturals. And the more she understood about bodies, the more she began to understand the potential of her own ability.

She'd always wondered if her ability could grant her immortality if she just figured out how to counteract the aging mechanism.

She'd always wanted to go to college, to study and learn from professionals, to research with proper machines, to publish papers and discuss her theories on unnatural traits with others in her field. But her mother had refused to let Nita go — said she couldn't be spared for some "waste of time and money." So Nita contented herself with her biology journals and her dissections.

But this wasn't dissection.

Outside, the sky was gray, sun barely visible. Nita walked out of her residential area, toward one of the main thoroughfares. People hung out the doors of small buses, calling out destinations to those on the street. Boutique stores and small cafés gave way to a wide plaza in front of Larcomar shopping mall, which hung off the edge of the bluffs. The open mall gleamed pristine and white, and beyond it, she could hear the gentle thrum of the ocean.

Nita crossed the street to the wide path that meandered along the cliffs and overlooked the ocean. It went all along the coast, but Nita's favorite part was the walk from Miraflores to Barranco. Just the sound and smell of the ocean hundreds of feet below her, and the steady rhythm of her own footsteps.

Nita wandered a while before taking a seat under a floripondio tree and watching the ocean. A couple nearby curled up together on the grass, whispering secrets to each other, and an old woman walked a tiny brown dog along the path.

Nita closed her eyes and savored the smell of crushed grass. Her pocket buzzed, and she pulled out her phone.

Her father had texted her. *You okay? I haven't heard from you lately.*

Nita let out a breath and leaned back until she was lying on the grass, staring at the sky. Her father was perfectly human, but some days she wondered if he didn't have some sort of extrasensory perception that knew whenever Nita was unhappy.

I'm fine, Dad. Nita hesitated, mind at war. She wanted so badly to talk about Fabricio with someone, but she knew they had to be careful with their personal phones. These phones were supposed to be safe, serving as a believable cover if ever they were caught by INHUP. No work stuff allowed. That was for their other email accounts on the dark web.

But she wasn't allowed to access those on her phone either. They had a computer for that kind of thing. One that her mother had been hogging lately.

Nita bit her lip and caved. She needed to talk about this. It would be even better to hear her dad's voice. But her phone plan didn't allow international calling. It didn't even have data. Mom was cheap that way.

If Nita didn't know better, she'd think her mother was trying to prevent her from talking with her father.

Did Mom tell you what she brought home yesterday? Nita asked.

There was a long pause before her father responded. *Yes, I heard. You have a new pet.*

Yes. It's very messy. Nita swallowed. How did she even begin to explain all the terrible, complicated feelings that were going on in her head? *I don't really like it.*

Understatement of the year.

Well, we're only taking care of it for a while. Don't worry, it'll have a new home soon. You won't have to deal with it again after that.

Yeah. Nita's fingers swiped across the screen. *I guess I just feel like it deserves better than we can give it.*

There was an even longer pause this time. Then, *A pet like that can't survive in the wild. Don't do anything stupid, Nita.*

Don't do anything stupid.

Nita took a deep breath, trying to blink away the angry tears pricking her eyes. She wasn't sure what she wanted her father to say. That her mother had gone too far? That there was a mix-up? That she could go home, and when she got back, all evidence of Fabricio's existence would be wiped away, so she never had to think about it again?

God, she was awful.

It took a special type of monster to dissect dead people and sell them without guilt. Nita was aware that morally speaking, she wasn't on the good side of the scale. In fact, she was probably closer to the serial killer side of the scale. Sometimes thinking that bothered her a little. But then she stopped thinking about it and the uneasy feeling went away.

Don't think about it was always a great solution. It had solved so many moral issues in her life.

It wasn't working this time.

How was Fabricio any different from Nita? Nita was sure her body parts would make a pretty penny on the black market too. She could just imagine the things her father could write to market her unique characteristics.

Nita, are you still there?

Angry, she wiped the tears away and replied, *I've got to go. Don't worry, I won't do anything stupid. I'll talk to you later.*

She pocketed her phone without waiting for his response.

Then she rolled over on the grass, pressed her hands into her face, and wondered what the hell was wrong with her.

SIX

NITA DID SOME errands on the way home before picking up fried chicken for her mother. Her mother was picky about food, which was a waste, because Peru had some of the best food in the world. Whenever Nita needed a distraction, she bought herself comfort food.

She picked up some *causa* (similar to shepherd's pie, but served cold, with tuna or chicken instead of beef), a *rocoto relleno* (a spicy pepper stuffed with meat), and some *picarones* for dessert.

She ate her dessert on the way home. The *picarones* had been served on a paper plate, and they were drizzled in a sticky sweet sauce. She ate the first one because she thought it would fall off, and then before she knew it, she'd eaten them all.

Best food in the world.

She entered the apartment, and her mother took the chicken out of her hands with a frown. Nita held on to her own food. "You got an awful lot."

"I got some for—" Nita caught herself before she said his name. Her mother would not appreciate that. "The boy."

Her mother slowly looked at Nita. Dark, thick eyelashes did nothing to soften the coldness of her eyes.

Nita swallowed and felt herself getting defensive. "Well, what did you expect him to eat? Dog food?"

Her mother raised her eyebrows. "Someone's not happy."

Nita sighed and deflected. "I heard some guy on the news talking about killing unnaturals."

"Ah." Her mother nodded. "UEA?"

The Unnatural Extermination Agenda was the biggest unnatural hate group in the world. And the most popular. Obviously there were other groups, but the power and influence of the UEA was a force to be reckoned with.

Nita's mother was a UEA member — not that the UEA knew she was an unnatural, obviously. She got updates on unnaturals found in her area that way, and then responded to them. Sometimes she got there before the UEA and took out the target. Sometimes she waited for the UEA to kill them, then stole the body, leaving the UEA members to be charged with murder. Nita had the UEA to thank for a lot of the bodies on her table.

"Not the UEA, just some ass who thinks we should eliminate unnaturals before they're born with genetic manipulation."

Her mother took a bite of chicken. "Interesting. I never thought of using genetic manipulation for anything like that." She tapped her finger against the table, her brow furrowing. Nita had a bad feeling she'd given her mother an idea for something, but she wasn't sure what.

"I'm going to feed Fa — the boy."

Her mother shrugged, eyes staring off into space, a small

smile curving her lips. Just great. Nita didn't want to know what her mother was planning.

Fabricio was curled up in his cage, but turned to Nita when she entered. She put a piece of chicken on a napkin on the floor, and then realized it was too big to get through the mesh of his cage. She wasn't really sure how she was going to feed him.

"She's going to take one of my eyes tomorrow." Fabricio's voice was soft, almost a whisper, but too croaky. All that screaming probably chafed his throat.

Nita flinched. "You don't know that."

"She told me so." He paused. "I think she likes to see me scared."

He was probably right.

"Then how do you know she's not baiting you?"

Fabricio met her eyes. "I don't. But you would. Is she?"

Nita looked at the floor. Her hands clenched into fists, and she could feel her scab tearing, little rivulets of blood leaking down her hand. She didn't fix it.

"No," she admitted. Fabricio was right. Her mother probably meant exactly what she said. "She's not baiting you."

Fabricio's jaw tightened. "How long? How long before every part of me is sold and you start in on the organs?"

Nita swallowed and did some math. The requests would start coming in faster as buyers learned what was on the market.

"A week. Tops." Nita nodded to herself. That sounded about right. Any longer than that, and her mother would probably kill him out of sheer frustration. An old friend of her father's visited once when Nita was a kid, and within four days,

44

her mother was close to murdering him. Not because he was particularly annoying or did anything wrong. Just because he existed in the same space as her mother.

"A week." He kept his eyes fixed on Nita. "And before then, how many pieces of me will be hacked off and sold?"

"I don't know."

He was silent, watching her.

Nita looked down at the chicken on the floor. Did it even matter if he ate?

"Nita," he pleaded.

"Stop it."

"Please, Nita, I don't want to die. Help me."

Nita got up and walked away, leaving the chicken on the floor.

She stood outside the door for a long time, shoulders shaking, eyes squeezed shut. She considered just shutting her amygdala off, but she despised the feeling of dullness that accompanied it, like she was lobotomized. So she tried to stem the flood of stress hormones on her system instead. Then she began increasing levels of serotonin and dopamine. She pulled the tension out of her muscles and focused on slowing her heartbeat.

Relax, Nita. You don't need to stress about this. Let it all go.

Nita let out a breath, swimming in a gentle high. Fear, stress, all of that was gone. Just peace.

Her muscles began to relax, knots in her shoulders and neck loosening. She hadn't realized how wound up she was about it all.

She's going to take one of my eyes tomorrow.

Her muscles tightened right back up.

She could imagine it in perfect detail. Her mother was probably still unhappy about Nita's behavior with the ear, so she'd make Nita do the cutting. Fabricio would be sedated, then strapped to a table. Her mother would make sure there was no way he could move. Then she'd wait for him to wake up to have Nita scoop out the eye.

Usually, Nita liked eyes, how they would pop right out and then you just snipped the optic nerve, like a strange umbilical cord. Her mother knew that. Nita would have bet the eighty-three dollars in her secret college fund that her mother would make her cut the eye out herself.

Fuck.

She couldn't do this.

She looked down at her sweaty palms and amended the thought: She *wouldn't* do this.

Hands trembling at her sides, shoulders tighter than ever, she resumed flooding her system with calming hormones. She would need to remain levelheaded tonight. There was a lot to be done.

Five hours later, in the middle of the night, Nita's high had worn off, and she was more terrified than ever before. One did not piss off her mother lightly.

She'd scoured the kitchen and living room for the keys to the padlock and handcuffs that held Fabricio, but her mother was probably wearing them around her neck like a badge of honor.

Nita ended up with a pair of crappy bolt cutters from the

toolbox her mother had bought to set up the apartment's soundproofing, and a pair of bobby pins. She'd never picked handcuff locks before, but she figured if it didn't work, she could just dislocate his thumbs and get them off that way. As long as she could make sure he didn't scream.

She closed the door to the dissection room behind her before she flicked on the light. Fabricio stirred, lifting his head from where it was curled by his knees. He blinked, eyes bleary from sleep. He sat up quickly when he saw the bolt cutters, causing his handcuffs to clink and the cage to rattle.

Nita put a finger to her lips and he settled down. His eyes were wide and hopeful, and a faint smile was trying to form on his lips. It caused the dried blood on the side of his face to crack and flake off.

Hefting the bolt cutters, she began making a hole in the cage.

Nita sometimes worried—well, not worried precisely, because it didn't actually *bother* her, but thought about in a concerned way—that she was a bit of a sociopath. She was socially inept, she hated people, and the only thing that made her feel calm and at peace was cutting up dead bodies. There was normal, there was abnormal, and then there was Nita.

But it was days like today, her heart pounding a frenetic, terrified rhythm as the bolt cutters snip-snip-snipped through the cage that Nita felt like things might not be as drastic as she feared. She did have morals. Not many, but she had some.

And she wouldn't let her mother cross them in front of her.

Her mother really should have killed Fabricio before coming home from Argentina.

47

Nita sat back and admired her work. There was a large, human-size hole in the cage. Fabricio crawled through it stiffly. His handcuffs caught on the bolt they'd been chained around, and Nita cut it with a final snap. Putting the bolt cutters down, she then took out the bobby pins.

"Do you know how to pick locks?" Fabricio asked.

Nita shrugged. "I read about it in a book once."

She tried shoving the pin in, but the weird little plastic globby thing on the end wouldn't fit. She cut it off with the bolt cutters and then inserted it into the handcuff lock, jiggling it around. The faint click of metal on metal was the only sound in the room. The handcuffs didn't unlock.

"Will the bolt cutters work on the handcuffs? Or at least, the chain between the cuffs?" Fabricio stretched his legs out as she worked, clearly glad to be able to extend them after being trapped in a cage since yesterday.

"I dunno. Maybe?" She put down the bobby pins and picked up the bolt cutters. The links between the two cuffs were large and thick, but it looked like the bolt cutters might work.

"Hold still," Nita said, using the bolt cutters to grip one of the links. Then she rose, and shoved down with all her might, trying to get the handles to close and the link to break.

Something did break — the bolt cutters.

Swearing as one half of the cutter clanked to the ground, Nita listened closely. Had her mother heard? Was she coming, even now, to punish them both?

Nita waited, breathing shallowly, head tilted to the side. Beside her, Fabricio watched her fear in silence, hands clenched into fists in front of him.

Finally, Nita turned back to him with a sigh. "I don't think I can break them. I'll have to dislocate your thumbs to get them off."

Eyes widening, Fabricio leaned back, palms facing her. "That's not necessary. I'll leave like this. I'm sure I can find somewhere to get them off."

"Your choice." Nita could have put his thumbs back in place when she was done, but she didn't think he'd appreciate her mentioning that.

Rising to his feet with much wincing, Fabricio headed for the exit. He paused, looking to Nita for guidance, and she quickly took the lead. They tiptoed across the kitchen together, toward the main entrance. Nita unbolted the door, and they slipped into the hallway.

She led him outside, and they walked down the street at a brisk pace. Fabricio trotted behind her. "Where are we going?"

"Bus station. There's a bus to Quito leaving in an hour, and you're going to be on it."

"Ecuador?" He hesitated. "Why am I going to Ecuador?"

Nita sighed. "Because we can't call INHUP here. Peru isn't a member country, so INHUP has no power. I don't know how the police here would react to your situation—or if my mother would just barge into the station to get you back. So. I'm putting you on a bus to Ecuador. If you can get there, INHUP will take you in and put you in the Unnatural Protection Program."

"Oh." He paused. "Where are we now?"

"Lima."

"Ah." He gave her a half-confused smile. "I thought we were still somewhere in Argentina. I mean, I remember the plane, I think, but the drugs made everything so hazy I wasn't sure it was real."

Nita spared him a glance, then turned her eyes forward and kept walking. "No. My mother only operates out of countries that aren't signed into INHUP these days. She collects from everywhere, but her base of operations is almost always in a non-INHUP member country."

"I suppose that's probably true for most of the black market."

"Depends. We operate through the internet, but there are actual physical markets where they sell unnatural parts. They're usually on borders, so people can enter the country, buy their illegal goods, use them, and then slip back."

Nita had been to one of the American markets when she was a child, but she didn't remember much about it except that her mother had held her hand the whole time and refused to let Nita go anywhere alone, including the bathroom. Sure, there might have been interesting things for sale there, but it didn't seem worth it. From what she'd heard, they made her mother's behavior sound saintly.

They came to the bus station. There were several double-decker buses preparing to leave, and a crowd of bored and tired-looking people milling in front of them. Most long-haul trips from Lima left at night so people could sleep half the time. It was a long ride to Ecuador.

Nita went into the bus station and picked up the ticket she'd ordered online an hour earlier, then came back out and handed it to Fabricio. His chains clinked as he took it. Nita frowned, took off her sweater and used it to cover his hands and hide the chains.

"This is your ticket. And here's some money." She gave him some Peruvian soles and some US dollars.

Fabricio stood there, shaking in the cool night air. There was still dried blood caked all over his face.

Nita sighed. "You can't ride the bus like that. We need to wash some of this blood off."

They went into the surprisingly clean bus terminal bathroom. Nita washed his face. He cried a bit when she approached where his ear had been, and she decided to leave it be. Sure, there was still dried blood, but his hair covered most of the wound. INHUP would have doctors look at it in eighteen hours or so. Nita didn't want to tear the scab and make it bleed again before he got on the bus. She didn't have any gauze or anything. And there was no time to get some, because the bus was already boarding.

They walked back out, and Nita nearly smacked her head. "You need to call INHUP before you reach the border. I don't have a passport for you. I booked your ticket to Piura, which is just south of the border, but the bus goes all the way to Quito. Just stay on. If you call INHUP in advance, they should wait for you at the border."

"How do I call?" His hands chinked as he moved. "I have no phone."

Nita hesitated. She only had her personal phone. The bus was boarding; there was no time. He was going to miss it. She looked down at her phone and bit her lip. On the front was a sticker, mostly rubbed off, of a human heart. Ventricles and capillaries colored blue and red, colors faded so they all seemed faint and monotone, a testament to how many years she'd had the small piece of technology.

It was just a phone, and he needed it more than she did.

She sighed, then she handed her phone to Fabricio. "Here."

"Thanks." He swallowed. "Five-five-two, right?"

"Yeah." INHUP numbers weren't like 911, changing between countries. They were standard worldwide. "You're going to miss the bus."

Fabricio gave her a strange look. "You're not coming?"

Nita blinked, surprised. "No. Of course not."

"You're not . . . going back there?"

Nita hesitated. The truth was, she didn't have any other option. For one thing, the bus ticket and few dollars she'd given to Fabricio had cleaned her out. All her pathetic college savings gone. Not that she'd ever had much to begin with.

Even if she'd had the money, she wouldn't go to INHUP with Fabricio.

Her parents always said you couldn't trust INHUP; they were as corrupt as any other police force. Her mother even claimed that an INHUP agent gave her tips on where to find unnaturals who were in hiding in the Unnatural Protection Program. Nita wasn't sure if it was true, but she had no doubt that INHUP couldn't protect her from her mother. Nita had too much valuable knowledge, the kind of things that could convict her parents in an instant, for her mother to ever let her escape.

Nita knew her mother loved her. But she also knew her

mother would kill her without a second thought if Nita became a serious threat.

"Nita."

"Yes, Fabricio?"

"Won't she . . ." He paused, shoulders hunched forward and eyes lowering in fear. "Won't she be mad?"

"Probably."

"Aren't you scared?"

Nita bit her lip, then nodded. "Of course. But it'll be fine."

He didn't look like he believed her.

"She's my mom. She can't stay mad forever."

The look in his eyes was pure pity. "I'm so sorry."

Nita bristled. She felt like he was insulting her. "For what?"

"You." Shaking his head, he turned and began walking toward the bus. Halfway down the street he paused, turned back, and whispered, "Thank you."

Nita didn't reply. She just started back home to await the fallout.

SEVEN

NITA HAD NEVER thought of herself as particularly
brave. There was never really anything to be brave
about. She'd never seen the sense in doing something you were
afraid of. Your brain was smart — it wouldn't send you fear signals without good cause.

So, although Nita was ready to cry from terror before she
even saw her mother, she still felt a little shred of pride. She'd
done something, something bad, because it was good. She felt
like someone had given her a particularly difficult test and
she'd passed. She'd done what a good person, a moral person,
would have done. There weren't many times she could say that.

She hoped Fabricio got to INHUP before her mother
caught up with him.

A strange realization hit her. Fabricio was the first person
she'd had a real conversation with besides her parents in almost
a decade. Of course, she'd ordered pizzas, and she'd asked for
change at the grocery store. But not had a real conversation.

When Nita first started going to school, she'd talked
like any normal five-year-old would. But one day, she'd said

something—Nita didn't remember what, exactly—that had made the teacher speak to her parents.

Her father sat her down and told her not to talk about anything she saw at home. Not the eyeballs in glass jars, not the shipments of white powder, not the small garden in the back where they composted what they couldn't sell online.

Then her mother sat down next to her. And smiled. Even as a small child, Nita had known that bad things were going to happen. After their conversation, Nita was quite certain that if she ever spoke to anyone besides her parents about anything again, she'd be the one in glass jars.

So she simply stopped talking. If she didn't say anything, she couldn't say the wrong thing, right?

Nita had to admire the wisdom of her child self. Even to this day, she mostly practiced that policy—though a good chunk of that was simply because she never really knew what to say to people. She couldn't think of anything to talk about. So she stayed silent. Life was easier, and more peaceful.

Unfortunately, her teachers hadn't thought so. And several years later, when her mother finally grew tired of getting calls that "Nita is antisocial" and "Nita is bright but doesn't participate in class," she pulled Nita from school.

After that, it was only really her parents in her life.

Nita's mother was waiting when Nita got home. Still wearing black pajamas, with bed head and no makeup, her mother regarded her from the kitchen table. Sitting on the table were the broken bolt cutters.

Nita paused, the front door still open behind her, offering a quick exit if things didn't go the way she hoped.

She had expected her mother to fly into a rage, for her to drop her voice to that frightening hiss and do . . . something. A punishment suitable for the crime. She hadn't thought much further than that. It was never a good idea to try to imagine what her mother would do when angry.

But her mother didn't do anything. She just sat at the table, hands at her side, watching Nita.

"How long?" her mother asked.

"How long . . . since he left?" Nita swallowed. "Half an hour?"

Her mother looked over her shoulder at the clock, probably estimating how long it would take Fabricio to call INHUP and then give them their address, how long it would take INHUP to realize that they'd caught a fairly big fish and to petition the Peruvian police to get involved.

Then cut that time to a quarter, because someone along the chain of command was going to be bribable and there was a decent chance they'd tip off one of her mother's rivals. Her mother had a lot of rivals — she was good at making enemies.

Her mother walked out of the room. "Pack your things. We're leaving in fifteen minutes. We won't be coming back."

Nita stared at the empty space her mother had just vacated. Where was the anger? Where was the reaction? An uneasy feeling began to creep through Nita. What was going on?

Nonetheless, Nita did as she was told. She went to her bedroom, picked up her backpack, and started shoving things into it. Important things first, like the scientific magazine she was reading and her empty wallet. Then some clothes, since she wasn't sure when they'd be stopping next. Just her favorites, a few shirts, some underwear, and a pair of jeans. She'd only just moved in and hadn't collected much from Peru yet, so she didn't feel any qualms about leaving things behind.

She hesitated a moment before pulling a college textbook out from under her mattress and stuffing it into her backpack too. She hoped her mother wouldn't look in her bag.

Nita brought her bag to the kitchen and found her mother eating leftover pizza cold from the box. Nita looked over her mother's shoulder, but there was none left. Her mother didn't offer anything else, so Nita scrounged. She found a carrot, which she washed and ate.

Nita swung her backpack over her shoulder and moved to check for messages on her cell phone before realizing she didn't have it anymore. Her mother, hair now combed but makeup still not applied, led them out the door and into the night.

They could've taken a cab, but her mother didn't like leaving traces, and besides, taking a cab in the dark in Lima wasn't always safe. So they walked. And walked. And walked.

Nita kept a wary eye out as they went, worried about being followed. Her mother's caution had rubbed off on her.

Nearly an hour later, her mother checked them into a hotel in San Isidro. It wasn't a crappy hostel, nor was it the Hilton. Livable, certainly, but not nice. The room was small, and Nita lifted the mattresses to check for bloodstains. There were none. That was a relief; Nita hated bedbugs.

Her mother put her bags down on the bed and checked her phone. She frowned, then glanced at Nita. "I need to go change some shipping addresses. I don't want anything of ours reaching that apartment after the police arrive."

"How are you going to change the address if it's already been shipped?" Nita asked.

"I'll have to find the person who delivers the mail to our building, won't I?"

Nita didn't respond. The cold condescension of the response made her throat close in on itself, like she was suffocating on words.

Her mother looked at Nita and then picked up her purse. "I need to take care of this now. I'll be back in a few hours."

"Okay." Nita swallowed, not liking that her mother hadn't addressed what happened at all. "Um . . . about what happened."

Her mother held up a hand. "Not now, Anita."

"But—"

"No." Her voice dipped low and cold. "You do *not* want me to talk about this now."

Nita quieted, but she couldn't stop her hands trembling against her sides.

Her mother slammed the door behind her without looking back. The reverberation caused the crappy flower painting on the other side of the room to rattle on its hook and fall off, smacking into the hard cement floor. The frame cracked audibly.

Nita flopped down on her bed and closed her eyes. It could have gone worse.

A newspaper lay on the bed beside Nita. Her mother had taken it from the lobby, more likely out of habit than to actually read.

Nita picked it up. On the front was a picture of the zannie she'd dissected earlier that week. The government confirmed his death, and the paper listed his crimes as well as some information on zannies. Nita let her eyes skim the article, eager for the distraction.

Native to Southeast Asia, zannies were skilled torturers, notoriously amoral, and universally despised. Over the years, zannies had spread across the world, and their small population made them highly paid and in higher demand. Every dictator and genocidal maniac worth his salt had a zannie on staff. Nita heard they also made particularly good mafia enforcers.

While Nita agreed zannies were evil, she wasn't so sure about zannies being on the list. It wasn't that she thought zannies weren't dangerous—she was firmly in the shoot-first, ask-questions-later camp on that. But the list contained creatures who needed to kill others for their continued survival, like unicorns, which ate the souls of virgins, or kappa, which ate human internal organs. Technically, people survived torture. Occasionally. So zannies didn't need to kill. Just, you know, cause the kind of horrific pain only found in torture.

Technicalities like that bothered Nita. They needed to redefine the mandate of the list so that zannies fit in there properly. What if someone tried to challenge the letter of the law and a zannie walked free?

Nita sighed, dropping the paper, unable to bring herself to care at the moment. Her mind wouldn't focus.

She bit her lip, fingers hovering over her pocket for a moment before she sat up. She found her mother's bag and pulled the laptop out, logged into her email, and composed a message to her father. *I think I did something really stupid. I'm scared. I've never seen Mom like this before.*

There was no response. But then, there wouldn't be. Dawn was just breaking outside, and there was no way her father would be up yet. The US had just started daylight saving time, which meant she was in the same time zone as her father. The same far-too-early-in-the-morning time.

Nita closed the laptop. She really wanted to talk to him.

Maybe she should just call and wake him?

But she had no cell phone. Ugh. She could Skype him, if he was awake. But the fact that he probably wasn't awake was the problem.

Nita rolled over and smushed her face into her pillow with a groan.

The snick of a key in the door lock made Nita sit upright in bed. Was her mother back? It couldn't have been half an hour since she'd left.

The door didn't open.

Nita's heart began to race. This wasn't her mother. She didn't know why or how she knew, but she could feel it, as surely as she could feel the itchy polyester blanket on the bed beneath her.

Shit. Had they been followed?

Getting to her feet as silently as she could, Nita looked around for a weapon. Her eyes skittered from one corner of the room to another, but all she saw were pillows, blankets, and a backpack full of clothes. Creeping forward, she picked up the broken picture from the floor. The frame was made of some sort of wood — *or cardboard painted to look like wood*, the cynical side of her said. But it was all she had.

She watched the door, trying to keep her breath shallow and quiet. Waiting. The door creaked open an inch, and Nita took a step back, picture frame at the ready.

She was so focused on the door in front of her, she didn't even notice the person come in through the open window behind her. Not until a needle stabbed into her shoulder and she spun around to see a young man's blurry face. Black hair, dark eyes, white smile.

Nita could feel the chemical sliding through her body, and she tried to prevent it from slipping through her bloodstream by blocking receptors and flinging white blood cells at it. But it was too fast, skipping through her body and attaching to the glutamate receptors in her nerve cells.

Nita swung the picture frame at the face in front of her, but her arms were too heavy, and she couldn't lift them more than waist height. He blocked her easily, and she stumbled back, trying to get away. If she could just reach the bathroom, she could lock herself in and wait for her mother to return. Her mother would take care of these people in minutes.

No matter how she strained, her legs wouldn't obey her, and instead, her knees folded and she fell to the floor.

She felt like her heart should be speeding up to match the panic jittering through her skull, but everything was slow and blurry. Her chest hurt like it had been hit with a meat tenderizer. Only her breathing obeyed her, coming fast and harsh, and she made a sound somewhere between a gasp and a sob.

How had they found her? She'd thought they hadn't been followed.

Her whole body began to tingle and go numb, until she couldn't even feel where the needle had gone in. She struggled to crawl away, desperate to stall for time until her mother got back, but she only managed to creep a few inches. The sound of shoes on floor reverberated in her skull as her face pressed into the ground.

The world spiraled into copies of itself as her vision doubled, then tripled. A few seconds later, everything blurred into darkness.

EIGHT

NITA'S HEAD HURT. She thought she might be awake, because it hurt, but she wasn't sure, because the ground was buzzing, and she was twitching, and someone was singing, but maybe that was just a dream and when her eyes opened the world was a Dalmatian. Before she slid back into unconsciousness, she realized the roar and the shaking might be from an engine. A really loud one, like on a plane.

Or muscle spasms and a headache.

When she woke up next, she thought there was sky above her, but she also thought she was on the sky, or maybe falling into it, and the clouds seemed to copy each other. There was still a roar and a buzzing, so maybe she was still on the plane. If there was a plane. Did planes have sky? Was that sky?

Obviously you're looking out the ceiling window of the plane, idiot.

Planes don't have ceiling windows, idiot.

But then the blue resolved itself into gray, so maybe that wasn't the sun, but the overhead lights.

Before she could follow the train of thought any further, she lost consciousness again.

This time, when she woke, she stayed awake. Her head throbbed, and her breathing was short and rapid, like she'd been running. Her skin was clammy and itchy with dried sweat. Her T-shirt stuck to her body where she was lying on the cot. Some of her hair had glued itself to her forehead, and she raised a trembling hand to peel it off.

She held out her arm in front of her, but it wavered and twitched. She tried to raise herself onto her elbows, but felt dizzy and had to lie back down. What had they given her?

Nita squeezed her eyelids together to prevent the tears burning behind them, but there was no moisture left in her body to cry with.

What were they going to do to her?

Her imagination supplied her with all sorts of ideas.

All. Sorts.

Panic tried to claw its way up her throat, but she choked on it with a croaky gasp that should have been a sob.

Calm down, Nita. You won't do yourself any favors panicking. You don't even know where you are. Assess. Analyze.

Calm. Right. She could be calm. Panic could come later, when she realized the scope of her situation.

She tried to concentrate and push the drugs out of her system—after all, what was the use of having the ability to control your body if you didn't use it? But it was too hard; Nita couldn't focus well enough to do anything, and trying just worsened her headache.

Swallowing with a dry throat, she tried to gauge how long she'd been out. A while. She turned her head to get a better view of where she was, but her vision was still double and the world was tilted sideways, making her nauseous. She closed her eyes, hoping it would pass.

Trying to relax her breathing, Nita focused on pulling her thoughts together. She'd been kidnapped, that much was clear. The major question was: Was this a random kidnapping, or had she been targeted?

If random, then they would be holding her for ransom. And while her mother could pay the money, Nita thought she was more likely to track down the kidnappers and slaughter them. You didn't get to be a professional unnatural hunter without some detective skills.

If the kidnapping wasn't random . . . that would be bad. For them to have found her at the hotel, it meant they'd been watching Nita's apartment, tracked her to the hotel, and waited until her mother had gone. That implied some knowledge about who Nita and her mother were, and whatever these people wanted, they'd be suitably careful with Nita's mother involved.

A nasty thought tickled Nita's brain. *What if this is Mom's punishment?*

Nita shied away from that idea, not wanting to believe her mother would go that far.

There was a click of plastic against concrete, followed by a scraping sound. Nita forced herself to lift her head and locate the source. It was hard to focus, with everything splitting into two and combining all the time.

She managed to locate a water bottle a few feet away and crawl over to it. She unscrewed the sealed cap and then paused, wondering if it was drugged.

"Why aren't you drinking?" asked a voice. Female, with an unfamiliar accent to her Spanish.

Nita blinked, attempting to focus her vision on where the voice was coming from. There was a glass wall in front of her, and then there was another glass wall and there was a blurry pink-gray person on the other side. Nita closed her eyes and opened them again, hoping that would clarify things. It didn't.

Nita's voice was scratchy and hoarse. "Drugged?"

The girl snorted. "They don't bother."

Why? And who are "they"? Nita wanted to ask, but at the moment she had more important concerns. She was thirsty, and the confirmation that the water was safe was enough for Nita to start chugging immediately. After it was gone, she was still thirsty.

The water helped clear her mind where her ability couldn't, and her vision settled a bit. Nita was pleased that while a little blurriness remained, in general her sight was much improved. She was in the equivalent of a glass box, about six feet by six feet, with an eight-foot-high ceiling. One wall, the farthest one, was concrete instead of glass. Someone had painted it white, but running her hands across it, Nita was easily able to chip chunks of paint off. She knocked against the concrete. It was solid.

There was another girl in a similar glass box across from Nita, and there were several other empty glass boxes in the room.

The girl's skin was a grayish-pink that didn't look entirely human, but other than that she seemed normal enough on the outside. Her hair was long and straight, and the same color as her skin, as were her eyes. She had a small, flat nose and a square face with strong cheekbones.

"Who are you?" Nita asked.

"I'm Mirella. And you are?"

"Nita." Nita squinted at the other girl. She was wearing shapeless sweatpants and a baggy T-shirt, so it was hard to tell, but her voice sounded young. "How old are you?"

"Sixteen. You?"

Nita licked her lips and ignored the question. "What's happening here?"

"We're prisoners."

Well, duh. Nita resisted the urge to roll her eyes. This was why she hated people.

She continued her examination of the room while Mirella watched. It was good to move. Moving, doing things, analyzing her situation kept her calm. She felt like if she sat down and let her thoughts percolate more, she'd start to descend back into panic.

Panic wasn't productive. She needed to keep it at bay. If she'd been at full strength, she could have just suppressed all the chemical impulses that stimulated it, but she wasn't. So she had to do it with sheer willpower.

But her hands wouldn't stop shaking, no matter how she tried.

Focus on the room, Nita. Look at it. Can you escape? Can you use anything?

There was a mattress on the floor, with a single blanket on it. The floor sloped to a drain, and a ceramic squat toilet sat against the wall. Nita looked up. A showerhead stuck out of the ceiling, too high for Nita to reach. A white plastic tarp hung on a hook that had been drilled into the wall. Nita picked it up and looked at it.

"It goes around and hangs on the hook on the other side. It's like a shower curtain."

Nita turned to Mirella with a bitter smile. "It's awfully nice of them to give us privacy."

"Yeah, right." Mirella laughed. "It's so you don't get the futon wet. They grow mold super fast."

"I see."

Nita walked over and pressed her fingers against the glass in the front of her cage. It was cool to the touch, which made sense, since now that she was thinking about it, she could feel the air conditioning on full blast. She tapped it, but it felt solid. Then she rammed her whole weak, still-drugged body into it, and it felt even more solid.

Bruised and feeling a little stupid, made worse by Mirella snickering in the background, Nita sat down and examined where the water bottle had come from. There was a ceiling-high door in the glass wall, though there was no handle on Nita's side. Beside it was another, smaller glass door in the wall that connected to a box on the other side. It reminded Nita of prison movies, where they slid food in through little holes in the door. Except everything here was clear or white, not gray, like in prisons.

Sitting back, Nita felt another trickle of unease slide through her. This was a state-of-the-art facility—not the kind of thing she'd expect from random kidnappers. This felt more like the kind of prison you found in Bond movies or space-ships. Not real.

The point was — it looked expensive to build. That was a bad sign.

Nita clenched her muscles, trying to stop the shaking that had started in her hands and crawled up her arms and now spread through her body like a disease.

On the other side of the room, Mirella watched Nita. "There's no way out of the cage."

Nita ignored her. She could hear something. Voices? People, lots of people. It was muffled by the concrete walls, but it was there. It sounded like there was a gathering outside.

"Hey!" Nita screamed, banging on the concrete wall. "Let me out! Can anyone hear me!"

The voices didn't even pause in their conversations.

Nita took a deep breath to yell again, but Mirella inter-rupted. "You're wasting your breath."

"Why?" Nita spun around. "They can't hear me?"

Mirella looked at Nita like she was an idiot. "Of course they can hear you. They just don't care."

Nita paused, a slow, horrifying thought coming to her mind. "Mirella. *Where are we?*"

"You don't know?" Mirella looked baffled. "Everyone else who's come through here has always known."

Nita glanced at the empty cages, and wondered what had happened to these *everyone else*s.

No. Not a good thought. It made the shaking worse.

"Mirella." Nita's voice dipped cold, a subconscious imitation of her mother. "I have been unconscious for God only knows how long. I know *nothing*."

Nita didn't like the way Mirella's face twisted into an expression of pity and guilt.

"I'm sorry." Her voice was a whisper, and she wrapped her strange pink-gray arms around her knees. "We're in Mercado de la Muerte. Death Market. The biggest market for unnatural body parts in the world."

NINE

D EATH MARKET.
Nita had heard stories, and not just from her
mother. While her family operated mostly online, many of the
older, more established black market families still clung to the
physical market structure. They were of the opinion that you
had to see a product in person to ensure its quality. Especially
the people who sold living unnaturals — it was hard to ship living people in the mail.

The biggest physical market in the world used to be on the
East Coast of the United States. Nita had gone there as a child,
closely supervised by her parents. An INHUP raid a few years
ago had caused it to move, and she'd heard it was somewhere in
the Midwest now.

Death Market was somewhere along the Amazon River,
though Nita wasn't sure where. Definitely on the Peruvian
side, but close to the Colombian and Brazilian borders. People
would fly in to small airstrips in Colombia and Brazil and boat
down the river, crossing the border to visit the market for the

day. Or the night. Supposedly, the market offered a lot more than body parts.

Nita swallowed. This was bad. Really, really bad.

Nita was on the wrong side of the cage in a market famous for selling body parts of people like her, hundreds of miles away from anywhere familiar. How long did she have before they started cutting her up?

"There must be some people not part of the black market here." Nita's voice ticked higher as she spoke. "Police? A nearby town?"

Mirella snorted. "No, this town was constructed specifically for the black market. I've heard the market tried to settle in other places all over Latin America. People think they can just come to Peru or Brazil or wherever and throw their money around and do anything they want. But we won't put up with that. I heard last time, the market bribed the local governments and police so it could set up in the Andes, but a small farming town nearby found out what was happening and snuck in during the night and burned it all down."

Nita couldn't imagine it — people would never take action like that in the US markets. There, after the dealers bribed the shit out of the authorities, the locals just looked away and pretended nothing was happening. They didn't want to see the darkness, refused to believe that their country could have such an ugly underbelly.

They thought because the US was a "first-world country," they didn't have black markets or human trafficking.

Idiots.

Mirella waved her hand. "This town? The reason it's this

far out is so no locals can get to it to drive it away like before. And in Peru, if you clear the land in the Amazon and settle it, you own it. The market owns this town." She frowned. "This place isn't a town—I shouldn't call it that."

Mirella tilted her head, considering. "It's a shopping mall. And the only people here are the buyers, the sellers"—she met Nita's eyes—"and the products."

Nita opened her mouth to respond, then closed it.

She was so screwed.

A door opened somewhere nearby, and Nita paused, listening. The creak of the door ushered in the noise of the market outside, the crowded chatter of people, interspersed with laughter and shrieks. Underlying it, she could also hear other sounds, sounds she didn't recognize. A plop, like someone had dropped a raindrop on a megaphone. Caws of birds and a hum of what she thought might be cicadas.

Then the door closed with a clunk, and the sounds became muted. They were replaced with a new sound.

Footsteps.

Mirella's eyes widened, and her body seemed to shrink as she wrapped her blanket around her shoulders. Her long hair fell over her face, making Nita think of an ostrich sticking its head in the sand. If you can't see them, they can't see you.

Voices echoed against the concrete, one male, one female.

"That's my point." This from the male voice. "How am I supposed to do any of those things when I don't speak Spanish?"

"You'll manage." The woman's voice was clipped and cold.

As they approached, Nita startled, realizing that they were

speaking English, both with American accents. The man's had a hint of something East Coast in it, and the woman's had that slight upward tick that Nita sometimes heard in eastern Canada and parts of the Midwest.

There was a frustrated sigh from the man as they came around the corner and into Nita's view. They both stopped to appraise Nita, who stared right back at them.

The woman was wide. Not in the sense that she was fat — she wasn't, but she had broad shoulders and an hourglass figure just beginning to thicken with age. Gray streaked her severely tied-back brown hair, and her face was the mayonnaise-white that made it clear this woman rarely saw the sun.

In contrast, the young man standing beside her looked no older than his early twenties. He had warm brown skin, a wiry frame, and dark hair and eyes. Shorter than the woman beside him, and probably an inch or so shorter than Nita, there was something about the way his eyes flicked around the room, the way his mouth twitched like it wanted to half smile that felt *wrong* in some way.

"Well." The woman spoke, her expression remaining somewhere between neutral and bored. "It's awake."

Nita rose and tried to keep her chin high to hide her fear. She ruthlessly stopped the trembling her muscles were attempting and tried to limit the adrenaline, cortisol, and other fear hormones breeding like horny rabbits. She quickly gave up the task as futile. She let her hands shake.

The woman turned to the young man. "Go on then, Kovit."

The young man — Kovit — turned to Nita, and she took an involuntary step back. His eyes were dancing, and the smile that crossed his face was too excited, too happy, too crooked. He snorted when he saw her move and then rolled his eyes. "Relax, it'll be over soon."

He sounded disappointed about that.

The woman pressed a button, and there was a soft click as the door unlocked. Nita's eyes widened as Kovit approached.

"What are you doing?" Nita finally managed to squeak. Her voice was weak and stringy, full of terror.

No one bothered to respond to her.

Sighing with anticipation, Kovit pulled a switchblade out of his pocket. His eyes were soft, mouth slightly parted in a smile.

Nita didn't like that expression one bit.

He opened the door and watched as Nita took another involuntary step back. Behind him, the woman had pulled out and loaded a gun. She clicked the safety off, and then held it loose in her hand, waiting. Probably in case Nita tried to rush Kovit and escape.

She considered that option. The door was open. If she could get past Kovit and his knife somehow, and then dodge the bullets from the woman's gun . . . no. But what if she got the knife from Kovit and then threatened to kill him with it? Could she do that? Nita glanced at the woman's cold, bored expression and wondered if she would just shoot Kovit if it came to that.

This was all assuming Nita could overpower Kovit and steal his knife. Which was about as likely as Nita winning the lottery without a ticket, given both her complete lack of training and the drug still working its way out of her system.

Kovit took a step into Nita's cell, so his body blocked the

door. He gave her a lopsided grin and twirled his knife, eyes never leaving her face. He looked . . . hungry.

Nita's throat closed up, leaving her lungs burning for air.

Oh, God. What was he going to do?

One moment, Kovit was giving her a warped smile from a pace away; the next, he moved, snaking forward with an athlete's speed. Nita raised her arms to protect her face out of instinct more than anything else as she stumbled back. The knife lashed out, slicing into her arm and turning, so instead of going deep, it went wide. Like she was being skinned.

And it *hurt*.

Kovit gasped, whole body shuddering, a twisted smile of pleasure crossing his face. His knife moved forward, ready to strike again.

Shrieking, Nita immediately disabled all nociceptors and shut off her ascending pain pathways for good measure. The pain vanished—or at least, her ability to perceive it did. Nita's mother had told her how to stop pain when she was seven years old, and her father had told her it was better to turn off her pain receptors only in emergencies. Pain was there for a reason, and it shouldn't be ignored.

Nita fell on her butt and scrambled backwards, fingers scraping the cement in an effort to put as much distance between herself and Kovit as possible. Her whole body was rigid, waiting for the next attack, but it didn't come. Kovit was standing there, frozen. His grin had fallen, and his face had transformed. He no longer looked cruel—he looked scared.

"You stopped it." His voice was stunned.

Nita swallowed, her breath still choking her. She clutched

her arm, heart pounding in her chest like it was trying to break out and flee on its own. Blood spattered onto the floor. A chunk of skin hung from Kovit's knife. She redoubled clotting efforts. Her head throbbed in protest — she'd overused her ability today, and she still wasn't at full strength.

"Stopped what?" Nita asked, voice trembling.

Kovit's eyes were large and worried, his face tilted at an angle so that only she could see him. His voice was barely louder than a whisper. "You stopped the pain."

How the hell could he know that? Unless . . . "You're a zannie."

He scowled. "I hate that word."

She noticed he didn't deny it. Nita licked her lips, searching for an appropriate response. It didn't come.

This situation had gone from bad to worse. One of her kidnappers was a pain-addicted torturer. And it seemed like the woman was Kovit's boss.

Nita was so fucked.

Nita had almost forgotten the woman until she spoke. "Come out now, Kovit. You can play with it later. We have what we need."

Kovit backed out slowly, never taking his eyes off Nita, who lay curled on the floor. The door closed behind him, and the automatic lock bolted her cage closed.

The woman seemed pleased. "Look at how fast that wound clotted. It looks days old already. Exactly as promised."

Blinking, Nita looked down at her arm. She'd been repairing it as she watched the two of them, and indeed, it had scabbed over quite thoroughly. It was at the scaly, flaky stage of scabbing. A few more hours, and she'd be ready to start growing some new skin over it.

"Good job." The woman nodded at Kovit. "The angle is exactly what we needed. It's all on the camera."

Nita looked up at the small black ball with blinking red light in the top corner of her room. It would have had a perfect view of the attack, but never captured Kovit's face.

Kovit nodded, but his hair fell in front of his face, obscuring his eyes. Then he took a short breath, as though collecting himself, and turned to the woman with the wide, twisted smile Nita had seen earlier. "Oh, Ms. Reyes, it was my *pleasure*."

The woman — Reyes — twisted her face in disgust. "I'm sure it was."

Then she turned and left the room, leaving Kovit smiling at her back. When she was gone, his face resumed the thoughtful, anxious expression he'd worn earlier. He appraised Nita for a moment with dark eyes before following Reyes out.

After he was gone, Nita let out the breath she'd been holding. Her lungs felt scorched, like she'd been trapping fire. Her whole body shook with fear. The shaking got worse until Nita realized that she wasn't just shaking, she was sobbing. Her nose began to stuff up, and great gasping breaths caused heavy tears to cut their way down her face.

She tried to tell her body that it was having a delayed reaction, that the danger was over now, but it wouldn't listen to her. Wrapping her arms around her legs, she pillowed her face in her knees and sobbed until her shirt was damp.

It wasn't just that she'd been kidnapped, or that one of her captors was a pain-eating psychopath.

It was the fact that they knew what Nita was — knew that she could control her body, and were expecting it. Had clearly targeted her for it.

There were only three people in the whole world who knew what Nita could do — Nita, who certainly hadn't sold herself. Her father, who would never, ever betray Nita this way.

And her mother. Who'd promised Nita a punishment like nothing else last time Nita disobeyed her.

Nita felt a wretched sob curl out of her body. There was no other possibility.

Nita's mother had sold her to the black market.

TEN

NITA WASN'T SURE how long she cried. It felt like hours, but it could have been minutes. There was nothing to mark the passage of time, and even if there had been, Nita wasn't sure she was in a good enough state of mind to notice it.

How could her mother have done this to her? Sure, Nita had done something wrong. Yes, it had probably cost them millions. But . . . it was just money. It wasn't like they were broke. They had nearly a dozen bank accounts Nita knew about, and she was sure there were some she didn't. They'd been laundering and hiding money from their black market sales for years. They were not doing poorly.

Plus, her father had a real person job too, with a salary and tax forms and everything. Their finances were not in trouble.

What had her mother been thinking—that Nita would spend several terrifying days in captivity, learn her lesson, and then her mother would come rescue her?

Nita clung to that faint hope. It was exactly the type of punishment her mother would devise.

"Are you okay?" A small voice came from the other side of the room.

Nita turned away from Mirella. "I don't want to talk right now."

"I'm sorry. I should've warned you about the zannie."

"It's fine."

"Don't worry. Señora Reyes keeps a tight leash on him. Can't let monsters like that roam free."

Nita turned around to give Mirella a disgusted look. "Is that why we're in cages? Because monsters like us can't be trusted to roam free too?"

"No." Mirella rolled her eyes. "We're here because we're for sale. That's different."

For sale.

That's right, Nita was the one in the cage now. The one waiting for a sadistic monster to cut her ear off or tie her up to pull out her eye. Now it would be her blood spattering the walls, her screams waking people in the morning. The echo of Fabricio's pleas for help whispered in the back of her mind, and she wondered who she'd be begging for mercy.

Somehow, she doubted she'd get it.

Nita squeezed her eyes shut and curled up on her cot. All she wanted was to be alone with her thoughts. Mirella took the hint this time and let Nita lie down in silence.

She wondered what piece of her they'd cut off first.

Stop. Now. This isn't helping.

You want me to just ignore it?

A pause. *You're very good at that.*

She was indeed.

Nita imagined her dissection room. Her smooth metal dissection table was in front of her. There was a body on it—a zannie, like the one she'd dissected a few days ago, like Kovit. Nita approached and began procedures. She imagined the feel of the spoon in her hand as she scooped the eyes out. She imagined the texture of the heart through her gloved hands, placing it gently in a jar. Slowly, piece by piece, she went through the full dissection until there was nothing left unpackaged or unlabeled. Not even bones.

There. That felt better. She felt calmer, more in control now, ready to face the world.

Nita took a deep breath. She didn't know how far her mother would take the punishment, so she couldn't rely on her for rescue. Nita was going to have to break out on her own. Her mother respected that kind of thing. Maybe it would be enough to be forgiven.

And then you have a way out in case your mother never comes to save you, a small voice whispered in her head.

Shut up, Nita told it. *My father won't let that happen. He'd never have agreed to this. If Mom doesn't come for me, he will.*

"Are you feeling better now?" Mirella asked.

Nita looked over at the other girl. Lit by the fluorescent lights, her skin looked almost cracked, perhaps from the dryness of the constant air conditioning.

"Fine."

Mirella smiled softly. "No one's fine."

Nita sighed, leaning her chin on her hand. If the other girl wasn't going to shut up, Nita might as well try and get information. "So, do you know what time it is?"

"Nope." She shrugged. "Fluorescents are on all the time. Food is delivered whenever. I've never really noticed a pattern."

Great. Nita wondered how long it had been since she was taken. Had her father heard yet?

"So, Nita." Mirella gave her a sideways glance that seemed more appropriate for a high school drama. "Your Spanish is . . . interesting. Where are you from?"

Nita shrugged. "My dad's from Chile, but I lived in Madrid until I was six. I'm from . . ." Where was she from? She was born in Spain, raised in the States, Germany, Vietnam, and now Peru. She didn't really feel a pull to any of those places, though. Well, a bit to Chicago because her dad was there. "I don't know."

"Uhhh. Okay . . ." Mirella stared and then tactfully changed the subject. "So, I saw you heal. That's pretty cool."

"Not really." Nita eyed the pink-gray girl. She didn't really want to talk about herself with a stranger. "So, what's your story?"

Mirella shrugged. "You ever hear of the pink dolphins in the Amazon River?"

"Yeah. I've heard. Scientists still haven't figured out why they're pink. I read one thing that said they were pink because of the minerals in the water, and another that said it was because of how close their blood vessels are to the surface of their skin." She'd actually wanted to go to the Amazon River and see the pink dolphins. She'd asked her mother to go for her birthday, but her mother had refused. No reason given.

"Actually, they're like flamingoes. They eat certain foods, and they get pink. Different foods, and they're gray." Mirella spoke slowly, as though to a toddler. Nita wanted to slap her. "But I was referring to the legend."

"No."

"Well, there's an old legend among the people who live along the Amazon River." Mirella settled herself, crossing her legs and tilting her head high. "A pale man in a hat will walk into a village, and try and sweet-talk the girls. If he manages to lure one away, he takes her back to the river to be his bride, and drowns her beneath the water."

Nita frowned. "Isn't that mermaids? The drowning?"

"It's both," Mirella admitted grudgingly. "The more popular version of the legend says the dolphins just get women pregnant and then leave the next morning. But I like the drowning one better."

Nita had to admit she did too.

Mirella resettled herself. "*But* if you take the pale man's hat off, he reveals his true form — a dolphin. Then he flees into the river and escapes to hunt for brides in another town. They say his shoes turn into catfish, and his belt is an eel and . . . Well, they say a lot of things."

Nita blinked. "So you can turn into a dolphin?"

"Of course not," Mirella snorted.

"Then where is this going?"

Mirella crossed her arms and scowled. "I was trying to give you background."

"Yeah, but that's just a legend." Nita tried to keep the irritation out of her voice. "I was interested in the facts. What are you?"

"I'm a human," she snapped. "Just like you."

Nita sighed.

Mirella continued to pout. "My pigmentation is like dolphins, though. I change color depending on my diet. Those stories were based on legends about my people."

Nita leaned against the glass wall of her prison. "Can you do anything else besides change color by eating?"

"No."

"No other adaptations?" Nita wasn't holding out hope for it. Skin color changed because of ingestion of carotenoids in food, and while prominent examples included flamingos, humans, especially babies, could also do this to some extent. She'd read about babies that turned yellow-orange from eating too many carrots, and the mothers always seemed to think it was jaundice. When Nita was much younger, she'd tried to change her own coloring, but found it was more complicated than she initially thought, especially since she already had a lot of melanin naturally in her skin tone.

She hadn't tried since, though she thought she might be able to manage it now. When she was twelve, it had seemed cool to be an artificial chameleon, but she just didn't really see the point of it now, especially since it wouldn't be terribly useful.

"Nothing I know of."

"That's useless."

Mirella glared. "Can you do anything besides heal yourself?"

Nita paused. Her mother could enhance her own muscles, give herself a strength that was almost superhuman. Could Nita?

How would she go about doing that? Could she cause muscles to build faster by artificially training them? And she wanted to speed up the process more, so maybe she could synthesize the effects of steroids. Her head began to pound as she worked — not hurt, because she had no pain receptors on, but pound, like there was a loud bass music only she could hear. It warned her that she'd been overstretching herself today, that she still had traces of a sedative in her blood. But Nita kept pushing, until she could barely lift her arm for all the muscles.

Then, stumbling to her feet, she swung with all her might at the glass wall.

It reverberated, but didn't break.

Three of Nita's fingers did.

Nita fell backwards and landed on her butt. Hard. She looked at her fingers, snapped, and her wrist, with torn tendons needing repair. If she could feel pain, that would probably have hurt a lot. Well, that was an unforeseen advantage to Kovit's presence.

Sighing, she used her other hand to set her broken fingers in the right positions.

Maybe she should have learned how to throw a punch first.

She groaned and leaned back against the glass and cut off the steroid synthesis. Then she relaxed her muscles, let the chemicals reabsorb. Her skin rippled as her artificial muscles faded back into her body. Clearly, this wasn't the answer.

Mirella stared at Nita with wide eyes. Nita ignored her.

Nita closed her eyes for a while, breathing. God, she felt awful. She shouldn't have tried that. She might not be able to feel pain, but she could still feel exhaustion, nausea, and the sensation of her bones grinding against each other in her broken fingers.

She groaned. She didn't even have the energy to mend her fingers.

There was a clunk as the door to the facility opened, followed by the click of footsteps on concrete. Mirella shrank under the blankets again.

Nita cracked her eyes open as Kovit came down the hall. He was carrying two plates of food and had bottles of water tucked under his arms.

He went to Mirella's cage first and slid the plate of food through the box in front of it. It looked pink — was he feeding her shrimp? That seemed decadent. But they were probably trying to keep the pink pigmentation to her skin for sales purposes. That was the sort of thing Nita's mother would have done.

Then he moved to Nita's cage. He placed the tray in the box and closed the door, which triggered a lever that opened a door on Nita's side. It was a clever little mechanism, so both doors could never be opened at the same time.

Nita reached in and pulled the tray out. Then she realized it wasn't a tray, but a large piece of bread that was hard enough to act like a tray. On top of the bread were a few spoonfuls of beans, some shredded chicken, and rice. There was no plate or cutlery.

The tray snapped closed, and Nita pulled her food close.

"Thank you." The words were automatic, out before she could catch them.

Kovit blinked, as though surprised she'd said anything.

Nita cleared her throat, then continued, "I was wondering —there's a shower mechanism here. How do I turn it on?"

She regretted the words almost as soon as they were out of her mouth, because Kovit's eyes focused on her in a not-entirely-sane way. His expression said he found something both hilariously funny and sort of sad at the same time. Nita had a feeling it was her. She didn't like it.

But she really, really wanted a shower.

Finally, he responded, flicking a hand as though to dust her question off. "You can't."

"Oh."

He continued to watch her, head tilted slightly to the side, expression unreadable. "But I can."

Nita tilted her head to one side.

"I'll be back."

Kovit turned and left, and Nita watched him go.

After a moment, Mirella, still wrapped in her blanket, leaned forward and whispered, "You *talked* to him!"

"Yeah. You haven't?"

"Of course not." Mirella swallowed, squeezing her eyes shut for a moment before whispering, "He's a monster."

Nita wasn't going to contradict that. "I wanted a shower. I won't get one if I don't say anything."

Mirella picked up her food and began nibbling it. "You're mad."

"Possibly."

Ten minutes later, Kovit returned. He had a towel in his hands, as well as a folded pair of sweatpants and an oversized T-shirt. Nita sat up in the cot, silent with surprise as he dropped them into her food box and slid them through.

"I'll turn it on in two minutes, and then off ten minutes later."

He turned to leave, and Nita called out, "Thank you."

He paused before rounding the corner and looked up at her with those dark, slightly crazy eyes. And smiled.

It was not a nice smile.

Nita matched it with her own smile, thinking of the zannie on her dissection table. She imagined sliding the scalpel through his flesh, how there would be resistance, and then it would come easy once it had parted. Like the surface tension of water.

Kovit laughed, a more genuine, less harsh sound than she'd expected. Then he gave her a crooked grin that, while still ever so slightly crazy, didn't seem to have any menace in it.

"You're welcome."

ELEVEN

NITA WANTED TO take a long, leisurely shower. But the water was ice-cold and, combined with the constant air conditioning, made for an unbearable situation. She hopped in and out of the water for a while, before biting the bullet and just showering cold.

Shivering, she dried off and put on her new clothes. But she was still cold, so she wrapped the towel around her hair and curled up in her blankets. She wished they'd turn the air conditioning off.

Nita almost forgot about the wound Kovit gave her until it started trickling blood on her cot. She examined it. It was about three inches by two inches in size, but not deep at all. Really, it was just the skin peeled off. Nita almost admired how expertly it had been done. It took a lot of skill to skin a moving, struggling person so cleanly. Kovit must have had a lot of practice.

That was not a thought Nita wanted to pursue.

Shuddering, she lowered her arm, careful of the wound. On a normal person, an injury like that would take several months to heal fully. Whether it would scar or not depended on the person. If Nita focused on it, she thought she could probably have it cleared up in another day or so. She'd make sure it didn't scar.

She settled herself on her bed, careful of her broken fingers, bleeding arm, and injured wrist. She couldn't feel pain now, so there was a danger she'd damage them by rolling over in her sleep. She briefly considered turning her pain receptors back on to avoid further accidental damage, but discarded the thought before it had even fully formed.

First, turning them on would hurt. Nita had only turned them off once before in her life, when she'd been in a car accident and sliced her arm open. But turning those receptors back on had been the most painful thing she'd ever done in her life. It was like her body had completely rediscovered pain and had to make sure every pathway was working.

She'd never felt pain like that before or since. She wasn't eager to repeat it.

That led her to the second reason. There was a zannie in the building. As long as Kovit was here, it was in Nita's best interests to keep all pain functions off. If she kept them off, she hoped he'd be less tempted to torture her.

For a moment, her mind flashed to the anxious expression on his face when her pain receptors clicked off. Why anxious? Anger or frustration, Nita could understand, but anxiety? She felt like she was missing something.

Well, she probably wasn't going to figure it out now, sick, injured, and head muzzy with exhaustion.

Nita let her eyes drift closed, blanket and towel wrapped around her, and slept.

She woke up sometime later. There was food waiting for her, bread and beans and chicken, like last time. Nita nibbled on it. Across from her, Mirella dozed.

Nita sighed, leaning back and watching the younger girl, glad she was asleep. Mirella annoyed Nita—she seemed to represent everything about people that Nita found annoying. Bratty, whiny, and helpless. Of all the people in the world Nita could have been stuck in a cage with, why did it have to be a snotty sixteen-year-old?

She rested her head against the glass, and focused on healing her body. First, she welded the bones in her fingers together, knitting them until the breaks were fully fused—they weren't healed, per se, but more like three weeks along in the healing process instead of eight hours. The tendons in her wrist were trickier, but when she was done, they were mostly healed. And she got her body to start growing new skin on her cut.

Nita rose. Now that her body had been taken care of, she'd slept, and she'd eaten, she could start thinking of a real plan to get the hell out of here.

She wasn't planning to get out through the glass walls now —she'd learned her lesson. It might have been possible for her to get out that way by enhancing her strength, but she simply didn't have the training to know how to make proper use of that strength.

The food door was too small to crawl through, even if she could make it open on the other side. The walls of her prison went up to the ceiling, which was around eight feet high.

So the only way out was through the door that opened from the outside.

If they opened her door again, did Nita have anything she could fight them with? She glanced around. A cot. A towel. A blanket. Could she strangle them with the towel?

Nita snorted. Not likely. How would she even get it around their neck?

She sank down, restless and bored. There was a weird sense of tension. She knew something was going to happen soon—she could *feel* it—but until it happened, she just had to wait. And Nita hated waiting.

She supposed she could talk to Mirella.

Ugh.

As if on cue, the girl stirred and woke. "Morning."

"Is it?"

"I dunno."

Nita sighed. Was there anything useful she could get out of Mirella?

"How long have you been here?" Nita finally asked.

"Around two weeks, I think." Her voice was soft.

"And have there been other prisoners?"

Mirella stiffened. "Yes."

Nita waited for her to elaborate. When nothing came, she prompted. "What happened to them?"

Mirella looked away. "Can we change the subject?"

Nita didn't like that response. Not at all.

"Have you ever been to Iquitos?" Mirella jumped in before Nita could press the issue.

"No. Where's that?"

"Upriver. Northern Peru." A small smile crossed her face. "It's my home. It's the most beautiful city in the world. My brother thinks it's backwards and wants to move away, but I wouldn't trade it for anything."

Nita blinked. "Brother? Is he . . . like you?"

"No, I'm the only one"—she waved an arm, gesturing to herself—"like this. My mother says my great-grandfather was too, but he's been gone a long time. My cousin was also like me, but she disappeared when I was young."

"Ah." She'd never considered the idea that Mirella had a family. It seemed an obvious thing, but for some reason, Nita was surprised.

Mirella wrapped her arms around her legs. "I miss my family. My parents. My cousins. My grandparents, especially my grandma. Her family, the side with the dolphin genes, they're from the Brazilian part of the Amazon. She always wanted us to take a barge back to her hometown for a visit, but we never have . . ." She blinked a few times and smiled softly. "I even miss my stupid older brother. He's always showing me all these pictures of other cities he wants to move to. I think he can recognize any city in South America now, even though he's never left Iquitos."

Nita cringed as Mirella hid her face in her hands. She was glad for the glass barrier between them, otherwise the other girl might expect her to hug her or something equally unpleasant.

Nita sighed and wondered what it would be like to have a family like Mirella's. She didn't actually want one—she'd seen enough telenovelas and sitcoms to be glad she didn't have to deal with that. But sometimes she wondered about her parents.

Her father had told her he was from Chile, but he'd never say where. When she was younger, it had been a challenge to figure it out. Spanish had such intricate regional dialects she'd been sure she could narrow it down by how he spoke. Nita recorded every idiom, every turn of phrase, hoping one day she could take these fragments of pieces to build an outline of the puzzle that was her father's origins.

It hadn't worked. There just wasn't enough information. His accent was too influenced by his years in Madrid. He'd never told her bedtime stories that weren't from Barnes & Noble. He never took her to church, even though he went himself every Sunday.

She'd always wondered why he hid his life from her. When she Googled the history of Chile, she found a sea of disturbing information about the years he was growing up, after a CIA-sponsored coup d'état put a dictator in power. She wondered if something so awful had happened he couldn't talk about it.

As for her mother . . . Nita always had the impression she'd just sprung out of thin air fully formed. And if her mother had a family, Nita wasn't sure she ever wanted to know.

Shuddering, she turned away from her thoughts and the quietly crying girl in front of her. Lying back, she looked up at the blinking security camera.

"Mirella."

"Yeah?" Her voice was soft.

"Do you know who watches the security camera?"

She shivered and whispered, "Kovit."

Nita raised her eyebrows. "All twenty-four hours a day?"

"I dunno."

Useless.

Nita looked up at the security camera again, considering. Then she rose and began waving wildly, gesturing for someone to come.

The light blinked steadily on.

"What are you doing?" Mirella yelped.

Nita ignored her. Heart racing, she waited.

She wasn't really sure why she'd done it. But there was something about the way Mirella had mentioned Kovit being on a tight leash and the implication that he was always on security duty that made Nita wonder how much freedom he had. And, more importantly, how bored he was.

On the one hand, having a zannie—especially a bored zannie—around was not ideal. However, he knew she could turn her ability to feel pain off now, so he probably wouldn't hurt her when he was hungry—but if he just liked to hurt people even if he didn't get food, she was screwed.

On the other hand, if he was bored, maybe he'd be willing to talk and she could fish for information.

Besides which, if she kept her requests small and innocuous, maybe she could keep getting things. A book and a towel by themselves were harmless. But a book wrapped in a towel was like a brick in a purse—a decent weapon.

He didn't come.

Nita told herself she should be relieved. It would be creepy if he were sitting there, watching her on the security camera all day. That wasn't something she wanted. She should take it as a good sign. Unless he was just ignoring her.

96

Sighing, she sank back on the bed, frustrated and bored. Mirella hid under her blanket.

A soft scuff was the only warning she had before Kovit walked into the room. He tilted his head and raised his eyebrows at her in amusement. "Did you want something?"

Nita blinked. "Um."

He put his hands in his pockets and watched her. She opened her mouth and closed it a few times.

"Did you wave me down here to admire me?" He laughed, and his smile turned into something mean and playful at the same time. "Or something else?"

Nita didn't like that smile one bit. It sent her heart skittering in fear and her hands twitching for her scalpel. She swallowed, trying to find the words to speak. They wouldn't come.

Kovit sighed and turned to leave, and Nita finally spoke. "Were you watching me on the camera?"

He snorted. "Someone always has to be watching the damn camera."

Nita wasn't sure if that was a lie or not. Probably not. But it being Kovit all day wasn't believable. So more than one person watched the camera. Good to know.

She held an image of her dissection table in her mind, using it as an anchor to calm her breathing and stay focused.

"I'm bored." Good, her voice didn't crack in fear too much.

Kovit glanced over at Mirella, cowering under the blankets. "You have company."

"She's—" Nita paused before she could say something rude, then something occurred to her. "Does she speak English?"

Kovit snorted. "Not a word. It's very annoying, since I don't speak Spanish."

"Ah." Well, that meant she couldn't understand Nita and Kovit's conversation. "Well, she's not exactly great company."

Kovit laughed, sharp and cruel. "And you want me to, ah, do something about that?"

Nita did *not* like the way he said that, full of dark and twisted implications. His eyes seemed to laugh at her, as though he could read her mind and knew exactly where her thoughts had gone, and he approved.

"No. I was wondering if you had anything to read."

"Nothing good." Kovit ran a hand through his hair and gave her one of his crooked smiles. Nita couldn't pinpoint what was wrong with the smile. It wasn't that he didn't look human, and it wasn't that the movement of the muscles in his face was altered, but there was something just . . . *wrong* in the way he smiled.

It creeped her out.

Nita licked her lips. "What about board games? Cards?"

He shook his head.

"Well, I guess a bad book is better than no book, then." Nita gave him a shaky smile.

He gave her a long look. "I'm not sure you'll say that after you've read it."

"I like to form my own opinion. I try not to judge before I read."

"Everyone judges."

"Fine. If I go in thinking it's bad, I'll be pleasantly surprised when it's decent."

He laughed, a short, surprisingly light sound. Then he shrugged. "All right. Sure. I'll bring it over."

"Thanks," Nita said, but he was already gone.

He came back five minutes later and slid a small, beat-up paperback into her food tray. Nita pulled it out and checked the blurb. It was one of those theory books on unnaturals, and supposedly provided in detail explanations of all the leading ideas.

"It doesn't look too bad."

"That's what I thought. Then I read it."

"Ah."

Nita put the book down, silent. Kovit lingered for a moment, watching her. He shoved his hands back in the pockets of his jeans.

Swallowing, Nita made a gamble. "You look like you want to ask me something."

He tilted his head so a few strands of his bangs fell in his eyes. It looked charming. Nita wasn't fooled. "I was wondering about the pain. You turned it off."

"Yes." Nita raised her eyebrows. "Wouldn't you have done the same in my situation?"

"Absolutely."

His answer was much faster and more decisive than Nita expected. He saw her surprise, and the corner of his mouth twisted upward. "I do know what pain feels like, you know."

"I'm sure you know exactly what it feels like," Nita agreed easily. Wasn't that the point? Zannies could feel other people's pain and eat it. She imagined it felt slightly better for them than it did for the person they were torturing.

Kovit rolled his eyes. "You do know zannies can't feed on their own pain, right? It just hurts us, like normal humans."

Nita hadn't known that, but she just gave him a long, cool look. If he was trying to look sympathetic, he was failing. There was plenty of pain in the world already—he could just go sit in a hospital emergency room to find it.

"Well, it makes them all the more monstrous, then." Nita was surprised how even her voice was. "After all, if they know exactly how it feels to be in pain but they still choose to inflict it on others for their own pleasure . . . well, that's worse than if they didn't feel pain at all, isn't it?"

She didn't expect Kovit to laugh. But he did, and it was long and light, almost like a child's laugh. He treated her to one of his too wide, crazy smiles as he said, "I completely agree."

With that, he turned on his heel and left.

Nita stayed where she was on the floor, trying to convince her body to move. But something about his laugh, his smile, had frozen everything in fear. Instead of the fight-or-flight response to terror, Nita had gotten the freeze response.

After a long mental session at her dissection table, she managed to crawl over to her bed with the book.

Kovit was right. It was awful.

TWELVE

NITA PUT THE truly awful book down. She was only halfway through, even though she'd received it yesterday and had nothing better to do than read. It was because she kept flinging it away in disgust, then getting desperately bored and reading another chapter, only to fling it away again.

It had started out fine. It was going to outline a history of how unnaturals were explained at different periods in time. It talked about how the Catholic Church had coined the term "unnatural" in the eleventh century because they thought unnaturals were the spawn of demons breeding with humans. Which of course was ridiculous, and the book acknowledged that.

And it covered the Church of the Resurrection, a modern spinoff of Christianity that believed Jesus had been a vampire, and was still alive and would return to save them. They had a very literal version of the Eucharist.

But then the book decided to explain its theory: alternate realities. The book was trying to tell Nita unnaturals had come from another world and then interbred with humans.

Aside from the obvious questions — How would something from another world be genetically compatible with people from this world? How did they cross between universes? And where the fuck was any evidence of this shit? — Nita wanted to know who this book was funded by. These things were always advancing someone's agenda.

She'd heard about a big lawsuit recently, where a major fur company had paid researchers to publish scientific papers claiming chinchillas were unnaturals. They were hoping it would reduce public backlash on chinchilla fur farming.

Nita looked down at the next chapter. It was all about the ghoul controversy. Ghouls, who needed to eat human flesh to survive, had been flagged as a possible species for the Dangerous Unnaturals List. Until a major incident three years ago where a family of ghouls had been stealing bodies from a crematorium — not killing people, the media liked to point out. The son of a person "cremated" found out what was going on and took a machine gun to the whole family while they were eating his dead father for dinner. The court case was a mess.

But ghouls hadn't ended up on the list. Because that one well-publicized family had proven that they could live without killing people and that there were ghouls doing exactly that.

They were the opposite of kappa in the media.

A string of prominent murders, mostly of children, in rural Japan decades ago had thrust river-dwelling kappa into the world's eye. At the time, it had just been another unnatural murder, not worthy of too much publicity. But a few years later, the story was made into a popular horror movie, *Watering the Kappa*. Suddenly, kappa were a thing. Everyone knew about them. People put pressure on INHUP, and next thing anyone knew, kappa had made the Dangerous Unnaturals List.

Nita had done quite a bit of kappa study and dissection and wasn't sure she entirely agreed with that assessment. Yes, kappa lived on human organs. Their saliva contained a chemical that liquefied organs, which they would then slurp up like a soup. But nothing in their biology that Nita had discovered indicated that they couldn't eat cow, pig, or any other kind of organs either.

They just chose not to.

The creak and clunk of the door opening to outside distracted Nita from her thoughts. The sounds of the market filtered through, the hum of voices, punctuated by sharp laughs and shrieks. The caws of an angry bird rose as though it were approaching the open door and then faded as it passed by.

Nita paused, edging closer to the glass wall of her prison. There were voices — multiple voices, mixed in with the clomp of boots and the thunk of a heavy door closing. A gravelly laugh, a nasal snort. Definitely not Kovit or Reyes.

Nita listened as the footsteps drew closer, and felt slightly uneasy. That was a lot of footsteps. What did this mean? What was happening?

Across from her, Mirella pressed herself into the corner of her cage, her fingers curled against the floor.

"Mirella?"

But the girl didn't respond, her blanket wrapped tightly around her body.

Nita edged to the back of her cage.

"This way." Reyes' voice, short and clipped.

The *clack-clack-clack* of boots on the cement flooring felt like a drumroll as a tall man rounded the corner. For a moment, the silhouette looked like her father, and Nita licked her lips, wondering if he'd come to rescue her.

Then the man turned and she got a good look at him—pale, dark blond hair, mild sunburn. Definitely not her father.

She pushed away the rush of disappointment. How long did her mother plan to leave her here? Nita was beginning to have a fluttery feeling whenever she thought of her mother, like the butterflies in her stomach got caught in her throat when they tried to escape and choked her. It was fear, not unlike the way her heart skipped in terror when Kovit walked into the room.

A fear that this was permanent. That her mother had no plans to save her. That Nita had finally pushed her too far, and the only purpose Nita had left was to make her mother some money to atone for the fortune she'd lost freeing Fabricio.

But even though the little voice in her head kept hissing that she'd been abandoned, Nita was reluctant to believe it was true. Not out of any logical reason, but just because she didn't want to believe it.

Nita was very good at ignoring truths she didn't want to see.

Reyes walked beside the blond man, trailed by two men in identical white shirts and slacks. Sweat stains under their armpits attested the reason for the constant air conditioning. One of them was tall and sniffling, and kept touching his cheek and then looking at his fingers. The other was short and square, as though his whole body had been built around Legos.

Bodyguards? But for who — Reyes or the man? Reyes hadn't had bodyguards before, but then again, she hadn't been escorting strangers in either.

Nita barely noticed when Kovit slunk in after everyone else.

The man turned to Mirella's cage. He flashed a smile that gleamed like the polish on his black business shoes. "Hello, little one. Remember me?"

He spoke in English with the standard American accent, no hint of regional intonation slipping in.

Mirella stayed huddled under her covers, not moving.

The man *tsk*ed, and then said in clipped, heavily English-accented Spanish, "Ah, I forgot. Well, it's nice to see you again."

Mirella's lips pressed into a thin line and her jaw clenched, but she didn't respond.

His smile didn't change, but his gaze was flat and cold. "I have to say, I've been looking forward to seeing you again. I was too busy with the others earlier to give you the attention you deserve."

Mirella flinched, and Nita wondered if this man was what had happened to all the previous tenants of the cages.

Reyes raised an eyebrow. "I've heard it's bad form to play with your food, Boulder."

The man — Boulder — chuckled. "But that's half the fun."

"If you say so." Reyes' voice was bored. "Which part are you interested in?"

Boulder smiled, his eyes running over Mirella and lingering on her face, the curtain of hair only partially masking her toxic glare. "I've heard if you look at the person you want through the eye of a dolphin, they'll fall in love with you."

Reyes nodded. "I've heard that legend too. Do you have someone you'd like to fall in love with you?"

He snorted. "Of course not. But I have to wonder what kind of power eating an eye like that would give you." Then he grinned with bleached white teeth. "And eyes are such a delicacy."

Nita stared, frozen, as a small, light butterfly crawled up her throat and choked her. How could she have not seen this coming? She knew people liked to eat certain unnaturals "fresh." The same kind of people who ordered pieces of Fabricio.

Mirella turned around, but didn't respond. She just bared her teeth, but Nita could almost see the magma just beneath the surface of her skin, waiting to erupt.

Nita was surprised by how fast her heart raced. She was scared. Not for herself, but for Mirella. For what this man wanted to do. Nita didn't even like Mirella—but whatever was about to happen, she wouldn't wish it on anyone.

Then Boulder turned to Nita's cage.

Nita's heart stopped. He wasn't going to . . . she wasn't going to—

"What's that one?"

"Ah." Reyes smiled, teeth showing. "That is our latest acquisition. It arrived yesterday. It can heal itself. We've posted the video online. Have you seen it?"

"Ah, yes, I heard. There's been quite a bit of chatter." Boulder raised one hand and rested it on the glass of Nita's cage. "Tell me, have you removed any parts of its body to test their effects?"

"We're analyzing the composition of some of its skin now, but we haven't removed anything else yet."

Wait. Yet?

"Of course." He shifted to stare at her. "You think that some of these healing properties will transfer themselves over when her body is consumed?"

Consumed.

"We believe so, yes, based on how other unnatural flesh interacts in humans. However, we have no conclusive proof."

Consumed.

They were going to sell Nita off to be eaten.

"What about cutting parts off? Can it regrow severed body parts?"

Reyes smiled. "We're monitoring the progress of an injury it's healing. We hope to gain relevant data from how it heals, and potentially extrapolate."

Nita's heart slammed in her chest, and she opened her mouth to say she most definitely could not regrow severed body parts, but her throat was too tight, and nothing came out.

"Hmm. I'd love to see a demonstration."

Reyes' eyes flicked to Kovit, and her voice turned cold. "Go have fun."

Kovit gave the woman an impassive, bland face. No twitching smile, no crazy eyes. It made him look almost normal—tense, but normal.

The blocky bodyguard pushed the button to unlock the door, and the sniffly one hovered threateningly. Just in case Nita decided to run past Kovit and make a break for it? Not likely. Not with that many people.

Nita's eyes returned to Kovit. He'd pulled his switchblade out and opened the door. While last time he'd come in, grin wide with anticipation, this time there were circles under his eyes like he hadn't slept, and he seemed dissatisfied with the whole affair.

He was probably unhappy he couldn't make her scream. She had no sympathy for him.

Kovit took a step toward Nita, and she backed away.

He stopped, arms falling to his sides. "Are we going to do this the easy way or the hard way?"

Nita licked her lips, glancing around the room. "What are my options?"

"Option one: you hold out your arm, and I cut you." Kovit twirled his switchblade and gave her a half grin. "Option two: you struggle until Reyes' men hold you down, and then I cut you."

That wasn't much of an option. Nita held out her arm.

The switchblade was fast and sure across her skin. A piece of skin came off with his knife and stuck to the blade. Blood welled up and began a slow slither down her arm from the cut. Kovit took a step back. Everyone outside the cell turned their attention to Nita's cut, waiting.

After a minute, Boulder turned to Reyes. "Why isn't she healing?"

Reyes looked to Kovit, who shrugged and said, "Ask her."

Turning her attention to Nita, Reyes smiled. "You're slowing your healing on purpose, aren't you?"

Nita didn't respond.

Reyes' smile remained firmly in place. "I see. You don't like the little demonstration. But you see, I need you to be a good girl and heal it up. If you don't, I'm afraid things will get . . . unpleasant."

Nita's gaze flickered to Kovit.

"Oh, no, don't worry about him. He's not reacting to you, which means you can't feel pain, can you? I bet you can turn that ability off. Clever girl." Reyes folded her hands behind her back and took a pace forward. "I'm sure pain won't motivate you. But you see, there are a great many other things that will."

Nita watched, wary of her smile. What did she have planned? If she couldn't hurt Nita, what would she do? Nita resisted the urge to let her eyes flick to Boulder.

Reyes turned to Kovit.

"Cut her fingers off. We'll see if they grow back."

Nita's body stiffened, and her mouth was moving before her brain had time to connect to the words. "I'm healing. Right now. See, look — healing."

As she spoke, her mind was already focused on clotting blood, knitting skin back together. The wound dried up and scabbed over. It slowly began to close, and within five minutes, the shallow cut was a thin red line on her arm.

Boulder hissed in pleasure. Reyes' smile had never left her face. "Good girl."

Nita tried to swallow her fear, but couldn't, because it was leaking out her eyes.

"How much?" Boulder asked.

"We're hoping to auction some pieces later this week. There

are a great many buyers interested, and several already have plans to fly out and view it. You're welcome to participate in the auction."

He took a step forward and brushed his fingers over the glass wall that separated him from Nita. "Would you be willing to sell me that fresh strip of skin?"

"For yourself?"

"Yes." He licked his lips, turning his attention to the piece of skin on Kovit's knife.

Reyes considered. "You know how valuable this one could potentially be. It won't be cheap."

"Name your price."

"I want the name of your contact in the FBI. The one you bribed, who made the human trafficking charges against you disappear."

Boulder pursed his lips, eyes narrowing. "Very well."

Reyes nodded to Kovit, and he held out the knife. Boulder strode over and plucked the strip of skin off it.

And ate it.

It was gone in one swallow, Nita's blood not even touching his white, white teeth. "Immortality awaits."

A piece of Nita had just been eaten.

She hadn't really thought about the part of being kidnapped where they made money. Part of it had been a childish belief that she would be rescued before she had to worry about it, or maybe even escape on her own. But the bigger part, she had to admit to herself, had known what all this meant, but hadn't wanted to acknowledge it.

After all, this was Nita's job. Except this time, she was the one lying on the dissection table.

Someone, maybe this man, maybe someone else, was going to buy her. Then they were going to drink her blood, cut out pieces of her, and see what happened. Certain unnatural body parts had properties. Kappa body parts were a deadly poison. Zannie body parts could be used for pain relief and as an anesthesia. Unicorn bone caused people to get high.

What would pieces of Nita do?

This man at least seemed to think they'd give him immortality. Nita wasn't so sure about that, but it seemed plausible. Plausible enough that she was sure an awful lot of other people would be interested to find out as well. And see how extensive her powers were.

Nita felt nauseous. Someone was going to cut her up and eat her. Boulder had already started. Was this some sort of karma?

No, you can't think like that. They were already dead when they got to your table. You couldn't have done anything else, her mind insisted.

Yeah, and when there was a live captive, you set him free, another voice agreed.

Why, you're a regular saint! a third chimed in.

Is it healthy to have this many voices inside your head? Nita wondered.

"Time will tell." Reyes pursed her lips, examining Mirella and then turning to Boulder. "I'll have my people remove the eye here and bring it to you. In the meantime . . ."

Boulder nodded, eyes never leaving Mirella. "I'll have my people bring the money. Same as last time. And I'll get you the name and contact details."

"Excellent. We'll bring it to your office."

Boulder tore his eyes from Mirella long enough to shake hands with Reyes and leave.

His footsteps echoed on the concrete as he departed. The sound of the door opening hadn't even registered before Reyes swung over to the sniffly bodyguard. "Lorenzo."

Lorenzo turned to her and swallowed. "Yes, Señora?"

She glared. "Look at me when I'm speaking to you."

Reyes switched to Spanish easily, and it sounded just as smooth and native as her English, though it was an accent Nita was unfamiliar with.

Lorenzo swallowed and looked up.

Reyes' eyes narrowed. "You've been sampling the product."

Nita could see it now. His pupils were dilated, and his breath came too fast. His sweat glittered like tinsel.

He was high on powdered unicorn bone.

Nita was surprised to see someone using unicorn bone here. It was more of a problem in Europe and the States—unicorns were from western Europe, after all. After Nita's mother had cleared out hundreds of unicorns while they were living in Germany and the US, she'd flooded the market. It had lowered the price of the drug to something affordable, and now it was considered a major epidemic in several states.

Her mother was holding on to a huge stash, waiting for the product to become scarce after the glut of new addicts so she could parcel it out, bit by bit, for crazy-high prices.

"Ah . . ." Lorenzo looked away.

Reyes' voice dropped low and cold. "If I ever see you using while you're on the job again, I'll give you to Kovit. Understood?"

Lorenzo's eyes went huge, and he nodded, body shaking slightly as his eyes flitted to Kovit, who smiled at him with undisguised hunger. Finally, he lowered his head and whispered, "Yes, Señora."

"Good." Reyes turned away and waved her hand at the two bodyguards. "Bring the girl to the workroom."

Lorenzo pressed the button on the wall, and Mirella's cage buzzed open. As they stepped in, Mirella screamed and threw her blanket at Lorenzo, and then tackled the short, blocky guard.

He stumbled backwards, howling, but Lorenzo grabbed her arm, tossing the blanket off, and smashed her against the glass wall. He twisted the arm behind her back and pulled until she howled. But still she struggled, kicking backwards at him, tears making her face squeak as it slid along the glass.

Nita met Mirella's eyes, saw the rage and panic there. Reyes nodded to the guards, and they dragged Mirella out, still struggling.

Tears rolled down Nita's cheeks as Mirella's screams echoed through the building. Her throat closed in on itself. She fought between the desire to cry out for all of this to stop, and the urge to stay quiet and invisible so Reyes wouldn't notice her.

Silence didn't save Nita from Reyes' attention. She examined Nita with a cool eye. "Are you upset about your cellmate?"

Nita's jaw clenched. "Her name is Mirella."

"So it is." Reyes smiled slightly, and made to walk away, but paused. "Ah. There is the matter of your troublesome display."

Nita stiffened.

"Kovit, I gave you an order."

Wait. Reyes couldn't mean . . . No. This wasn't happening. She'd done what Reyes told her to!

Her breath coming in harsh gasps, Nita stumbled back, remembering Fabricio's screams as her mother sliced off his ear. Nita imagined herself screaming as her fingers came off one by one and Boulder popping them into his mouth like mozzarella sticks. She thought she might simply die of terror from the culmination of everything she'd seen. She'd heard about that happening to people. If ever there was a time in her life, now would be it.

Kovit blinked and looked up at Reyes. "She can't feel pain."

"So? What does that have to do with cutting off her fingers?" Reyes raised her eyebrows.

Kovit shifted, clearly uncomfortable. Reyes laughed and turned to Nita.

"I'll give you a choice. You can either lose three fingers, or you can turn your pain back on and let Kovit have his fun for an hour. It's up to you."

Kovit and Nita stared after Reyes as she strode after Boulder and the bodyguards, and then Kovit turned to her. Nita skittered to the back of the cage.

What a choice. Be tortured or lose your fingers.

Nita thought about it for a moment, but the conclusion was an easy one to come to.

"I'm not turning my pain circuits on." Her voice trembled.

Yes, she would lose her fingers. And she didn't dare even attempt to grow them back—not that she even thought she could—because Reyes might get ideas. But she had no guarantee Kovit's torture wouldn't do more damage than just losing her fingers. Besides, they were planning to cut her up anyway. Reyes had just said so—they were selling pieces of her. If it was going to happen no matter what, why would she also add torture to her list of horrors to endure?

More important, if Kovit thought he could threaten her into turning her pain circuits on, what was to stop him from doing it again? He could threaten to do almost anything to her if he thought she'd turn her pain circuits back on. She didn't dare give him that kind of blackmail.

Kovit looked at her for a long moment. Nita met his gaze head-on, trying to summon the bravery to go through with her choice.

He sighed and pocketed his knife. "I wouldn't in your situation either."

He left her cage and locked the door behind him. Nita stared at him for a moment. "You're not—"

"No."

He watched as she collapsed onto the ground, beginning to sob in great heaving breaths and rocking. Nita knew she should do or say something, but she'd been so *scared*. And now that Reyes was gone and Kovit was out of the cage, all she could do was cry in remembered terror.

Then Kovit left, his passage marked by the distant screams of Mirella as she was dragged away.

THIRTEEN

KOVIT BROUGHT HER meal and a bottle of water at some point, but Nita didn't touch them, too terrified he'd change his mind and cut off her fingers like Reyes wanted. Her body shook—she couldn't seem to stop it. Not even when she went and tried to calm the muscles, tried to stimulate hormones for happiness and relaxing. Nothing helped.

Her mind simply couldn't seem to stop whirring, desperately attempting to process events. What had happened. What was going to happen. It was one thing to be locked in a cage. Nita was familiar with the black market—she knew how the processes went. In a sense, the situation felt familiar, even if the roles were reversed. More unnerving, like looking at a picture that looked slightly off but you couldn't pinpoint why.

This, Nita realized with a sudden, painful clarity, this was what the black market really was. Her mother had in some ways protected her, kept her away from the messy, living parts of it. Nita had only seen the aftermath, the bodies. And those were easily taken apart and forgotten.

She thought of Fabricio, screaming, body curled in the fetal position because he couldn't stretch out, fighting as her mother hacked away at him. How many people who ended up on her dissection table had experienced that? How many had her mother tortured for information, trying to find more potential victims? Had her father known and participated? Casually cut off the fingers of those who wouldn't cooperate?

Nita buried her face in her sweatpants, letting the fabric soak up the moisture even as the air conditioning dried it right off her face. She had spent her whole life aiding and abetting this industry. Cutting up bodies and shipping them off. And she had enjoyed it.

Her fingers twitched, reaching for a scalpel that wasn't there. If someone had put a body in front of her and asked her to dissect it, she would still have enjoyed it. It was too integral to who she was now. She liked cutting people up.

She didn't want to stop.

But when—if—she ever got out of here, she'd never be able to work in the black market again. It was a slow, sad realization. Memories of smiles shared between her parents, dissections to Disney songs, and brushing sweaty hair out of her face after labeling the last jar of the day took on a dark tint. The memories didn't feel happy anymore, overshadowed with the knowledge of what had gone into them.

Eventually, she managed to cry herself to sleep.

Her dream started out well. Nita was standing in her white lab coat, and there was a body on the dissection table in front of her. Sighing in familiar pleasure, Nita picked up the scalpel and began the first incision. She worked at it for a time, taking out body parts, weighing and labeling them. Then she went to scoop out the eyes.

The body had Kovit's face.

His eyes were closed, but she didn't hesitate to pry them open. It was the fuzzy way of dreams that all she could think at the time was she was dissecting a zannie, and everything was fine. But then she scooped his eyes out and took a closer look and found that they were golden-brown.

They were her own eyes.

The face on the table was Nita's face, and suddenly she was seeing the room through the eyes dangling from her hand. Except it wasn't her hand anymore, it was an older woman's hand and when she looked up, Reyes smiled back.

Nita woke screaming.

Thrashing around on the cot, she kicked off her blanket and clutched at her hair, as though she could pull the dream right out of her skull.

Her screams eventually faded into sobs as Kovit ran into the room, wearing black sweatpants mismatched with a button-up pajama shirt. His hair was mussed from bed, but his eyes were wide and nervous as they flicked around, trying to see what was panicking Nita.

He hesitated. "Nightmare?"

Nita nodded, not trusting her voice.

Kovit looked at Nita, but she turned her face away, wondering what kinds of things he'd done to Mirella before Nita came here. Maybe that was why Mirella had been so scared of him.

He didn't say anything, just padded away and left Nita alone again.

That was okay. She liked being alone.

Or she had. Now there was an empty space across from her where Mirella had been. She still hadn't returned.

Nita was surprised when Kovit came back a few minutes later. He looked even more tired, if that was possible, with tight lines around his mouth and heavy bags under his eyes. But he gave her one of his characteristic, slightly-off grins that made something inside her wriggle with fear.

Maybe she was becoming accustomed to him, though, because this time she didn't feel quite as scared. Or maybe fear was like tears. Once you cried too much, it was hard to cry more. So if you were permanently scared, you just became numb to it.

He plopped himself down cross-legged in front of her prison box, the stupid device through which she was being fed every day. He took a stack of pieces of paper tied with an elastic band out of his pocket. Snapping off the elastic band, he began shuffling.

"What kind of card games do you like? Poker? Big two? War? Solitaire?"

Nita stared at the small pieces of paper in his hand. "Did you make those?"

Kovit laughed, showing her a card. It was a badly cut out piece of printer paper with a heart and a three scrawled in ballpoint pen. "It didn't take long." He continued shuffling. "Let's play poker."

Nita nodded, not trusting her voice. Her throat felt scratchy and rough. He passed her cards through the food tray, and Nita picked them up with unsteady hands.

She put the cards in her lap and looked down. "Why are you doing this?"

"I'm bored." His voice was flat. "There's no internet and no books. Reyes only lets me have a cell phone from the dinosaur age with her number in it, and I hate going outside in this shit-hole market."

Nita didn't respond.

Kovit sighed. "I thought you might be bored too. Shall I leave?"

"No," Nita whispered, for the first time in her life wanting company, even if it was a psychopath. "Let's play."

She ignored his victory smile. It was too creepy, too hungry, for her to look at.

They played a few rounds in silence. Nita lost most of them. She hadn't played much poker before. As they continued, she started to do progressively better. They played in silence for a long time before Nita finally felt like she could speak.

"So . . ." Nita tried to think of a conversation topic. Since she had Kovit here, she felt like she should fish for information. But for the life of her, she couldn't think of a single thing to say.

He raised his eyebrows and smirked. "Yes?"

"You haven't cut my fingers off."

"No."

"Are you going to?"

He was silent for a long time. Nita raised her eyes to find him watching her. She shifted in discomfort.

"No," he finally said, looking over his cards.

When he didn't continue, Nita fidgeted. Part of her told her to drop it—she didn't want to push. What if he changed his mind? But the rest of her wasn't smart enough to listen, so she asked, "Why?"

He shrugged. "It seemed like a waste. All that pain and suffering, and no one to benefit from it."

Nita stared at him. "You didn't do it because you couldn't eat it?"

"Of course." He looked away.

Nita licked her lips. "Liar."

He laughed. "Maybe. I do lie."

"Everyone lies. That's not saying anything."

"Exactly."

Nita shoved her losing hand back through the food tray device thingy.

"Well, whatever your reason. Thank you." Nita brushed a hair out of her face. "I didn't expect that kind of thing from a zannie."

Kovit scowled. "I hate that word."

"You mentioned that before." Nita folded her hands in her lap and watched him. "Why?"

"It's one of those Englishisms that really annoy me."

"Oh? That's not what you're called?"

Kovit shuffled the cards and shook his head. "It's from back in the eighteen hundreds when European countries were

121

doing all these land grabs in Asia. The British had what's now modern Malaysia and Singapore, and the French took over Vietnam and Cambodia. Thailand, called Siam at the time, worked hard to remain independent, both politically and militarily. To make a long story short, there was a 'zannie' who, uh, enjoyed the conflict. No one's sure whether she was hired by the Siamese government or not. I dunno myself, I think there's a good case either way."

Kovit gave her a tight smile. "Anyways, the French nicknamed her 'Sang'—which means blood." He shrugged. "Someone along the line miscommunicated the nickname to the British, and it became 'zannie.'"

"I never knew that." Nita shifted position. "So what are zannies really called?"

He hesitated. "There's a debate. I mean, these days because zannie is what INHUP calls them, it's sort of a standard. But some people say we're actually *krasue*."

"What language is that?"

"Thai." He brushed a hair out of his face. "But there's names in other languages. *Kasu* in Lao and, uh... *ahp*? In Khmer. I think the Malaysian name starts with a *p* sound, but I can't recall it right now."

Nita folded her cards on her lap. "I've never heard these names before."

"You wouldn't." He shrugged. "I mean, traditionally, those names only refer to women."

"Oh?"

"Well, people thought that *krasue* were floating women's

heads with a bunch of internal organs hanging down. They left their bodies behind and came into town and ripped unborn children from their mothers' wombs, eviscerated people, ate their flesh, you know." He smirked. "Some people say it was just 'zannies' who went a little overboard back in the day and used to loop people's digestive tracts around their necks like scarves."

"That's unsanitary." Nita cringed at the mess.

Kovit laughed. "Not disgusting?"

She shrugged. They were just organs. "So why did people think there were only women *krasue*?"

He winced at her pronunciation. "Because the men joined whatever army or dictator was around, or even outlaws and such. In other words, groups where . . . the kind of behavior we exhibit would, uh, not be uncommon. I guess we blended in." He snorted. "But there were no career paths open to women that could explain them torturing people. So people tended to notice more when women came into town eviscerating people than when men did the same thing."

"Interesting." She wondered how many other oral legends about unnaturals had been blurred or warped because the lens they were being viewed through was wrong. She pursed her lips. "But this is all a theory."

"Yes."

Nita tilted her head. There was something in the way he said it that made Nita think it was more that he *wanted* to be connected to these legendary monsters than any real evidence he was.

She could understand that. There were no traditional legends about whatever she was. She didn't even have a name. None that she could find, anyway. She'd always felt a little jealous of all the legends and hype surrounding vampires, and the near reverence that Chinese dragons received. There was something appealing about belonging to a tradition like that, being included in something with so much history and culture.

"How popular is the theory?"

"Somewhat." He shrugged. "Some people think *krasue* are a different species entirely. One that's been very good at keeping off INHUP's radar or blaming other unnaturals for their . . . messes."

Kovit's smile seemed to conjure images in Nita's imagination of what those messes would look like.

She shoved them aside and changed the subject. "So, you speak Thai?"

"Yes."

"First language?"

"Mm-hmm."

"Were you born in Thailand?"

"Yes. I lived there until I was ten."

"Then what happened?"

Kovit stopped shuffling the cards and put them down. His fingers lingered on them. "My mother was captured by INHUP and executed."

Nita blinked, opened her mouth, and closed it. She'd lived her whole life in fear of INHUP, worried they'd come and arrest her parents, take them away to be charged with crimes against humanity or some such thing. She imagined them as towering men in dark suits with glasses, blank stony faces devoid of sympathy as they tore apart her life.

If she ever got out of this cage and got cell phone service, they were the first people she'd call.

She wished they were here right now — or even better, that she'd gone with Fabricio when he left Lima to meet up with them. She wouldn't even have minded if they arrested her mother anymore.

Well, maybe a little.

"I'm sorry." Nita hugged her knees to her chest and rested her chin on them. "I guess your mother was a zannie too?"

"Yes."

"How did they catch her?"

Kovit raised his eyebrows, and his mouth formed into a twisted smile. A self-deprecating, I'd-love-to-comfort-torture-you smile. "I called them and told them about her."

Nita stared at him. "What?"

He shrugged, but she could see the tension in his shoulders. "I called them. My sister was furious. She hid me under the floorboards of the house so INHUP wouldn't find me."

"Wasn't your sister worried about herself?"

He snorted. "Hardly. It's not like she's a zannie." Seeing the surprise on Nita's face, he continued, "It's a recessive gene, like blond hair. My mom had it, and I got it. But my father was human, so my sister didn't end up like me."

Nita wondered what it would be like to grow up in a household where half the people were zannies and half weren't. She couldn't imagine zannie children were nice. Had little baby Kovit toddled around stabbing his father in the shins and ripping his sister's hair out?

Actually, that probably wasn't too different from other children.

"Where's your sister now?" Nita asked.

"No idea. I haven't seen her since INHUP took her away." His voice was casual, but she had a feeling he'd been closer to his sister than to his mother. Since he'd called the police on one and the other had protected him. "I was ten so that was . . . ten years ago?"

Nita wasn't sure if she was supposed to express sympathy here, or how to express it appropriately. "I'm sorry."

He waved it away. "It was a long time ago."

Nita hesitated, wondering if she should let the topic drop. But she wasn't sure if Kovit would ever talk about himself like this again. She wasn't sure why he was talking now. "Why did you turn your mother in?"

Kovit met her eyes. His were black, iris and pupil, and seemed to go on forever. It was like looking into a well leading deep into the earth. You could fall in if you wanted, but at the bottom, there'd only be a painful landing followed by a slow, agonizing death.

He smiled. It was charming. Nita was more terrified of it than his creepy smiles. Then he deftly changed the subject. "What about you? Who betrayed your trust and turned you in?"

Nita dropped her eyes and looked down, a sudden stab of hurt slicing up through her rib cage. She pressed her nose into her sweatpants and whispered, "My mother."

126

"Sorry? I couldn't quite hear that."

Nita raised her chin, almost defiant. Her voice didn't even tremble. "My mother."

"Ah." His smile fell, and he just looked tired. Even more tired than before. "Mothers, eh? Never like the movies portray them."

Nita had to laugh at that, just a little. It was a sad laugh, but it was something.

They played a few more rounds of cards before Reyes interrupted them. Kovit rose and went to her immediately when she walked into the room.

Behind Reyes, the two bodyguards from earlier dragged Mirella between them. Her feet stumbled as she walked, and her gaze was fixed on the ground. A large patch of white gauze covered one eye. Or where one eye had been.

Kovit hissed softly as she passed, his eyes slitting in pleasure. Nita felt sick.

Mirella was deposited back in her cell, where she curled up under her blanket. Reyes nodded to the men, and they departed. Then she turned to Kovit.

"We have the first group of customers coming in to see our newest product."

"Now?" Kovit sounded surprised.

"Yes." Reyes turned and smiled at Nita. "I'm sure they'll be very interested by the demonstration we're going to provide." Then she looked back at Kovit. "I see her fingers are still attached."

"She opted for torture."

"You don't look like you ate much."

Kovit shrugged, and Nita wondered how Reyes could tell. "I ate when you left. That was hours ago." A small, twisty smile snaked across his face. "Though if you want me to eat more, I'd be *delighted* to oblige."

Reyes smiled. "Good. I was hoping you'd say that."

Kovit brightened. "You have someone?"

"After this batch of customers, I have a treat for you."

Watching Kovit's face was like watching a child opening an unexpected present. First surprise, then disbelief, then growing excitement as Reyes' words penetrated, until a huge grin plastered itself across his face. His eyes danced with madness.

"All mine?" Kovit pressed, leaning forward in anticipation.

"For an hour or so. *After* we get through this demonstration."

Reyes turned and walked away, waving for Kovit to follow.

Kovit stood there for a moment, staring after her. Then he turned to Nita, ratcheted up his grin a few notches, and gave her a slight, almost mocking bow. "Thanks for the entertainment. But I'm afraid dinner awaits."

Then he spun around and half skipped, half walked away.

FOURTEEN

"Mirella, are you okay?"

Mirella lifted her head up in the cage on the other side of the room and gave Nita a poisonous look. It highlighted how puffy the skin around her eyes—eye—was from crying and the sickly grayish tint to her skin. The white gauze seemed to stare at Nita.

"What kind of stupid question is that?" she snapped. Then her voice lowered into a cold hiss. "One day, I'm going to kill him."

Nita blinked, but couldn't think of anything to say in response. Mirella didn't seem to expect anything and proceeded to curl up under her blanket. Nita was beginning to learn that bad things always happened when Mirella pulled that blanket over her.

The voices Nita had heard earlier rose, and Reyes and Kovit reappeared a few moments later, along with the two bodyguards and four other people. One was a tall woman whose face was veiled by a mosquito net—ever hopeful, Nita wondered if it was her mother, but was quickly disappointed to see it wasn't. Her voice was too breathy, and she didn't walk right. There were two older men with rheumy eyes and wrinkled skin in polo shirts and slacks. They whispered to each other in French and ignored the other people.

The last person was a vampire.

Despite Nita's lack of familiarity with vampires, she knew one when she saw one. His hair was brown, but there were bold streaks of perfect white—an unnatural white that shimmered slightly and shifted colors in different light. It looked like he had a weird brown baby zebra on his head. Nita had heard it was impossible to dye the white part of a vampire's hair, that the dye didn't stick, but also that young vampires didn't have a drop of white in their hair. They could walk in the sun, and they were insanely strong, to the point where taking on a baby vampire was considered to be a form of suicide in some parts of the world. As they aged, their hair began to get white streaks in it. The more white streaks, the weaker they became, and the less tolerant of sunlight. It was a tradeoff—the oldest vampires were close to crippled, unable to move or even feed themselves sometimes, but they had to be crafty to live that long. They tended to like heading organized crime—then they could maintain their power and have other people do their dirty work.

Nita wasn't sure how old Zebra-stripes here was. Vampires could live around seven hundred years before their bodies became too frail with age and they died. Based on the amount of white in his hair, Nita decided this one was probably older than a hundred, but less than three.

Arguably, the most dangerous time to be near a vampire. Still strong, but with experience and cunning the young ones lacked.

When the vampire moved, there was no sound. There was something smooth, almost liquid about his motions, as if instead of joints, he had water. He flowed. Almost like a dancer.

It didn't look natural in the slightest.

Nita didn't realize she'd started backing away until her shoulders pressed against the wall. She folded her hands in front of her to hide the tremor. Not that anyone in the room cared.

"This is it?" The woman waved at Nita, but her face was turned toward Reyes.

She gave the veiled woman an insincere smile. "Indeed. Would you like a demonstration?"

"Please."

Kovit came into Nita's room, and she held her arm out, mute. She'd learned her lesson. She wouldn't defy Reyes in public again.

Afterward, the woman in the mosquito-net veil turned to Reyes and clapped her hands together. "A superb display."

One of the older men nodded. "Indeed. I hadn't quite believed — you know how good video editing can be these days."

Reyes gave them all a small smile. "Of course. It's no trouble. Perhaps we can retire to my office and discuss this creature. No one has ever sold anything like this before — it's completely unique. We haven't even taken samples yet."

Pleased murmurs accompanied this.

Suddenly Zebra-stripes the vampire was in front of her cage. Nita hadn't even seen him move. One second he was beside the woman in the veil, and the next he wasn't.

"What's your name?" he asked in English.

Nita blinked. "Me?"

"Yes. You."

She hesitated, wondering if this was some sort of trick. "Nita."

His eyes were pale, irises almost fading into the whites. "Nita."

She didn't like it when he said her name.

"Tell me, Nita, have you met other people with the same ability as you? A relative? A friend?"

Nita didn't respond. The only person she knew of with the same ability was her mother. But she certainly wasn't going to tell him that, even if her mother had betrayed her.

"I'm sorry." Reyes took a step forward. "If you wish to question the subject, you'll have to purchase her first."

Zebra-stripes turned around slowly to face Reyes. It was a deliberate movement, not unlike a horror film, where the head keeps turning until it goes all the way round. Zebra-stripes' didn't turn 360 degrees, but Nita was no less creeped out by it.

"How much?" His voice was soft, almost friendly.

Reyes' smile never faltered. "We can negotiate."

The other people in the group made noises. They weren't going to let Nita go to someone else easily.

Zebra-stripes paused, then turned back to Nita in that same slow motion. "Tell me, have you ever met a woman who goes by the name Monica? She may have called herself something else. She's white, about five foot seven. Last I saw her, she had chin-length black hair with red streaks. She has the same ability you do."

Nita felt a chill make its slow, deliberate way up her spine, like there was an army of ice ants crawling up her back. Nita's mother occasionally went by Monica, among other names. And the description fit to a tee. Though really, any description with brightly colored hair and makeup would have. Her mother liked to make herself distinctive, so that when she actually needed to disappear, no one could remember anything about her except her hair color.

Nita's face must have shown something of recognition, because Zebra-stripes flashed her a smile. "Tell me, what do you know about Monica's current whereabouts?"

"I'm afraid you've been warned." Reyes nodded to her guards, who each took a step forward. "If you wish to speak to the merchandise, you'll have to buy it."

Zebra-stripes moved. One moment he was pressed against the glass of her cage, and the next he was in front of unicorn-bone addict Lorenzo. It was the same as when he'd come to her cage. Nita couldn't follow his motions.

They were prepared for vampires, though. As Zebra-stripes approached, both guards turned on flashlights that had been hanging in their belts. Under the UV light, Zebra-stripes let a slow hiss out through his teeth and took a step back, into the shadows. Nita had a brief glimpse of the sudden blistering burns that had developed on one side of his face, like melted candle wax. On the other side of the room, Kovit also hissed, his eyes turned up to the ceiling, body rocking with ecstasy. Nita had to look away.

"You were warned." Reyes linked her fingers together.

Zebra-stripes glanced at the flashlights, still on, though not pointed at him. Nita could almost see him calculating his odds. Then he turned his head and looked toward the hall, clearly thinking of some other factor outside. The sun? Or maybe leaving once he killed everyone.

Zebra-stripes came to a decision. He inclined his head ever so slightly to Reyes and said, "Of course. We can discuss purchase options."

Reyes held out an arm to indicate the door. "Shall we depart, then?"

Zebra-stripes cast one last look at Nita, clearly wishing to break into her cage and shake some answers out of her. But then he turned away and disappeared down the hall.

Trembling, Nita sank to the floor, feeling like she was sinking deeper and deeper into some quagmire of disaster with every hour.

A vampire was hunting her mother. He'd come all the way out here on the chance that Nita might have some information. His voice, when he spoke of her mother, promised the kind of horrors only a vampire—or maybe Kovit—could deliver.

What had her mother *done*?

How many of her mother's sins was Nita going to have to pay for?

Nita wrapped her arms around herself, feeling the grief, the betrayal at her mother grow and morph into something different. How *dare* she sell Nita? For one mistake? One act of defiance?

Nita had thought her mother loved her. Believed it. Believed no matter what, they were family.

Lies.

Anger flickered in Nita's soul, hot and all encompassing.

When next we meet, Mom, you better beware. I don't forgive.

The guards returned to the cell block and took Mirella out. Nita lifted her head and scooted forward. Mirella just looked at them, tired, and didn't fight. For the first time, Nita wondered if she'd been drugged. Her arms were limp, and her gaze was unfocused.

"What are you doing?" Nita snapped, pressing her hands against the glass.

Lorenzo looked at her, wiping his nose. His pupils were still dilated, but his sweat wasn't tinsel-like anymore. Dark circles nestled under his eyes. He ignored her and turned to the other guard. "Jorge, can you close the door?"

Blocky Guard—Jorge—left Mirella in Lorenzo's arms and closed the cage door.

"Where are you taking her?" Nita repeated, pressing her fists against her sides.

"The workroom," Jorge answered absently.

Nita felt her stomach contents shift. That was where they'd taken her to remove her eye. "She's going to be cut up again?"

He shook his head. "Nah. But she fought back against Señora Reyes and one of her clients. They even had to put her under to remove her eye. That never goes unpunished."

"Too true," Lorenzo whispered, shivering.

135

"What will her punishment be?" Nita asked.

The guards looked at each other. Lorenzo looked vaguely sick, and he kept rubbing his nose, but it was Jorge who spoke. "Kovit, of course."

They dragged Mirella off, and Nita remembered Kovit's delight and excitement at the promise of someone to torture after the customers left. Nita hadn't thought it would be Mirella.

A few minutes later, the screaming started.

FIFTEEN

THE SCREAMING SEEMED to go on forever.

Nita sat curled on her cot, trying to cover her ears, but nothing she did blocked out the noise. The screams were often punctuated by sharper, higher screams or lower, broken sobbing howls. Nita wasn't sure if Mirella wept that loud or if the sounds were coming in through the ventilation. Sometimes, the screaming would stop for a brief respite, and Nita would hear wretched, choked weeping, interspersed with hiccups that sounded more like cries for help.

Nita thought she might be going mad imagining Mirella thrashing as Kovit—no, Nita didn't want to think of the specifics of what Kovit might be doing. Bad brain. No.

Sometimes, even if the real-world Mirella stopped screaming, the echo of her cries lingered in Nita's mind until she couldn't tell which cries were real and which were just her mind supplying her with memories.

One thing, however, became crystal clear to Nita: Kovit was a monster.

Oh, she'd known that. She'd been scared of him. But

knowing and seeing—or hearing, in this case—were two very different things. She'd allowed herself to relax a little around him, even if subconsciously. He'd saved her from being mutilated; he'd played cards with her.

And he was torturing Mirella in the other room.

If Nita hadn't turned off her pain receptors, that person would have been her.

It wasn't as hard as Nita thought to reconcile the two images. After all, her mother used to take her to rides on her birthday and chase her around the house spraying her with Cheez Whiz. But her mother also killed people and then sold them.

Sold Nita.

People were never just one thing. Nita had let herself get lulled by the less monstrous side of Kovit, if only a little.

The screams echoing through the building corrected that for her. So did the laughter that accompanied them.

Nita had stalled long enough: it was time to leave, no matter what the cost. She'd been waiting to seize an opportunity, but it was clear to her that she was going to have to make her own.

Nita needed an offensive move. She closed her eyes and focused. She simulated the effects of being struck on different parts of her back and neck, trying to find the spot that would cause her opponent to fall with the least effort. Knocking someone out was notoriously difficult, and how long they stayed out for could be unpredictable. Nita wanted to eliminate as much of the danger as possible, so she practiced on her own body and healed it. What would happen if you hit someone there—would it cause them to collapse, or did you need to do something that would cause permanent damage in order for it to be effective?

Her limbs gained and lost feeling in a repeat pattern as Nita damaged and repaired her spine and head. Soon everything had a strange, tingling feeling to it, like a mild version of the pins-and-needles sensation that came when you got feeling back in a numb limb.

At some point, the sounds changed, as though Mirella's throat had been damaged from overuse, and the noises she made were closer to scratchy gasps than screams. Each time Nita heard one, she imagined the pressure of the scream ripping the skin of her throat until it bled. That was just what it sounded like.

Nita cried at one point. Not sobs, just sad tears that leaked out of her eyes as she stared at the ceiling.

Nita decided to make a weapon. At first she thought she might be able to make a knife out of the paper from the book — if paper cuts were sharp, could she make something equally sharp, but sturdier?

She couldn't. Maybe an expert could have figured something out, but Nita was no expert.

Then she tried doing something with the plastic water bottles. It took ages to bend the plastic enough that it snapped so she could rip a good-size hunk out. It was kind of sharp, but not really. And it was bendy and pretty flimsy. Still, if she made the blade super short and held tight to her "handle," she might be able to get a solid jab in.

Not likely.

Nita examined her blanket. If she twisted it up, she could

use it like a noose. But it would be really obvious she was up to no good if she had a twisted roll of strangling blanket in her hand at all times. Ditto to folding the book up in the blanket and fashioning a makeshift mace.

But still, they were options.

Nita closed her eyes and wished she had a scalpel and a dead body. What she wouldn't give to be in her workroom, taking someone apart piece by piece. She wanted to feel the press of the knife on skin, the weight of the organs in her hands, trace the curvature of the ribs in the gaping chest cavity. She wanted the single-minded clarity that came when she was dissecting, that state where she could forget about everything and only focus on the task at hand.

When Kovit came back with Mirella, Nita was shocked by his changed appearance. He *glowed*.

Not literally. He wasn't bioluminescent or anything. But everything about him just seemed to shine. It was like when pregnant women got all those random hormone glands working overtime and they always looked unnaturally beautiful and healthy. Better hair, better skin. Kovit was like that.

The dark circles under his eyes were gone, and the tired lines were smoothed out. His hair, which hadn't been anything special before, looked like the kind of hair that should be in a shampoo commercial.

Nita realized that Kovit probably hadn't eaten since before she came. Had he been starving? She had no way to know when his last meal had been. How often did zannies need to eat pain anyway? How much pain did they need — she knew it was a lot, but how much was "a lot"? How did you even quantify something as subjective as levels of pain?

Not that his hunger excused anything. Especially with the clear, maniacal glee he took in hurting people.

Mirella was walking on her own, but Kovit held tight to her arm. She stumbled, favoring one leg. Nita couldn't see any obvious physical marks on her, and she seemed to have all her body parts, which was a relief.

Nita hoped Mirella would take the opportunity to break away from Kovit. He only had her by one arm, and there wasn't anyone else there. But one eye was glued to the ground, and the other was leaking blood, and she sagged.

Once she was back in her cell, she curled up underneath her blanket and didn't move.

"Kovit."

Nita's voice was soft, and it came out hoarser than she intended.

He turned to her, and the contented smile on his face fell. His jaw tightened, and his shoulders tensed, as though he expected Nita to challenge him. She could almost see him bristling, ready for a fight.

"Can I have some water?"

He blinked, fists unclenching and hands falling loose to his sides. He hesitated, eyes running over Nita, confused. "Sure."

While he was gone, she used a piece of broken plastic bottle to wedge her food tray shut. She wiggled and pushed at it, but there was no way the little door was working.

Kovit returned with a water bottle. He tugged on the tray,

and when it didn't open, he kicked at it in frustration. Then he looked to Nita.

She made a show of tugging and pulling from her side, but then raised her hands in defeat. "I think it's broken."

Kovit's brows drew together. "We'll have to move you to a different cell while we repair it."

"Oh."

He moved to leave, and Nita's heart stuttered. He wasn't supposed to leave now! That was *not* part of the plan. "Wait, Kovit!" He turned back and Nita pressed her palms to the glass. "My water."

Blinking, he looked down at the water bottle in his hand. He examined her cage, his face tight, clearly considering.

Come on, Kovit, I know you want to give me the water. You're not that type of monster—you won't deny me. Torture me maybe, but deny me water, no.

He sighed. "Fine. Back of the cage, hands where I can see them."

Nita did as ordered, dragging her feet in her blanket so it came with her, fighting back her grin.

Kovit buzzed the door so it unlocked and pushed it open.

Nita didn't even wait until the water bottle was in the air before she moved.

Kicking up the blanket from the ground, Nita threw it in front of her as she powered forward. The blanket half landed over Kovit, obscuring his view and mobility. He flailed, arm reaching to tear it off.

Nita launched herself on top of him, arms wrapping around Kovit and trapping him in the blanket. It looked like a child's attempt at a ghost costume with a sheet, except some-one forgot to cut the eye holes. Nita pumped her body with adrenaline, tightening her bear hug as they both fell.

Kovit hit the ground hard and grunted as Nita landed on top of him. His hands scrabbled to remove the blanket, even though his arms were pinned. Nita heard the swish of a switch-blade release mechanism, and her heart rate sped up. He must have had it in his pocket.

Kovit's head reared out from the blanket, and Nita finally struck.

Swinging her arm around, she clocked him in the temple. He cried out, turning his head away and stretching forward, giving Nita the perfect angle to smash the knuckle of her middle and index fingers into Kovit's vertebrae. She was glad there were no differences in spinal structure between zannies and other people, because if there were, she would have been screwed.

He went instantly limp, paralyzed. Permanently or tempo-rarily, Nita didn't know.

Nita stumbled over him, terrified the blow wasn't strong enough to immobilize him for long. She nearly fell on the ground as her feet caught in the blanket while she launched herself out of the cage. She clawed at the door and slammed it shut, trapping Kovit inside.

Nita stood there for a moment, breathing. Kovit lay in a puddle on the floor, blanket still half covering him. Behind her, Mirella's face pressed against the glass, eye wide in shock.

Nita had done it.

She was free.

SIXTEEN

NITA STOOD THERE for a few moments after her escape, just breathing.

You actually did it. Nita's inner voice sounded shocked.

Nita's heartbeat smashed in her chest.

Kovit didn't move, and Nita's throat began to tighten, making it hard to breathe. She hadn't wanted to kill him.

She peered closer. Her shoulders loosened and her chest unclenched. Kovit was breathing. His chest rose and fell in the slow, deep rhythm of sleep.

She closed her eyes, swamped by relief. She wasn't a murderer yet. But then again, if he were dead, she could have dissected him.

"Hello? Nita."

Nita spun around. Mirella's whole body was pressed against the glass as though she could push through it like a ghost. Her pink-gray hair was tousled, and she was licking her dry, cracked lips. Her eye was bloodshot, and combined with her pink iris, made her eye look like it was bleeding color, like a runny watercolor painting.

"Are you going to let me out or not?" she rasped.

"Oh, right." Nita went to the control panel she'd seen Reyes use to release the locks before. There was a line of buttons, small and black, with numbers beside them. She found a small white number painted into the concrete beside Mirella's cage and pressed the corresponding button.

The cage door clicked open, and Mirella slipped out. She padded over to Nita's cage, leaning heavily on one leg, and looked in. "Is he dead?"

"No."

"Good."

Nita raised her eyebrows. "Why?"

Mirella turned and gave Nita a twisted look, mouth curling somewhere between a sneer and a snarl. "Because I want Reyes to find him. I know however Reyes chooses to kill him, it will be worse than anything we could do."

Nita just blinked, and Kovit stirred in the cage. "Reyes will kill him?"

Mirella spat on the floor in his direction. "Definitely."

Well, that wasn't Nita's fault, was it? And she'd be gone by then anyway, so it didn't matter.

Nita took a breath and put Kovit's impending demise from her mind. She turned to Mirella. "Come on. Let's go."

Nita's body resisted, still high on adrenaline and panic. Part of her wanted to sit in a corner and cry tears of relief. But the rest of her wouldn't let that happen. She wasn't out yet, and she couldn't afford to stop now. So she pushed everything away and focused on her escape. When she was far away, when she was safe, she'd let herself feel every moment of fear, but right now, she needed to stay calm and focused.

The end of the hall had three doors. Mirella limped to the largest one, but Nita held her back.

"You're limping."

Mirella leaned against the wall, panting, and Nita stepped forward, reaching out to see the extent of Mirella's wound.

Mirella pushed her hand away. "I'm fine."

Nita looked away, secretly relieved. She didn't actually want to know what had been done.

Mirella was leaning heavily against the wall, and Nita cast a critical eye over her. She wasn't going to be able to walk without help. She was going to slow them down.

Nita glanced to the doors, torn. She wanted to rip through them, but she needed to be practical. Mirella was a problem.

"What's behind there?" she asked, gesturing to the door Mirella had been heading toward.

"Escape." Mirella's voice was sad. Nita would have expected the younger girl to be more excited or scared, but she just seemed small, eye glassy and distant.

"The market?"

"Yeah."

"Okay." Nita frowned. "What about those doors?"

"I don't know that one." Mirella pointed to the door open a crack, before shifting her attention to a closed one, then quickly turning away. "But that one is . . . there's nothing helpful in there."

It took Nita a moment to clue in. That must be the

"workroom," where Mirella had just been tortured. Nita had a feeling Mirella wouldn't be too keen to explore it, so Nita resisted the urge to peer in and let the white walls and surgical implements calm her. There were more important things to do.

Nita pushed the other door open and peeked in, body tense, waiting for someone to jump out at her, but the room was empty. Her shoulders relaxed, but her heart rate remained high.

"Mirella, find something to help you walk." Nita eyed the other girl's pink hair and gory shirt, stained from the blood that periodically dripped down the side of her face from where her eye had once been. "And change into something less conspicuous."

The security camera feed from the room with her and Mirella's cages was displayed on a screen on the far wall. There were no other screens with security footage. Did that mean they had no other security cameras? That seemed a little unlikely, given that this was clearly a pretty sophisticated compound. But maybe there was a general security room, and this was just for whoever was watching the prisoners?

"Do you know how many other rooms are in this building?" Nita asked.

"None."

Nita blinked. "This is it? Where do Reyes and the guards stay?"

Mirella shrugged, and Nita rolled her eyes. Well, at least they were alone here. For now.

She wasn't sure how long that would last. She just needed to grab things and go. She wanted a weapon.

The room was unpleasantly small and cramped. An air conditioner and mini fridge were crammed against one wall, and a single chair had been used to anchor a line of laundry (probably Kovit's) to the mini fridge. A few of the pieces were on the floor, having fallen from the line. There was a small cot on the far side of the room, with rumpled sheets and blankets, and another basket of dry clothes.

Mirella hobbled in and started fishing through the basket of dry clothes, shoving aside jeans and underwear. She pulled out a reddish-brown T-shirt, and started wrapping her far-too-conspicuous hair in it.

"Does Kovit stay here?" Nita asked, eyeing the cot.

Mirella's voice was indifferent. "Does it matter?"

Nita sighed. "Of course it matters. If he's staying here, his money has to be around somewhere, right?"

That made Mirella pause and look around. "Good point."

Nita resisted the urge to roll her eyes again.

Before she started searching, Nita took one of Kovit's wet shirts and covered the screen. She didn't care about supervising her newfound prisoner—she just didn't want to see Kovit wake up and realize Reyes was going to kill him. If Nita didn't see him, she wouldn't have to think about the part she'd played in his death.

He's a monster. He deserves whatever's coming to him.

That may be true, but she covered the screen anyway.

Just below the screen was a small table with a power outlet. There was a shitty, dinosaur-age flip phone charging in the dock. Kovit's, she presumed.

She picked it up and checked. The signal was strong.

"There's nothing here." Mirella leaned against the fridge, her breathing still too fast and sharp.

She'd wrapped her pink hair in a T-shirt, like a terrible rusty toque, and had swapped her bloody sweatpants and T-shirt out for jeans and a different T-shirt. She looked even more conspicuous than before, if that was possible. But at least she didn't look quite so noticeably physically different. People would be too busy staring at that weird toque to notice how gray Mirella's skin was. Though there was nothing to be done about the eye patch.

"There's no point calling INHUP." Mirella noticed the phone in Nita's hands. "We're on the wrong side of the border. They have no power here."

"I know that. We can't call until we're in Brazil." Nita pocketed the phone and crossed the room to Mirella.

Mirella went to the door. "Are you coming?"

Nita hesitated. "Money?"

"I didn't see any. Who knows where he hid it. For all you know, it's in his pocket."

Nita nodded, trying to calm her racing heart. Why should taking that final step out of the building be any scarier than staying? She didn't know, but somehow it was.

Mirella was staring at her, and Nita took a deep breath. She'd delayed them long enough. They had no idea when

Reyes or her guards were coming back. Money or no money, they needed to get out of here. They'd figure it out as they went.

"Okay." Nita turned to the front door. "It's time."

She pulled back the deadbolt, took a deep breath, and opened the door.

SEVENTEEN

NITA STUMBLED BACK as she slammed into a wall of humidity. She blinked, suddenly sweating despite the air conditioning at her back. She barely noticed, too caught up in staring at the spectacle in front of her.

Buildings made of wood and mosquito netting squatted in rows down the street. Interspersed blocky concrete structures with — was that woven giant reeds on the roof?

There weren't many people on the street, though she could hear them, the babble, the incessant chatter, from close by. She was probably on a side street.

A monkey sat on one of the roofs, watching her. It was soon joined by another monkey. And then a third. They stared at her for a while before one of them jumped, whole body spread-eagling as he leapt into the forest behind him.

No, the *jungle* behind him.

The whole market — or at least, the part that Nita could see — was surrounded by rainforest. The trees were huge, towering up into the sky. The area around Nita had been cleared, and she felt like she was looking through a long wooden tube at the blue sky above. There were no clouds.

The trees were draped with wooden vines—were all vines wood? In movies, when she'd seen people swinging on them, she'd always thought of them as sturdy green plants, like giant dandelion stems. But these looked more like trees that had gained the power of movement, wrapping and weaving and choking the other trees in a throttle, wooden boa constrictors.

Smaller trees with huge leaves, shrubs, and sticks packed the area closer to the ground. It looked impassable, like the thorns around Sleeping Beauty's castle. Except with more spiderwebs and giant bugs.

Beads of sweat trickled down Nita's forehead and into her shirt. Sweat stains began to appear under her armpits.

Mirella pushed past her, unaffected by the surroundings. "The pier is this way. I remember from when we arrived."

Nita took a step outside and then realized she was barefoot. The ground was littered with rocks and tree roots, and she thought she saw pieces of glass from shattered bottles.

"We need shoes."

Mirella paused. Then she began to shake, her whole body trembling like the beginning of a seizure. "I'm not going back in there."

Nita's shoulders tightened, and she found herself agreeing with Mirella, stupid as it was.

Mirella turned back to her with large pink eyes. "The only pair of shoes in there is probably on Kovit's feet."

Good point.

Mirella crunched across the gravel. Her tiny feet left small droplets of blood behind with each step. Sighing, Nita followed. She started killing and layering the skin on the bottom of her feet, trying to create a thick callus. She hoped it would be enough.

Since Mirella actually remembered her journey here, Nita was inclined to trust that she had a better idea of where to go.

"You mentioned a pier." Nita trotted to catch up with Mirella. She was moving faster than Nita would've thought possible, considering her limp. "Any other way out?"

Mirella shook her head. "No. It's too hard to carve paths through the jungle for cars for long distances. Same with airplane landing strips."

Too bad. Though stealing a boat might be easier than a car. "Do you know how to operate a boat?"

"No." Mirella shrugged, then winced. Her voice went a little too high. "How hard can it be? You just row, right?"

Nita didn't respond, mostly because she didn't actually have any more knowledge than that either.

They crunched around a corner, and all thoughts fled as Nita stared at the scene in front of her.

There were hundreds of people. Nita hadn't really understood the sheer scale of the market before.

Small huts and two-story wooden buildings lined the street, but most wares were set up on tables in front of the buildings. Jars with eyes and tongues in formaldehyde sat next to slabs of meat. Little bags of powdered unicorn bone and bundles of phoenix feathers dangled from the woven-reed roofs of the makeshift shops like tassels from graduation caps.

Other stores had cages with live creatures in them. A large sheeplike creature with fangs gnashed at the bars of its cage. In another, a small fluffy animal huddled into itself, puffy black fur twitching when people got too close. One pen held a massive serpent with horns like antennae. It watched as people passed, tongue flicking in and out, tasting the air.

But what gave Nita pause was that most people seemed to be speaking English. She caught American accents as well as British. There was Spanish in there too, but the sea of faces throughout the market was more white than brown.

Not that there weren't white people in South America. The demographics were actually pretty similar to the States, with large white, black, indigenous, and Asian populations. And like the States, the majority of the ultra-rich—the type of people who could afford the delicacies the market had to offer —were middle-aged white men. So seeing a lot of rich white people in a market like this wasn't surprising.

But the amount of English being spoken was.

Nita had made the very stupid assumption that because she was in Peru, the dealers and the buyers would mostly be from Latin America.

They weren't.

They were from everywhere, and the universal thing they had in common was money. It showed in their tailored clothes, bleached smiles, and the sharp-eyed bodyguards flanking them. These were the exploiters, the people who felt like they could come into a country and do whatever they wanted.

Conquistadores in suits.

"Come on." Mirella tried to take Nita's hand and pull her forward, but Nita shifted subtly away.

"Yeah. Coming." Nita swallowed, eyes still absorbing the scene before her.

Mirella strode down the street, stumbling through the crowd. A fine layer of sweat covered Nita's whole body, and glued itself to other people she brushed past like Velcro; when she peeled herself off, there was a wet smacking sound.

Ugh.

The whole place smelled like rotting fruit, but also faintly of formaldehyde, which she found comforting. Food shops offered lunch and fresh fruit, but they often smelled worse than the body parts for sale, which was never a good sign.

Nita kept her head down as she walked. Not too far down —that would be suspicious—but she avoided meeting the gazes of other people in the market. She was hoping to avoid attention, but it would be hard with Mirella and her pink skin, red toque, and limp. Nita almost wished she'd left Mirella to fend for herself. But that wasn't a nice thought, so she tried not to have it.

They passed one group of tourists, with large floppy sun hats and cameras hanging around their necks. It made her feel sick. This place wasn't some side spectacle you could watch and then go home and tell your family about like it was a great adventure.

As Nita and Mirella got closer to the pier, the towering trees disappeared to reveal blue sky.

Stumbling down the path to the pier, Nita caught her first glimpse of the Amazon River.

She'd never been more happy to see a body of water. It promised freedom, a way out of this corrupt market and back to the real world. She imagined getting in a boat and rowing all the way home to Lima. Which was ridiculous, because the Amazon didn't go anywhere near Lima.

A wooden pier stretched out into the river, with several stairs scattered at different intervals to get down to the boats. Nita assumed that was in case the water levels rose during rainy season, and she wondered if the market ever flooded.

Guards were stationed along the pier, most of them wearing camo pants and T-shirts or tanks. In their arms, they cradled large, mean-looking guns. Not the little handguns her mother favored, but the long, military ones that looked like they belonged in a terrorist compound. Was that what a machine gun looked like? Or a submachine gun? What was the difference between those anyway?

Behind them, the boats were tied at the dock. While a few were wooden, more rowboats than anything else, most of them were made of fiberglass and metal, their surfaces stained from the dirty water and years of use. Even from here, Nita could see their engines. And where there were engines, there were usually keys. Or she thought there were. She'd never actually been in a boat—except, she assumed, when she'd been brought to the market, unconscious. At any rate, hot-wiring was not one of Nita's skills.

Her hand moved against her leg, trying to make a Y incision with a nonexistent scalpel.

Maybe the boats didn't need keys. Engines didn't necessarily mean keys, right? And those wooden ones with the paddles would work regardless—but if she ran off with one, she would bet the fiberglass ones could catch up in minutes. Not much of a getaway boat.

She swore, then turned to Mirella, who was eyeing the guards nervously.

Nita pursed her lips. "Do you know how far Brazil is? Can we swim?"

"No way." Mirella's body was hunched, as though curling up while standing would somehow alleviate whatever wounds lurked under her clothes. "It's a four-hour motorboat ride. Swimming? It'd take you days. And there're snakes in the water. Piranhas too, though those won't be too dangerous in the river itself; they're fairly well fed. It's the isolated ones trapped inland by the dry season you have to watch out for."

Nita massaged her temples. "All right. What about going through the forest itself?"

"Are you kidding?" Mirella gave Nita an appalled look. "You need a machete just to hack a trail through the underbrush. There're spiders in there that eat *birds*. We wouldn't last a day, especially with no supplies."

Nita clenched her jaw. Out of one cage and into a bigger one.

The smartest thing to do would be to simply buy passage. If there was anything else she needed, she could bribe the guards into ignoring it. Money solved all problems in the black market.

Problem: she had no money.

She wished she'd stolen those stupid tourists' cameras. Maybe someone would have taken them in trade.

She hovered at the side of a building, looking down at the pier, trying to figure out how to proceed. Mirella stood beside her, face blank.

If they waited until night, they could slip into the pier under the cover of darkness. But even if they did make off with one of those crappy-looking rowboats, heading down the river at night didn't particularly seem like the smartest plan. Aside from caimans and anacondas and who knew what else in the river, she doubted she'd be able to see well enough to know where she was going. She wasn't even sure which direction she should go. Maybe Mirella knew?

"We should just steal a boat." Mirella's eyes were fixed on the dock. "There's no other way out."

Nita licked her lips. "There's a lot of people here."

"That's not going to change anytime soon."

Nodding slowly, Nita looked around at the crowds. "What we need is a distraction."

"Any ideas?"

"Maybe." Nita unstuck a strand of hair from her sweaty forehead and eyed the various stalls by the pier. "Go find a boat and untie it. I'm going to make sure no one's looking."

Mirella gave her a mock salute before limping toward the pier.

Nita headed into the crowd, squeezing between sweaty people and stalls. Her eye found a stall full of various feathers, all wrapped with twine and tucked in baskets. Perfect.

As she passed, she slipped her leg out and kicked hard against one of the table legs. It didn't budge. Swallowing, hoping no one noticed, she kicked again, harder.

It buckled, sending the table, and all its feathery contents flying through the air. Phoenix tail feathers stuck to the sweat of random passersby and glued themselves to their skin. The air was a flurry of exotic colors, and the ground was patterned by the softest-looking leaves imaginable.

The stall owner cried out and ran around trying to grab feathers. Some of the passersby pocketed the feathers stuck to them. Others brushed them off. No one moved to help the lady.

No one even paid attention to the brightly colored fiasco.

Nita looked around at the oblivious people and realized any distraction she made would have to be much more noticeable. Short of burning a building down, she wasn't sure what would take people's eyes off the pier.

So, where could she find a match?

She looked around, hoping to find someone with a cigarette, but her eyes were instead drawn to the dock, where Mirella had already crept from the shadows and started walking toward the pier.

The guards were talking to another man, who had his back to Nita. But when he turned, she caught a glimpse of his face in profile.

Boulder.

The man who'd bought and eaten Mirella's eye.

And he was staring straight at Mirella.

Nita opened her mouth to cry out, but there was no way

her voice would carry over the crowd and reach Mirella in time. She felt like Cassandra of Greek myth, seeing the future but unable to do anything about it.

Boulder raised a gun.

Nita took a step forward.

Too late.

The bullet hit Mirella's stomach, shoving it backwards even as the rest of her kept moving. It was like watching a cartoon, but with more blood — as though she had run into an invisible table in the middle of the street, her top and bottom shot forward while her middle caught. Her whole body spasmed from the opposing forces, and she stumbled into the dirt.

Her fingers clutched at her wound, but the blood seemed to be leaching out of her at an alarming rate, pumping through her fingers and soaking everything around her a deep, vivid red.

Nita's brain, ever the analyst, determined that Mirella was as good as dead with a wound like that in these conditions. No medical attention. That pier was filthy, ripe for infection. There were men with guns who might very well shoot her again.

Nita resisted the urge to go to her. She couldn't be caught in this. Mirella was gone, and something as silly as pity or sympathy wasn't going to make Nita go over there and get shot too. There was no way to save Mirella.

Still, Nita had to cling to the side of the building, holding it like an anchor to prevent the stupid part of her from ignoring logic.

Mirella opened her mouth, but only a hoarse croak came

out, as though she'd used up all her screams during her time with Kovit.

Boulder put his gun away and turned back to the guards he'd been talking to, dismissing Mirella. It was like the man she'd seen last night had been there for pleasure, on his off time, and Mirella was his sport. But now that it was daylight and he was working, he didn't have time to care about his hobbies.

Something left Mirella when he did that, something in his casual dismissal of her. Her whole body seemed to shrink, shoulders slumping, chin falling, muscles losing their tension. Nita saw the moment when Mirella gave up.

One of the guards said something, and Boulder laughed and began walking toward Mirella. He hefted his gun, and Mirella rolled away, bloody fingers scrabbling on the wooden slats of the dock. With one final heave, she pulled herself over the edge and tumbled into the waters of the Amazon River below. There was a splash when she landed, then silence. No thrashing. No voice.

All around Nita, the market continued. The stall was standing again, the feathers collected. People had glanced over to see what Boulder had shot at, but then turned away when it was over. Boulder continued talking to the men on the dock before leaving with one. He walked right across the bloodstained pier and descended into a small boat at the end of the dock.

The river continued to flow, absorbing its gift, the red of the blood mixing into the water and disappearing.

No one would be selling any part of Mirella ever again.

161

EIGHTEEN

NITA FLED.

She pushed her way down the streets, using her elbows to jab people out of the way. There were too many people, all of them sweating and laughing and touching her, arms brushing hers as they moved through the market. Bodies stuck together and peeled apart. The air was hot, too hot, and Nita was a fever, consumed by heat and sweat and sickness.

She broke out of the market area and into a colorless cramped street not much better than an alley. Sweat glued her baggy T-shirt to her body. Part of her wanted to rest against the side of a building, but the other part didn't want to touch anything, even a piece of wood.

Her breathing was harsh and ragged, but she didn't cry.

Nita had never seen someone die before. Sure, she'd seen dead bodies, but she'd never seen the moment when a person went from alive, breathing and speaking and living, to dead. Silent. In her mind, living and dead people were almost different species, completely disconnected from each other. The idea that Mirella's life had been snuffed out, her annoying, whiny voice silent forever—it didn't seem right. And then Boulder just boated away.

In movies, whenever the bad guys fell, it was "what they deserved" and "karmic retribution." The thought had crossed Nita's mind that she deserved this after everything she'd done in her life. But that wasn't true. There was no karma; there was no balance. Nita wasn't making amends for her actions by experiencing this. She was experiencing this because her mother had betrayed her. There was nothing deeper.

If there had been deeper meaning in the world, Boulder would be the one at the bottom of the river, not Mirella. Heck, this whole market wouldn't exist.

But it still felt like a revelation to Nita. Because, on some childish level, she'd expected Mirella to get her justice. Because that's what happened in stories—the good guys reached their goal before they died. It was a rule. But it was a rule of fiction.

Stories here didn't get neat endings tied up in a bow.

Nita breathed, and let herself grieve for a girl she barely knew, who had the worst life Nita could have imagined. She remembered Mirella's squeaks as she hid under her blankets and the rage on her face when she saw Boulder. Nita closed her eyes and watched her sink into a watery grave.

Waste of a body.

Nope. That was not how you grieved. You did not imagine the person's dead body up for dissection.

The hum of cicadas mixed with the chirps of crickets and laughter of people. A bird soared the sky above, nothing more than a colorful speck. A toucan or a macaw. It was too far to tell.

Nita took a deep breath and examined her surroundings. Casinos lined the street, glittery neon lights switched off in the bright daylight. A sign on the building beside her advertised pishtaco liposuction services. It promised pinpoint precision body shaping as only a fat-eating unnatural could do. Nita remembered wishing for a pishtaco to dissect. It felt like a different lifetime.

Nita's fingers curled into a fist, and she slammed the wall of the building next to her, her breath hiccupping into a frustrated sob. She pressed her forehead against the wood. What was she going to do?

Not steal a boat, apparently.

Trying at night would be no better; navigating a boat in the dark was a recipe for failure. Perhaps she could go into the water and hide under the boat as it went away. She'd need to figure out how to hold her breath for an extended period of time —she figured if she increased hemoglobin levels in her blood and slowed her heart rate, she could up her lung capacity to maybe twenty minutes, but beyond that, things got doubtful. And how would she hold on to the bottom of the boat while it was moving? She might just slide off.

No, none of this was worth the risk. Failure meant instant death. She wouldn't make the same mistake twice.

So she would have to buy passage. And possibly bribes too. For that, she needed money.

Where was she going to get this money? She could attempt to pickpocket people in the market, except that she'd never stolen from anyone and was pretty sure she'd be caught.

Nita pressed her hands to her temple. She needed a way out

of here, and she needed it fast. Who knew when Reyes would come back and notice Nita's escape? If she deployed the guards, Nita would have no hope of escaping by boat.

Her breath caught. Reyes.

Reyes had money — the woman was running an unnatural-trafficking ring and selling body parts. She *had* to have money.

Nita could steal from her.

If Reyes hadn't already discovered Nita's escape, that is. If she hadn't, then Nita could go back to the compound, lay a trap for her and her bodyguards, rob them, and flee.

Nita didn't fool herself. It wasn't the best plan. It was high risk. But she was desperate, and it was better than going back to the pier and ending up like Mirella.

What if Reyes was already there when she got back?

Run. Nita would just run straight back to the pier and take her chances swimming. It might be a four-hour boat ride, but Nita could enhance her muscles. She might make it. Maybe.

It was better than the alternative. Nita wasn't going back in the cage.

The stones crunched beneath her feet as she wound her way through the market. It seemed endless, each street a copy of the last, like a video game that had reused the same background design in a repeating pattern. Dips in the ground collected water and made surprisingly deep puddles. Sometimes people had put planks of wood across the puddles to walk across, and sometimes they hadn't bothered.

In the depths of the market, Nita started seeing other signs, not for hotels, but for "curiosities." Come see the creatures for only a small entry fee. If you like them, you can buy them, or even just rent them. Other signs advertised places of entertainment for the more exotically minded. Sometimes there were pictures of women with scales or scantily clad girls with tails. Sometimes there were just directions.

Hawkers held up mummified limbs and waved bags of powders. A living shadow sat in a glass box, while a group of gawkers poked at the glass, watching it skitter away from their fingers. Nita turned down another street and found it crowded with produce and fish. She relaxed a little until she passed a stand that had a large yellow nectarine-like fruit with eyes. They blinked.

Nita looked away and picked up her pace.

She passed a man wearing a University of Toronto T-shirt, and her heart clenched. For years she'd been saving up for college. She wanted to be a researcher, to have people pay her to dissect bodies, legally. Like the people whose articles she read in scientific magazines. She wanted to go to conferences, to present research to her peers.

And she suddenly realized she couldn't. Ever.

Reyes had taken that from her too.

Her face was all over the internet, in all the wrong circles. Even if she escaped from here, even if she managed to get to safety, what then? Say she managed to get a new identity and afford college. What about when she started presenting about unnatural biology at conferences? Only a fool would think the black market didn't keep an eye on all the newest information. And then they would see Nita, and all her hiding would be for nothing. Because pictures on the internet didn't just disappear, and someone as potentially valuable as Nita wouldn't be for-gotten.

And then this would happen all over again.

Nita would be leaving a conference one day, and someone would try to grab her. And she'd just end up back in the cage, cut up for customers, pieces of her hacked off and sold.

Reyes and her promotional video had ruined Nita's life.

Nita's jaw clenched. She wasn't going to end up like Mirella. She was going to escape, to survive, no matter what the cost.

NINETEEN

IT TOOK NITA longer than she expected to find the concrete building she'd been held in. Partly because the sun was
setting, and it was hard to see. There were some electric lights,
but almost all of them were in the gambling areas, which were
behind Nita. The rest of the market was dark. Darker than
anything Nita had experienced before. It seemed to absorb the
light, suck it in and create only a void—she couldn't even see
where buildings ended and the jungle started.

Nita used the cell phone flashlight to pick her way through
the streets, cautious of dangers. A lot of monsters lived in this
jungle, and that didn't even count things like jaguars.

Even though it was darker, it wasn't any less humid. Nita's
shirt was actually dripping, and her baggy sweatpants clung
to her like skinny jeans. Wet, sticky, skinny jeans. The sweat
snuck through her hair, sort of dried, only to be layered with
more sweat, making her scalp ridiculously itchy. Or maybe
that was the mosquitos.

When she finally found the building, she resisted the urge

to fling herself inside. She had to be cautious. She didn't know if Reyes had discovered her escape yet.

She watched the building for ten minutes, but saw no sign of anyone. Silent, careful, she pulled open the door, still unlocked from when she left. She slipped inside and closed it gently behind her.

Air conditioning is the best invention in the world.

Nita paused after she closed the door, listening. There was no sound except the hum of the air conditioner. She closed her eyes and opened them again, trying to adjust to the sudden brightness of the fluorescents after the darkness outside.

She crept into the first room, the dissection room. It was cramped, with white walls, a tray of implements, and a metal cart in the middle. The room was empty.

She didn't see any scalpels, but there was a large pair of scissors, so she took that for a weapon. Just in case.

Next, she went to the security room, with its hanging laundry and mini fridge. She glanced in the washroom. Empty. Nita took a deep breath and removed the T-shirt from the monitor—dry now, which was probably why Kovit was hanging his laundry in here instead of outside.

Kovit was lying on the cot, arms above his head as though reaching for the ceiling. He seemed bored, his eyes occasionally flicking to the security camera.

Nita sank down in the chair in front of the monitor. No Reyes. Not yet, anyway. The cameras covered the whole cage room, and this was the only other room in the building. Nita was safe.

She closed her eyes, and relished the air conditioning. She could see the glow of the fluorescents through her closed eyes, but they didn't bother her. Despite the heat and exhaustion, she wasn't tired. Her body was still wired with adrenaline.

Before she could forget, she rose and locked the entrance to the building. She was sure Reyes had a key, but at least Nita would have some warning. She should start setting her trap immediately, so she'd be ready.

But she stood there, hesitating. Then she took Kovit's phone out of her pocket and finally did the thing she'd been both dying to do and dreading.

She called her mother.

The phone didn't even ring, just went straight to *the customer you are calling is unavailable.* Nita hadn't really expected anything else. Her mother had probably ditched her phone after Fabricio left and Nita was kidnapped — sold.

Part of Nita was glad it hadn't connected. She didn't know what she'd do if she were in front of her mother. That rage still smoldered just beneath the surface, ready to explode at the slightest provocation.

What about her father? Could Nita call him?

She considered the shitty keypad phone. It wouldn't have international calling, right? But it didn't hurt to check, so Nita dialed her father's number.

And it rang.

Heart leaping, she pressed the phone to her ear with both hands, trying to keep her arms from shaking. If she could just get him, he could rescue her. No need for elaborate plans to steal money. As long as Nita could stay under the radar for a day, he would have enough time to come pick her up. Nita closed her eyes, almost tasting freedom.

"Hello."

That was not her father's voice.

"Who is this?" Anger and confusion crept into her voice. Had she dialed the wrong number?

"This is Sergeant Mike Blaswell of the Chicago Police Department. To whom am I speaking?"

Nita's throat dried. Police. What was her father's phone doing in the police department?

A terrible thought occurred to her—had her mother done something to her father to prevent him finding out about Nita?

Nita realized the sergeant was waiting for her response. If she stayed on the line, she'd incriminate her father for sure. She didn't have any confidence in her subterfuge skills. If she hung up immediately, she might make him look equally suspicious. What to do?

"Oh. I must have the wrong number. I'm sorry."

Nita hung up before she could hear the response. She closed her eyes, head lowered. She was sure it looked horribly suspicious, but she wasn't the best at improvising.

After the phone clicked off, she realized she could have fished for information. She could have asked to speak to her father, seen what they said. Though that might have made things worse, depending on why the cops had her father's phone.

Well, she wasn't calling back now.

Turning her head to look at the video screen, she found Kovit waving up at the monitor. He must have heard her call.

Nita watched him for a moment, debating whether to go over to the cage. He stopped waving and sat back down with a sigh, but his eyes were still on the camera, as though he was watching her.

I gave you a book when you were in the cage and bored, and you won't even answer me, his eyes seemed to say.

Not that Nita actually felt guilty. She could still hear Mirella's screams. And Nita's wound from when she first met Kovit was still scaly and half healed. Her fingers danced over it, pausing on the rough edges, remembering. She could heal it fully now. She was feeling well enough. But she hadn't, focusing her energy on her myriad other injuries. And perhaps a little bit of her wanted that physical, tangible reminder of why she needed to be careful with Kovit.

But she got up and went down the hall to his cage. She had to go there eventually anyway.

As Nita rounded the corner, Kovit got to his feet. "Hey."

Nita ignored him and started examining the angle of the entranceway. If she stood just here, Reyes wouldn't see Nita when she entered. If Nita had some tranquilizer, she could take the woman down before she knew what was happening. There probably wasn't tranquilizer. But a rope? Choke her until she passed out? But what about Reyes' gun? Maybe a blunt object to the temple was better.

"Uhhh, Nita?" Kovit called, as though she hadn't heard him the first time.

Nita turned to him and crossed her arms. "Yes?"

He gave her his best aren't-we-friends-I'm-not-crazy smile.

She ignored how it made her heart rate spike with fear. Screams echoed in her mind.

"You sticking around for the night?" His voice was smooth and friendly. Not his casual voice, like when they'd been playing cards. This voice was fake somehow, like a used-car salesman.

"Yes."

"Where's the dolphin wannabe?"

Nita looked away.

He raised one eyebrow and quirked a smile—something Nita had seen people do in movies, but never in real life. "All right, fine. Keep your silence. But would it be too much trouble to feed me?"

Oh. Oops. Nita had forgotten about that. She wasn't good at remembering to do things for herself, never mind taking care of other people. She was not going to make a very good captor.

"I'll get you something." Nita paused. "I didn't see bread. Where is it?"

"Bottom shelf of the fridge."

"You keep your bread in the fridge?"

He shrugged. "It doesn't mold that way."

Nita didn't argue. She turned around to find food, when Kovit stopped her. "Water too, please, if you don't mind."

Right. People needed water.

Nita fetched a bottle of water and a piece of bread from the fridge and put some beans on it. She took a detour to check the dissection room for tranquilizer, but there wasn't any.

173

However, she did find a hammer. If she swung it at Reyes' spine, she could paralyze the woman.

Or kill her.

But then how would Nita find out where the money was? Not ideal. Best to avoid that.

Nita pocketed the hammer anyway, along with a piece of twine that was holding a crate closed. It looked good for strangling. She didn't want to be unprepared if Reyes arrived while she was feeding Kovit.

Nita brought Kovit his food and put it on the tray, but it stuck. Of course it did. Nita hadn't taken out the piece of plastic she'd wedged in there.

"If you want food, you'll have to get rid of the thing I shoved in the mechanism," Nita told Kovit.

He felt around a bit before pulling the piece of plastic out. The food and water slid through.

Kovit gave her his only-a-little-crazy smile. "Thank you."

"You're welcome." Nita backed away. She hesitated, then asked, "Is there itch cream?"

Kovit looked up at Nita and laughed. She rubbed her mosquito-bitten arms, and then lowered her hands. Scratching would only make the bites worse. She could have just healed them, but it was like using a hammer to snap a cookie in half. Itch cream would do fine.

"No." Kovit gave her a self-deprecating grin. "Reyes wouldn't let me bring anything like that. She's quite strict about what can and can't come here."

"Why?" What was the harm in itch cream?

Kovit shrugged. "Beats me. She probably wants me to suffer."

Nita gave him a dubious look, and Kovit laughed. "You didn't think I actually wanted to be in this horrid shit-hole market, did you? It's miserable and hot. Counting you and Reyes, I've spoken with four people since I came here."

Nita wondered about that—she didn't think it was a language barrier problem, since she'd heard so much English on her way to the pier. So why hadn't he been speaking to others?

"And," he went on, waving one hand in a chopping motion, "there's no internet here, and Reyes won't let me use hers. Who in their right mind would want this position?"

Nita hadn't actually thought too much about it. But it was odd, now that Kovit mentioned it. Why send a zannie to do a job anyone could do? Zannies were coveted by corrupt governments, mafias, anywhere torture was useful. Even having one on staff and using it as a threat was effective. Putting one in the middle of the jungle, to guard prisoners, was an absolute waste. Sure, Reyes did use him as an enforcer—for the prisoners. Anyone could do that.

And why had Kovit agreed to come? Zannies really could get hired anywhere. They could charge insane rates for their services. Ending up in a cage in the middle of the jungle was not something she thought any zannie, especially Kovit, would want.

"So why are you here?" Nita asked, arms crossed.

"Why does anyone get the shitty posts? By screwing up."

Kovit's voice started out amused, but lost its humor by the end of the sentence.

Nita tilted her head to the side. "Reyes doesn't seem like the type to give second chances."

Kovit laughed, but there was something like fear in the sound. It made Nita flinch. Then she straightened her back. She had nothing to fear from Kovit. She was on the outside of the cage now.

Finally, Kovit calmed and gave her a sad look. "No, she doesn't give second chances."

Nita clenched her teeth. He was trying to remind her that Reyes would kill him when she returned.

So what? Nita thought. She needed to escape, and no matter what, he'd be punished for it. And Nita was much fonder of her own life than she was of his.

Kovit looked at her, and she wondered, *Isn't it better for the world if he dies?* Zannies were on the dangerous species list for a reason. If he lived, he'd keep hurting people.

Mirella's screams echoed through her memory.

Exactly.

Then, a terrible, wonderful thought occurred to Nita. Her fingers twitched with the need for a scalpel. She felt like an addict, deprived for weeks.

You could do it, her mind whispered at her. *You could poison the food or water. Something simple, tasteless. This is the Amazon, surely you can find something poisonous. It would be a mercy, compared to what Reyes has planned.*

I could, Nita agreed, licking her lips. *And then I'd have a body.*

Her hands ached for a scalpel, but she could use Kovit's

switchblade. It wouldn't be quite the same, but she could make it work.

Nita didn't realize that she was pressed against the cage, a hungry expression twisting her features, until she saw movement out of the corner of her eye.

Kovit had backed up to the other side of his cage, and was staring at her with wary eyes. "What are you doing?"

Nita's voice was almost dreamy. "Thinking of how I could dissect you."

"What?"

Nita smiled, a small, slightly crazy smile not dissimilar to some of Kovit's. "I like to dissect things. I *need* to dissect things."

Kovit stared at her, fear creeping into his voice. He wasn't smiling anymore, his mouth downturned, brows drawn together. "What . . . what are you?"

"Me? You know what I am. But what I do? I dissect people." Nita's fingers were warm on the cool glass. "My mother used to bring me bodies. Lots of bodies. Kappa and mermaids and unicorns. Zannies too." Her smile widened as she looked over at Kovit. "Lots of zannies."

Kovit was staring at her, his expression morphing into something nervous and definitely frightened. Nita wasn't sure when they'd well and truly switched positions. Nita on the outside, the psychopathic captor with the crazy smile that kept on stretching. Kovit on the inside, afraid of the implied threat and his own powerlessness.

That made something skittery and unhappy bounce around in her chest, like a marble had gotten loose and it was hitting strange things inside of her. She didn't want to be that person. It was too much like her mother.

This was different, though. Kovit really was evil.

You're just making excuses to justify your creepy craving, a snide part of her mind commented.

Shut up.

You're really going to go there? Murder someone and then dissect them? When did you cross into serial killer territory?

SHUT UP.

Silence, except for the heavy sound of her own breathing. Finally, Nita rose and schooled her expression.

She couldn't dissect Kovit. She ought to—he'd tortured Mirella, he'd killed who knew how many people. The only thing that awaited him was a horrid death. But she couldn't.

She remembered his face over his homemade playing cards, talking her through her fear. She flexed the fingers she still had attached because he hadn't gone through with Reyes' orders. She thought of the shitty book he'd loaned her.

She couldn't dissect him, because she knew him. She didn't dissect people she knew.

Her fingers twitched for a scalpel.

Coward, her mind sneered. *You can't even be honest with yourself about your own decisions.*

Nita ignored it.

Kovit watched her with wary eyes. "Have you decided to dissect, or not to dissect?"

"Was that an attempt at a *Hamlet* reference?" Nita gave him a confused look.

"No. I didn't even think of that until you mentioned it."

"Oh." Nita swallowed.

He watched her with wary eyes. "Well?"

"No." Nita let out a breath and lowered her hand. "I'm not going to dissect you." Then she turned and walked away. "I'll let Reyes decide what to do with you."

"Is that supposed to cheer me up?" Kovit called out, but Nita had already gone.

TWENTY

NITA DOUBLE CHECKED that the front door was locked, not because she believed it wasn't, but just because she felt comforted seeing the lock and knowing there was an obstacle between her and Reyes.

Then she checked Kovit's phone—Reyes' number had to be in there. Maybe Nita could text her and lure her into a trap.

Nita found a recent text from Reyes. It read *Customers coming at noon tomorrow. Have everything cleaned up.*

Nita hesitated. What was supposed to be cleaned up? And how would Kovit respond to this? Nita opted for a simple *Understood.*

Then she put the phone down and plopped onto the chair. The phone vibrated, and Nita picked up again.

I will be there at eleven to make sure there's no repeat of last time.

Nita wondered what happened last time, but she didn't type anything except another *Understood.*

The phone didn't buzz again.

Well, that was fine. Nita had a timeline. She could do this.

While she considered more effective ways to incapacitate

Reyes besides a hammer or rope, she decided a shower would be good. She felt disgusting.

There was a tiny bathroom attached to this room. It was so small the showerhead was above the toilet bowl, and Nita had to straddle the toilet while she showered and still barely had room to turn around. She stepped into the shower fully dressed. She peeled off her clothes underneath the ice-cold water—what a fantastic idea. Who needed hot water out here anyway?

Once she was scrubbed and had fished her shirt out of the toilet—stupid design—she stepped out. She couldn't find a towel, so she dried off with one of the shirts on the laundry line. They smelled clean—dirty things were very obvious in this kind of heat. She took a different black T-shirt and put it on.

Most of Kovit's T-shirts were black or dark red. *Probably to hide the bloodstains,* Nita thought, and then pushed that idea away. She didn't want to think about that.

She stole a pair of his jeans too, glad that he was skinny and lean. The waist was a bit too big, but the pants stayed up because she had hips where Kovit didn't. The rest of it was a little baggy, but not ridiculously so. The legs were a bit short, stopping just above her ankles, but Nita didn't care too much.

Finally clean, Nita lay down on the bed. She tried to think of a way she could lure Reyes into the cages instead of just hitting her, since that seemed fraught with dangers, but she was too exhausted and her mind so muddled that her eyes drifted closed before she could think of anything.

She didn't realize she'd fallen asleep until she dreamed of

Mirella's death. In the dream, the scene where Mirella's body was slammed into the ground by bullets was overlaid with the screams as Kovit tortured her. Her pink-gray hair stuck to her face, and her eyes stared out at Nita, wide and accusing. *Why didn't you help me?* they asked.

Nita woke up silent. No screaming. No crying. Just woke.

She let out a breath and rose. She checked the phone. The middle of the night.

Sighing, she leaned back. She didn't want to be left alone with these thoughts.

Unbidden, her eyes turned to the screen, where Kovit was still awake. He was making origami cranes with the pages of the terrible book.

She tapped a finger on her leg, then rose and went to see him.

He looked up when she approached. "Still here?"

"Obviously."

He shrugged. "If I were you, I'd have been long gone by now."

"I would too." Nita sat down in front of his cage. "If only I had some money to pay for my ride out of here."

A look of understanding crossed his face. "That's why you came back." Then he frowned. "I don't have any money."

"Really?"

"You already suspected as much, or you would have asked me earlier." Kovit shook his head, then tilted it to the side. "You're after Reyes' money, aren't you?"

Nita didn't respond.

Kovit sighed. "Why? Just go pickpocket someone."

"I don't know how to pickpocket. And there's no guarantee the amount would be sufficient."

He frowned. "I think you're making excuses."

Nita was silent.

Kovit was quiet for a long time. Then, in a soft voice, he asked, "What happened?"

"Mirella is dead." Nita's jaw clenched.

"Oh."

Nita raised her eyebrows, but Kovit's expression was going vacant. "Oh? That's all you have to say?"

He gave her a poisonous look, and then deftly changed the subject. "So now you want to target Reyes? Out of vengeance?"

"No." Nita pursed her lips. "Practicality."

"Hmm," he said, but it didn't sound like he believed her.

The hum of the air conditioning unit droned in the background, overlaid by the buzz of cicadas outside.

"So," Nita began, letting curiosity get the better of herself, "who did you piss off to end up here? I've been wanting to hear that story."

Kovit laughed. "Have you, now?"

Nita shrugged, not hiding anything.

His eyes sparkled. "Well, I'm happy to tell you the story. But" — his grin widened, almost like a snake — "I'd like to hear yours first."

"Mine?"

"Sure. How did someone whose mother gives her bodies to dissect end up on auction here?" He spread his arms, gesturing at the glass cage, like a square fishbowl.

Nita looked away, clenching her teeth. To tell him or not?

Did it matter? She didn't care what he thought of her, and she was curious to hear his story. She wasn't sure how much of his story she'd be able to believe, but she wanted to hear it anyway.

"Fine." Nita shrugged, feigning indifference. "It's not much of a story. My mom sells unnatural body parts online. I cut the bodies up for sale." She paused. "I used to cut the bodies up for sale."

Kovit leaned forward, waiting.

"One day my mom brought me a living boy instead of a dead one. He wasn't dangerous or anything, and I didn't particularly want to kill him, so I let him escape. Mom wasn't happy about it." Nita waved at the room. "And here I am."

"Your mom sold you?"

Nita was silent for a long moment. When the words came out, they were small and tight and angry. "Yes."

Kovit's expression had lapsed into something like a poker face. Nita had no idea what he was thinking.

She nodded to him. "Your turn."

Kovit was silent a long time, watching her. Then he smiled, but it was a sad, very sane, normal smile. "I'm afraid my story isn't too different from yours. I've been working for a certain crime family in the United States since I was about ten years old."

"Ten is awfully young."

He shrugged. "After INHUP arrested my mother and took my sister into protective custody, I was alone on the streets of Bangkok. Let me tell you, joining an organized crime syndicate in search of a zannie was by far my best option."

His smile was a little mean, like he was daring her to challenge him. She just waved for him to continue.

"Well, at any rate, I've been working for this family since I was ten." His eyes were off staring at a memory. "Mostly in the States. This is my first time working with their Latin American branch."

Nita had a good picture of the mafia Kovit worked for. Because many unnaturals were only found in certain places in the world, many criminal organizations required international partners or multiple branches to meet the growing demand for illegal parts.

She wondered which group he worked for. The only one she knew much about was the Chicago mafia. It was full of vampires who ran large underground auctions online every few years of all the different things they'd kidnapped, collected, and encountered in the course of their business. Everything from addresses of INHUP employees to interesting unnaturals.

"A few weeks ago, they gave me someone, and they told me I was to make an example of him, and then they were going to publicly kill him." Kovit ran a hand through his hair. "You know, people have this idea about torturing for information and all this kind of thing, but really, torture information is useless. The only thing causing pain is good for is punishing people and sending messages."

Kovit paused another moment. "Anyways, it was someone from the Family. Or well, another person in our organization. I'd known him for six years. He was only a few years older than

185

me. One of the few people who knew what I was and didn't avoid me."

Kovit laughed, sharp and cruel. "Obviously, he was being nice so that when this day came, he could try and use my sympathy to get out of whatever punishment was in store for him. It was a smart move—befriend the local monster so that if you're ever put in a cage with it, it doesn't bite."

"It worked, though, didn't it?" The words were out of Nita's mouth before she could stop them. They were gentler than she expected.

Kovit looked up at her, and she nearly flinched, heart slamming in her chest until she remembered he was on the other side of the cage.

"You're not pitying me, are you?" His voice was cold, angry.

Nita's heart continued to thunder. "Not really. But it's an ugly situation, whoever's in it."

Kovit pulled back, eyes still angry, mouth twisting downward. "It was. And afterward, you know what? Suddenly everyone wants to be my friend. They finally realized I'm a monster, but not the specific type of monster they thought. They think, 'If I'm nice to him, he won't torture me if I screw up.' And you know what happens then? The Family's punisher loses all his reputation and fear associated with him. And you know who else loses their reputation? The Family."

Kovit's jaw was clenched tight. "So they'll be needing a new zannie, one who isn't so easily bought. And in the meantime, it's not like they can just let me go, because I know too much. So here I am, in what must be the worst job in the industry, waiting for them to kill me."

Nita was silent a long time. That certainly wasn't the story she'd been expecting. She wasn't sure what she'd been expecting.

In a weird, twisted way, Nita almost felt like Kovit's and her stories were opposite facets on the same diamond. Different, sure, but similar in some fundamental ways. It made Nita feel . . . weird. Squiggly, not-quite empathy, but sort of fear-empathy . . . something. Nita couldn't put it into words.

She sighed, cupping her chin in her hand. "You're right."

"About?" He looked up.

"People thinking you're the wrong sort of monster." Nita looked down at her hands, imagining a scalpel in them. "I'm so very good at taking people apart. But that's because they're not people. I can't do it when they have a name or a face." She fisted her hands. "I was hopeless the minute that boy in the cage introduced himself."

"It's a dehumanizing tactic." Kovit shrugged, and Nita wondered if he would have been able to dehumanize Mirella so easily if they'd shared a language. "I don't hurt people I know. I've met zannies who can—those guys are so insanely obsessed with themselves and their own gratification, they can't even interact with the world normally. Nothing is real to them except themselves. I'm not like that . . . yet. Someday, probably."

"That's fatalistic." But Nita didn't disagree with it.

"Not really. Just truth."

Nita lay down on the floor, and stared up at the fluorescent lights. "You can't hurt people you know, huh? Am I included in that?"

He laughed, and it wasn't as dark a laugh as she expected. "You've been safe for a while."

"Forgive me if I don't turn my pain circuits on just yet."

He snorted. "You do remember that I'm on the wrong side of the cage now?"

She turned to him, and the floor was cool against her cheek. "I'm pretty sure we're both on the wrong side of the cage."

He smiled, and Nita liked the smile he gave her.

What are you doing, Nita? Are you sympathizing with this guy? Stop having a moment!

Screams echoed through her mind, Mirella's agonized cries. Nita felt her smile falling, and Kovit's smile fell with it.

"I'm sorry." Nita sat up, not sure why she was apologizing.

"It's fine." Kovit turned away. "I like it better when people remember what I am. The only thing I hate more than being demonized is when people actively ignore what I do or try to make excuses for it."

"I'm not."

"I know." His hand ran across the floor, making shapes in the nonexistent dust. "Have you ever seen those shows starring serial-killer main characters? *Dexter*? *Hannibal*? Some of those sexy vampire ones the mafia funds to lure victims to them? They make all sorts of excuses for the serial killers. 'It's okay, he's killing bad guys.' 'It's okay, because it happened offscreen.' I hate those. I hate when people do that to me. When they try to make me sympathetic, moralize all the decisions that aren't moral."

Nita swallowed and folded her hands in her lap, letting herself collect her thoughts. After a moment, she spoke. "No. I agree. That's wrong. Your actions aren't sympathetic. And I think the only person who tries to justify your choices is you."

He blinked, and looked up at her, uncertain.

"You torture people for a living. Not just because you need to, but because you *like* to. There is so much pain in this market — I'm sure you could find a meal if you walked around. But you choose not to. You choose to make your own meal." Nita met his eyes. "I don't think your decisions are moral or that they can be moralized."

He was silent before a cruel smile twisted his lips. "So you think I'm a monster."

"No."

His smile fell. "No?"

"I think Reyes is a monster. She lacks any form of discernible empathy for others. Not just her prisoners, but her employees. Even her customers, I can tell she'd kill them in a second. I don't think there's anyone in the world she cares for or any lines she wouldn't cross." Nita shrugged. "I've seen you. You have empathy. You just choose to use it selectively. That's a totally different thing. That's a human thing."

Nita rose and dusted herself off. She wasn't sure why her hands were shaking, but she tried to still them. Kovit watched her, face schooled to a forced neutral state.

As she turned to leave, Kovit called out, "Nita."

"Yes?"

He gave her a long look. "There's a gun hidden behind the

189

security screen. It's wedged between the screen and the wall. It's loaded."

She blinked, uncertain why he was telling her. "Oh."

He closed his eyes, lay back, staring up at the ceiling, and said nothing more.

TWENTY-ONE

THERE WAS MORE than just a gun hidden behind the screen. Nita also found another switchblade, which she pocketed, a crumpled beginner Spanish textbook, and a wad of American dollars that totaled just under forty.

Nita stared at the money a long time. Was it enough to take the boat out of here? If it was, she didn't need to rob Reyes. She could just leave.

Her fingers flicked through the money, counting it again. She didn't know if it was enough. It might be. Did she want to take the risk? She could leave at dawn, be on a boat, and be in Brazil by noon. And then call INHUP. Once she was in Brazil, she could request INHUP's protection until she could contact her father and go home. She could report every sordid detail about Boulder and Reyes so the police could arrest them next time they left Peru. Mirella would appreciate that.

She put the money down on the floor and sat cross-legged beside it. Why had Kovit told her about this?

And when he told her to look for it, he mentioned the gun,

not the money. She found that interesting too. She didn't know what it *meant*, but she found it interesting.

So. She might be able to leave. Nita checked the time. Almost dawn. The sun would be rising in the next half hour. She had enough time to go down to the docks, see if she could barter passage to Brazil, and if she didn't have enough cash, there'd still be time to come back, set her trap for Reyes, and rob her.

It was a good plan.

She grabbed the money and stuffed it in her pocket, and after a moment, she took the gun and shoved it in her other pocket. It made a big, distinctive bulge, but Nita figured it made her look more dangerous and less like a target for anyone who might be out and about at this hour.

Her hand lingered on the door far longer than it should have. She knew if she left and took a boat, she was essentially killing Kovit. Could she do that?

The door creaked when she opened it. Kovit wasn't her responsibility—Nita wasn't culpable for either his or Reyes' actions. Besides. She had time, if she changed her mind. Reyes wasn't coming until eleven.

She still didn't have shoes, which annoyed her. She didn't want to step on anything, but as Mirella had said, the only shoes in the building were on Kovit's feet. She wasn't willing to go back and ask for them. She didn't want to talk to him again. It might make her resolve waver.

Nita crept out into the predawn and clicked on the cell phone light. She tried to be careful where she stepped, because thick calluses or not, things would be unpleasant if she stepped on a poisonous caterpillar. But it was hard when she could barely see in front of her. She slipped in the gravel several times when she spun toward movement she thought she'd seen out of the corner of her eyes.

There was no one out. Nita wasn't sure what she had expected—dawn seemed like the sort of time that things came alive in the jungle. And indeed, the jungle around the market was coming to life. Crickets and cicadas were a background chorus to bird chirps and caws. Other noises too, ones Nita couldn't place. Sounds like sandpaper laughing. Something resembling bells scraping together. The shaking branches rustling against each other as things high above leapt between trees.

But the market itself was quiet. Dark.

Closer to the pier, neon lights still shone from the entryways to gambling dens and shady brothels. There were a few people passed out in front, but either the rest of the customers were still in there or they'd gone back to wherever they were staying for the night.

Nita took a deep breath before turning down the path toward the dock. In her memory, she could still see Mirella saluting her before marching down this path to her doom. Nita walked in the footsteps of a dead girl.

The pier still had its guards, but the sun was just coming up, and there were two other people doing things with boats. Getting ready for the first clients of the morning, she assumed.

The guards moved to block Nita from entry. She resisted the urge to turn and run, and instead forced herself to smile, and say in Spanish, "Good morning. I'd like to go to Tabatinga."

One of them raised his eyebrows, and looked her up and down, taking in her jeans, T-shirt, and bare feet. Nita hoped she didn't look like an escaped prisoner—was that what these guards were supposed to watch out for?

"I'm supposed to be picking something up," Nita continued, trying to draw off suspicion and not sure if it was making her seem more suspicious. "Since you guys see all the transactions that go on here, I wanted to know what time of day you thought I could get the best price."

Nita didn't want to just come right out and ask how much it would cost to get to Tabatinga. That would be suspicious . . . right? But time of day and price was less suspicious. Maybe.

She had no clue what she was doing.

But she must have been doing something right, because the guard said, "Probably around one p.m. That's when all the boats from Tabatinga who've brought customers in today decide they want to get back home before dark. They're more willing to go lower then."

Nita licked her lips. "How much cheaper is it, do you think?"

The other guard shrugged. "Maybe ten dollars cheaper? I've never seen them go below eighty, though."

Eighty dollars? What a rip-off! Fabricio's bus ticket from Peru to Ecuador had been half that, and it was a sixteen-hour ride, not a—what?—four-hour one.

But she was cornered—there was no other way she knew out of the market. Maybe that was why the boat owners could charge so much. They knew they could get away with it.

Or maybe the guard was testing her and was lying. How did

194

she know he was telling the truth? Was it paranoid to think he was lying? No. Better to assume everyone in the market wanted to scam you out of money.

"Eighty?" Her eyebrows rose. "I find that hard to believe."

One of them laughed at her skepticism. "Yeah, I don't think you'll get a deal that good."

She tried to smile. "Well, I'll see what they offer me."

By this time, one of the men who'd been working on a boat came over to Nita. He had a large belly and was smoking a nearly nonexistent cigarette.

Nita approached him. "I'd like to go to Tabatinga. Give me a price."

The man smiled and responded to Nita in heavily Portuguese-accented Spanish. "One hundred fifty dollars. Good price! Special price for a lovely lady."

Nita turned and walked away. Behind her, the guards chuckled, and the man chased her, trying to get her to bargain. But there was no point—there was no way his prices would go low enough that Nita could afford them with her forty dollars.

At least she still had her backup plan.

As she trudged back through the streets as dawn lit the crumbling jungle market, street vendors started setting up their tables, pulling jars from crates on dollies. The stench of formaldehyde and bug spray mixed together. A mosquito bit Nita, and she wondered if it carried dengue fever or malaria. She didn't have antibodies for either in her bloodstream. She was going to have to be careful and keep a close eye on her body's condition. She didn't need some tropical disease on top of everything else.

She turned the corner onto the street with Reyes' building and froze.

Reyes was on the other side of the street. Her hair was pulled back, and she looked unruffled in her business suit, as though she were frozen in stasis, doomed to look exactly the same for all eternity.

Nita watched in horror as Reyes walked over to the building and opened the door, six hours before Nita had been expecting her.

TWENTY-TWO

NITA FROZE, MUSCLES stiffening in the hope that if she didn't move, Reyes' eyes wouldn't be drawn to her.

What was Reyes doing here so early?

Something had changed, but what? Or had she lied in the text she sent to Kovit? Nita didn't know enough about their relationship to know if that was something Reyes would do.

It didn't matter why she was here. What mattered was that she was here, and she wasn't supposed to be, and Nita's plans had all become worthless because she hadn't prepared anything yet.

Fuck.

The door clanged shut behind Reyes, and Nita let out the breath she hadn't realized she'd been holding. Her shoulders sagged. Safe. For now.

But what should she do?

She wasn't in position. She had no way of getting Reyes out of the way. And in a few moments, Reyes would realize Nita was gone. Then what? Reyes might call Jorge and Lorenzo, who would start hunting Nita through the market. They might alert other people, like the guards at the pier, and arm them with pictures of Nita from the video clips.

Nita couldn't let that happen.

Money, escape, everything could wait. Nita had to stop Reyes.

Her feet were moving before her mind had time to form a plan, slipping across the street and up to the front of the building. Nita hesitated at the door, worried Reyes might be waiting on the other side.

Swallowing, Nita pulled the gun out of her pocket. It wasn't as heavy as she'd thought it would be, but there was a sense of weightiness to the decision to pull it out that she didn't like. But better to have it out and not need it than not have it out and need it.

Maybe she could use it to threaten Reyes into a cage. Then lock her in too—all her enemies trapped in cages the way they had trapped her.

What if she resists? part of her asked.

I'll deal with that if it happens.

The other part of her wasn't happy about that, but it quieted.

Nita took a deep breath and opened the door, gun raised high. She ducked her head and her gun through the door, and kept the rest of her body shielded behind it. She scanned the hall and the part of the security room she could see. No Reyes.

Nita slipped through the door and closed it as silently as possible behind her.

Breathing shallowly, the gun slippery in her sweaty palms, Nita edged forward and peered into the security room. Empty.

She checked the closet they called a dissection room. Also empty.

Faint voices drifted down the hall, and Nita realized Reyes must have found Kovit. Crap. Was she on the phone already, putting the guards on alert?

Nita crept down the hall, trying to keep her shaking hands from accidentally firing the gun. Nita had never used a gun before, and all she knew was what she'd seen on television and what her mother did. But her mother rarely brought her gun out around Nita, and on TV, guns either went off when touched by a feather or could withstand pretty much anything without firing. So she had no clue how a real one worked. Point and shoot. Turn the safety off.

Wait. What did the safety even look like?

Nita looked at her gun, but she couldn't tell if it was on or off. All she saw was the dark barrel and a lot of pieces of metal. It meant nothing to her. She hoped the safety was off.

As Nita approached, she could make out the conversation.

"Where's the merchandise, Kovit?"

"Gone."

"Where?"

"I don't know."

Nita edged closer and peered around the corner. She could see Reyes' profile, back straight, shoulders squared. Nita couldn't see the woman's expression, but she could see the gun hanging loosely in her hand.

Shit.

If Reyes was armed and already had her weapon out, it was going to be impossible to get her in the cage. Reyes was probably better with a weapon than Nita, and likely knew it. If Nita went in there screaming, "Drop your weapon," chances were good Reyes would just turn around and shoot Nita instead of complying.

While Nita was trying to puzzle out what to do, Reyes had continued moving. She walked over to the release button and unlocked Kovit's cage. There was a buzz and a click as the mechanism released and the door swung gently open. She gestured with her gun. "Out."

Kovit complied slowly. Each of his motions was calm and deliberate. His face was expressionless—not a poker face, but like all the things that usually ran through his mind were gone and there was only this moment left. It was a focused kind of expressionless.

Reyes kept herself at a distance from Kovit as he exited the cage. Close enough that any shot would hit, far enough she'd have time to shoot Kovit if he lunged at her.

"Where are we going?" he asked, but his voice said he already knew.

"Outside."

Kovit gave a bitter laugh. "Don't want to clean up the mess it would make blowing out my brains in here?"

"Yes."

Nita flinched.

They were making their way down the hall toward Nita. They'd be on her in a few seconds. She'd run out of time awfully fast. Her plan was crumbling around her, and she hadn't even started it yet.

Kovit was about to be executed.

Reyes had a gun and was about to see Nita, the moment she turned the corner. Then Nita would be killed too.

Nita had seconds to decide: What did she do now?

Nita raised her gun with trembling hands. Then she aimed it.

Reyes was only a few feet away. She couldn't see Nita around the corner.

Can you kill a human, Nita? You, who were so proud of those tiny little morals you found? Are you going to throw it all away?

Nita thought of Fabricio. She thought of how certain she'd been about herself, how right it had felt to free him. How she'd drawn a line that murder was on the other side of.

Was she willing to cross the line from being willfully ignorant, abetting murders, to becoming a killer who knows what she's doing?

If it's my life or Reyes', I choose mine, Nita responded. *And if it's her life or Kovit's, I choose Kovit's.*

When she raised the gun and stepped out from her hiding place, her hands were steady, no hint of the trembling that plagued her conscience.

Then she fired.

Nita's aim was good, but not great. She hit Reyes in the shoulder where it connected to her neck, causing her to tumble to the ground with a shocked cry that turned into a gurgle. Kovit gasped as Reyes fell, his whole body doing that creepy, my-drugs-just-kicked-in shudder of ecstasy as Reyes' pain flowed through him.

Nita swore, terrified Reyes would shoot back. She raised her gun to fire again, heart slamming in her chest.

Kovit moved at the same time, swinging around and tackling Reyes, motions swift and ruthless. He fisted one hand in Reyes' hair and used the other to grip her injured shoulder, tearing a shriek of pain out of Reyes. Her shoulder, the one hit by the bullet, popped right out of its socket with an unhealthy crunch. The gun in her hand tumbled to the ground. Kovit kicked it away.

Then Kovit twisted around, smashing Reyes' head against the wall. Hard.

Her skull cracked open.

Blood and pieces of hair clung to the cement, even as Reyes' body slumped to the floor, leaving a wet trail behind on the wall. It seemed like there was blood everywhere — the wall, the floor, and splattered like freckles across Kovit's cheeks.

Kovit sat up, breathing hard. Reyes was still. Nita had dealt with enough bodies before to know she was dead. Part of the head had clearly caved in. No one could survive that. Nita had knowingly killed another person.

No, Kovit bashed her head in.

Only because you couldn't shoot her first, Nita snapped back. *Stop it. I'm done shifting the blame. I killed her.*

The other voice in her head was silent for a long time before it said, *Yes. You did.*

And Nita finally saw it.

She was exactly the same as Kovit.

Kovit used the mafia as his excuse — *Oh, they're going to have him tortured anyways, might as well enjoy it.* And Nita used her mother — *Oh, he's already dead, might as well dissect him. Is that a bullet wound? Not my problem, too late, already dead.*

Neither of them had to do these things. They did it because they liked it.

Nita was exactly the same as Kovit.

The thought hurt. Nita wasn't a good person, but she liked to think she tried. But in the end, it really was all talk. Just empty platitudes to make her feel good, to try to justify her lifestyle to herself.

Nita's hands began to tremble and then full on shake. The gun clattered in her hand, and she forced herself to take her finger off the trigger for fear of accidentally firing again. She shoved the gun in her pocket, but it was still warm, and she could feel its heat, almost burning her skin through the thin material of her jeans.

Nita choked back a gasp. She was a killer. She wanted to scream. She wanted to cry.

Later, she told herself. *You can freak out later. Not now. You need to keep it together for now. You still don't know where you stand with Kovit. You don't know how you're getting out of here. You can panic later.*

Buoyed by the promise, she forced herself to try to see Reyes with the clinical detachment she used on the bodies she dissected. Forced herself to take a step back. That was just an arm. And a head. They were pieces, nothing more. Parts to be dissected.

It helped, thinking of it that way. It didn't make the panic attack building inside her leave, but it made it feel more manageable. At least, for the moment.

Kovit watched her face, searching for signs of . . . Nita wasn't sure what. Regret? Guilt? Was he worried Nita would shoot him next? That would be rather pointless, after the trouble she'd gone through to save him.

She tried to give him a reassuring smile, one that said, *I'm okay, I'm not going to shoot you.* What crossed her face was a warped grin, crooked and slightly off, though you'd be hard-pressed to say how.

Kovit didn't smile back. His face had the strangest expression, one that, if Nita had to guess, read *Is that how I look when I smile? Jeez, that's creepy.*

Kovit glanced over at Reyes, then back to Nita. "Why?"

"I owed you. For saving me from Reyes. I'm just returning the favor." Nita's voice was steady. Too steady for having just killed a person.

Kovit gave a soft, mocking smile. "And?"

"And I need help getting the hell out of this place." She hesitated. "You didn't seem too thrilled to be here, so I thought you might be interested in getting out too."

He looked to the floor, where Reyes' body sprawled. He stayed there for a few moments, and Nita wondered what thoughts were going through his head.

Finally, he seemed to come to a decision. He looked up and met Nita's eyes. "Yes. I'm interested."

Nita held out her hand. "Partners?"

He gave her a genuine, almost sweet smile and clasped her hand. "Partners."

TWENTY-THREE

KOVIT WAS THE ONE who scrounged through Reyes' pockets. He pulled out several keys, a second gun, and a cell phone. But there was no wallet, no money.

"She doesn't carry cash?" Nita asked.

He shook his head. "I don't know. Maybe she's so well-known she doesn't need it. People here are terrified of her."

Nita crossed her arms, examining the body with the clinical distance she'd learned in her dissections. "Why? I'm not saying she's not a scary woman, but this is a big market with lots of scary people."

Kovit grunted. "I've only been here a month, so I don't know the whole story. But apparently she deposed her predecessor. He was supposedly one of the most feared people in the industry. People called him the King of Parts."

Nita grunted. "I've heard of him. He used to kill his enemies and sell their parts to their families for burial, right?"

"Yup." Kovit sat back on the floor, examining the various keys from Reyes' pockets. "But I think he got his name from the unnatural body parts business. He just sort of . . . played it up when dealing with rivals."

"I see." Nita sat down beside Kovit. "I wasn't aware he was dead. The King of Parts."

"Yeah. About six months ago. I heard Reyes killed him, cut up his body, distributed a piece of him to every major player in the area, and told them the king was dead and there was a queen now." He shrugged. "After that, she just took over all his businesses and continued on with his work."

"She calls herself the Queen of Parts, and her name is Reyes? It means 'king.'" Nita snorted. "It can't be her real name."

"I'm pretty sure it's a pseudonym," Kovit agreed.

Nita looked over at Reyes. "So now that we've killed Reyes, does that make us the new King and Queen of Parts?"

"I think it just makes us the people who killed Reyes."

She laughed, then cut it short. She shouldn't be laughing. She'd just murdered someone, and not five minutes later, here she was, sitting in front of the dead body, laughing about her death.

Nita wondered if she was cracking.

Kovit was giving her a strange look, but she waved it away. "So, what are the keys for?"

"Well, this one"—he held up a standard, kind of old-fashioned-looking key—"is for this building."

Nita took it. "I didn't know this building could be locked from the outside."

"Yeah. Reyes locked me in the first few weeks I was here,

until she realized I hated the market and wouldn't go outside even if she kept it unlocked."

Nita blinked. "She locked you in?"

"She thought I would run."

"Would you?"

"Of course. I'm not an idiot. I knew I was in deep trouble with the Family—I don't even know how Reyes is connected to them. For all I know, the Family sold me to Reyes." Kovit's smile was bitter. "I thought they were going to kill me, you know. When I disobeyed . . . I thought that was the end. But they said this was a 'second chance' because zannies are valuable enough to get a second chance. They'd've just killed me if I were human."

Nita frowned. "Why haven't you left, then? The door isn't locked."

"Reyes brought me to meet all the guards at the port the first day I was here. It was made clear to them what kind of horrors would befall them if I left." He smiled. "I went to the port anyway. I tried to explain that the horrors of disobeying me would be far worse and far more immediate." His smile widened and warped a little, but then fell again. "It didn't make a difference. They were more scared of her than they were of me."

"Oh." Having heard the screams of Kovit's victims, Nita couldn't imagine what horror Reyes promised that could compare.

Nita's heart lurched suddenly, thinking of Mirella. What would she think of Nita teaming up with the man who tortured her?

*You gotta do what you gotta do. Kovit will help you escape. And
if anyone gets in your way, you can get him to do the killing while you
run off.*

Nita hadn't realized that her face had squished into a
frown until Kovit spoke.

"Nita?"

She hesitated, then shook her head. "Sorry. Just thinking
about how that changes escape plans."

"Ah." Kovit finished looking through Reyes' pockets and
rose.

"It's fine." Nita nodded to herself. "We just need enough
money to make the guards look the other way."

There were very few fears that a healthy dose of money
couldn't dispel. Her mother had taught her that.

Kovit tilted his head. "Or we could take a page out of Reyes'
book and give them her head, so they don't need to be scared
of her anymore."

"Also an option." Nita's finger's twitched for a scalpel. She
hoped Kovit wouldn't fight her for the chance to cut up Reyes.

"So." Nita looked at the other keys, trying to derail her
thoughts before they got too dark. "What are the other keys
for?"

"This one is her house." Kovit held up a square metal fob,
like a garage opener.

Nita blinked. "She has a house here?"

"Yeah. I can take you there. I've been a few times." He
looked over at Reyes. "It requires thumbprint access, though."

Nita shrugged, pulled Kovit's spare switchblade out of her
pocket, and removed Reyes' thumb. The switchblade didn't

like hitting bone, so Nita went a little deeper and dislocated the thumb so she only had flesh to cut through. It was a good feeling, sinking the knife into flesh. She always loved how skin resisted before it tore, but once you were in, the knife always just seemed to glide through. Well, until you hit bone. Or cartilage. Or other things.

Finally she stood and gestured to the door, still holding Reyes' thumb. "Shall we?"

Kovit watched her, dark eyes wide. An expression flitted across his face, too fast for Nita to read. Finally, his face relaxed into an easy, comfortable smile, and he rose. "Let's."

They locked the building behind them, just in case someone wandered in too soon and found Reyes dead. And since now there was a key in their possession, it only made sense.

Kovit stopped her as she was leaving. "Are you going out in bare feet?"

She shrugged. "No shoes."

Rolling his eyes, he ducked back into the building, and retrieved Reyes' shoes. They were a bit small for Nita, but the fit wasn't too terrible. Better than bare feet, so she put them on.

It was still early morning, and it was already too hot, in Nita's opinion. It wasn't long before a fine layer of sweat covered her body like a shield, protecting her from direct contact with the outside air. Mosquitoes buzzed around them, and Nita felt heavy, like the air was physically pushing her down.

They made their way through the market. Kovit took a meandering path that made them go around most of the major market streets, and sometimes other random streets too. He would pause occasionally and shiver like someone had dropped an ice cube down his back, before changing directions, veering around.

"Are you avoiding something?" Nita asked.

Kovit shook his head in a single jerky motion. "No. It's nothing."

"You sure?"

"Yes."

It took far longer than it should have for them to reach the other side of the market. Nita tried to press Kovit on why he kept detouring, but he ignored her questions.

He led her down a path through the jungle. It wound around enough that Nita couldn't see where it ended. Kovit started down it, his feet sure. Nita followed, careful to avoid the low-hanging branches and jutting roots.

The deeper she went, the more any evidence of human presence disappeared. If she woke up here, she'd never have imagined there was a market a few steps away. Even the sound was erased, no hum of generators or clatter of people. The jungle was too *loud*. Nita hadn't realized how the market muted things. She'd only faintly heard the noises of the rainforest. But here, between the trees, the level of noise was overpowering.

It didn't feel real, like she'd stepped onto the set of *Tarzan*, or some Disney movie. She almost expected to turn a corner and walk up to a pond covered in lily pads, with a singing princess lounging on a log.

As she continued into the forest, everything grew darker. It had been light when they left, but the canopy blocked out so much of the sun that it seemed like twilight in the jungle. Mosquitos buzzed, nipping as she went. Nita scratched absently, and then realized she could quell the allergic reaction causing the itch. She did so immediately.

She tried to be careful—she didn't want to dislodge some poisonous bug from a branch and have it fall on her and bite her. Everywhere she went, giant bugs hung on webs, sat on leaves, or scuttled across her path. And she had no idea which ones she was supposed to be wary of.

She was almost relieved when she saw a tarantula on the ground. Those, she knew, weren't fatally poisonous. Just big and gross. It was weirdly relieving to finally recognize something and know that it wasn't dangerous to her.

Ahead of her, Kovit moved with confidence. While he certainly wasn't vampire-silent in his movements, he was quieter than Nita. She tried to step where he stepped, but she seemed to make far more noise. Maybe it wasn't where he stepped but how he stepped? She wasn't sure.

Eventually, the trees thinned, and they appeared in a small clearing.

In the center was a mansion.

Made of a combination of wood, concrete, and something matte that might have been plastic, it looked like the modern version of the Swiss Family Robinson's house. Two floors, with windows shuttered and locked. The outside had mostly been left unpainted, except around the doors and windows, which were outlined in a pale blue.

Nita hesitated. Massive, and impressive, but she had to confess it didn't look terribly secure. Certainly not enough to warrant the need for a thumbprint scanner.

Kovit gestured for Nita to approach, and the two of them

picked their way over. Kovit was sweating as much as Nita, and his hair was sticking to the top of his skull and forehead. He wiped it back, and the sweat slicked his hair back like pomade.

They approached the front door, and Nita took out the thumb. "What do I do with this?"

"Place it here." Kovit flipped the wooden cover off a thumb scanner.

Nita did as instructed, and the machine beeped. There was a click, and a small green light went on. Kovit then took out the fob and pressed it. A second green light went on. Kovit opened the door, which didn't appear to be locked. Nita couldn't even see a bolt hole in it where the locking mechanism would attach.

"The thumb scanner isn't for the lock?" Nita asked.

Kovit shook his head. "No. The building's unlocked. The thumb scanner and key fob are to disable the mustard gas release mechanism. It kicks in automatically when any door or window is opened unless the thumb scanner is used to disable it."

Nita opened her mouth, then closed it. Of course there was mustard gas. Tear gas was just so passé. Why incapacitate your enemies when you could murder them?

Kovit led her in through the foyer. The room was sparse. A staircase led up, and other than that, there was a bookrack. Nothing more. It looked like a show home, brand-new and waiting for someone to fill it with life.

Nita looked around. "Where's all the stuff?"

"Upstairs. Reyes never left anything down here because she didn't want to get mustard gas in it if someone decided to break in."

"Has anyone ever tried?"

"Not that I know of." He shrugged. "Though I figure some-one must have a long time ago—there's too many contingen-cies in place for it to be entirely preventative."

Nita nodded absently, and then started up the stairs. Kovit followed.

She immediately regretted going first. She didn't like hav-ing Kovit where she couldn't see him. It wasn't that she didn't trust him—well, maybe a little—she just wanted him in her line of sight. This partnership wasn't exactly the most stable dynamic she'd ever had. But then again, she'd only ever worked with her parents. That wasn't a good baseline. Maybe everyone was scared of the people they worked with?

Not likely. Most people weren't working with people who reveled in the pain of others. Right?

The steps creaked as she ascended. On the second floor, there were several rooms. A bedroom, bed made, clothes in drawers and hung neatly in the closet. Not a mote of dust out of place. A mosquito net hung over the bed, and an air condi-tioning unit perched above the window.

The next room was a study, with a laptop and two screens. There were no papers, pens, or any other paraphernalia Nita associated with studies, though. The wooden chair had no cushions. Another air conditioning unit sat above the desk, though it wasn't on.

The third room was empty. Just bare wood floor.

Nita turned to Kovit. "Start with the computer?"

He nodded, and they retreated to the den. Nita flipped the laptop up, but was prompted for a password. She swore.

Kovit leaned over and squinted at the screen. Then he typed something.

You have entered the wrong password. Please try again.

He tried something else.

"Do you have any idea what you're doing?" Nita asked him.

"None." He grinned, a cheeky, childish smile. "But I might as well give it a shot."

None of his guesses worked, and they were locked out of the laptop. Nita closed the top, unhappy. She'd been hoping she could get internet, see if there were messages from either of her parents. Maybe check the news to see what her father had been arrested for, or if he'd been transferred to INHUP custody.

Nita frowned. She hadn't thought of that before. Why were the Chicago police holding him, and not INHUP? If they'd found out about her family's black market business selling unnaturals, then her father shouldn't be in Chicago PD custody. Maybe something else had happened?

Nita ran her fingers through her hair and gripped the strands just against her skull in her fists. She wished she knew. Not knowing was going to drive her crazy. She had no clue what had happened to her father, if her mother had done something to him, *nothing*. Once she escaped, how was she supposed to figure out what to do if she didn't *know*?

Rage at her mother continued to burble just under the surface, but she pushed it away. It wasn't productive to think about that now. Focus on escape. Then on everything else.

"Nita? I think I found a safe."

Kovit had pulled out a drawer with a small locked box in

it. It had a combination lock. Nita knelt beside it and listened. She heightened her hearing, trying to make it more and more sensitive. Then she turned the dial. She enhanced her hearing until she could hear the pins tumbling.

She closed her eyes so she could focus better, stopped at the click, then turned the other way.

A few minutes later, the lock box was open and the contents spread across the floor.

They were disappointing.

A list of sales ledgers that indicated Reyes was making a lot of money, but neither hide nor hair of said money. The printouts were dated the end of last month, and Nita wondered why Reyes even bothered with hard copies, until she realized they were in the middle of the jungle, which wasn't really healthy for electronics or a good internet connection. Kovit's passport was also there, but since it said he was born in Los Angeles, she figured it was fake. Kovit seemed pleased by its appearance and immediately pocketed it.

There was also a list of names, as well as dates and amounts. This was all handwritten, not typed. Nita wasn't sure what it meant. She showed it to Kovit, and he looked through.

"Bribes."

Nita blinked and took the list back. "How can you be sure?"

He pointed to the top of each page, where there was a single letter. One page was I, another PB, and another PP.

"I is for INHUP. PB is *Policía Brasileña*. PP is *Policía Peruana*." He flipped through a few other pages and paused on another one labeled F. "I bet this is FBI."

Nita ran her fingers down the names. "How can you be sure?"

"This one," he pointed to one of the INHUP names. "I know of him. He's in the zannie division, I forget which branch." Kovit gave Nita a crooked grin. "I like to know who to avoid. I track all zannie-related news and make notes on the agents involved."

"I see."

Of course there would be corruption in INHUP. There was corruption in everything. People had yet to design an incorruptible police force or government, or an incorruptible anything, really. You'd have to change human nature to do that.

Nita knew that better than most. Her parents paid multiple bribes to ship their products in the US. Half the American customs agents were probably in her mother's pocket. Not to mention the police officers and medical examiners she'd paid to let her take bodies. Nita remembered her mother paying a lot of money to a detective in Chicago when she was a kid to have a murder investigation go away after a job went wrong.

Nita hesitated, eyes running down the list. Had she accidentally sent Fabricio into the lion's den? She hoped not—it would make all she'd done for nothing.

Her fingers ran over the list of names, and she wondered how valuable a list like this would be.

Kovit sighed and leaned back. "There's nothing helpful here."

"We should check the other rooms. Maybe there's another safe or something?" Nita pocketed the paper.

Kovit nodded, and they decided to split up. Kovit took the bedroom, and Nita took the empty room.

She stood in the room, looking at the bare walls, the bare floor. She walked, listening for a change in the sound, indicating a cavity beneath the floor. But the boards were all uneven, and every step she took sounded different. It was hopeless.

Nita sat down and realized for the first time since she'd shot Reyes, she was alone. No Kovit. No one to see her meltdown.

But she couldn't seem to cry. Her eyes prickled, but the tears didn't come. Her chest constricted, and she folded over herself.

Nita had killed Reyes. She'd held the gun, and in full knowledge of what she was doing, she'd pulled the trigger. She'd never thought she'd kill someone. She'd said she wouldn't. What did anything mean anymore, now that she'd broken that rule?

Her mind swirled with memories, Reyes' blood on the floor, the look on the woman's face when the bullet hit.

You had to do it, Nita.

I know.

And she did, but it didn't make it any easier.

And then she was crying. It felt good to give the pain inside her a physical outlet. Not great wracking sobs, just sad, salty tears. She felt like if she could cry all her emotion out, the pain of what she'd done would flow out with it.

It didn't, but she still felt better afterward.

When Kovit barged into the room, Nita stumbled in her effort to stand up quickly and wipe her eyes, trying to hide what had happened. But he didn't seem to notice, his eyes wide with worry.

"We have a problem."

"What?" Nita's voice choked.

"Jorge and Renzo are here. They're walking up to the building now."

Nita ran over to the shutters and peered out in time to see Reyes' two guards approach the door and knock.

TWENTY-FOUR

NITA SPUN AROUND, eyes wide as she faced Kovit. "What do we do?"

Kovit's eyes darted around the empty room, as though searching for some clue that would tell him how to proceed. "I don't know."

"If we don't answer the door, maybe they'll go away?" Nita hedged.

He shook his head. "We disabled the gas. The security is green, and they'll be able to see that on the thumb pad. They'll know someone is here."

Sure enough, there was a faint scrape and the thunk of rubber boots on wooden flooring as the guards entered the house below.

Nita swore. What should they do?

Kovit pulled out his switchblade and eyed the gun in Nita's pocket. Nita's hand hovered over it protectively.

"You're not thinking about killing them, are you?" Nita asked. "I'm not a great shot."

The footfalls were starting up the stairs, and Kovit

hesitated before shaking his head. "It might work, but they're both armed and know how to use their guns." He looked pointedly at Nita's pocket, where her gun rested. She took it out and handed it to him. He shook his head. "I prefer my knife."

Nita snorted. "Are you really going to take a knife to a gunfight?"

"Yes." He fingered his switchblade. "I've never been good with guns. They lack finesse."

Nita rolled her eyes and kept the gun.

"If we attacked and even one of them got away, we'd be absolutely screwed." Kovit frowned. "Once he gets into the market . . . well, let's just say pieces of us would be for sale within an hour."

Part of Nita was relieved, and part of her was panicked. It would be so much easier if they could just get rid of the guards, once and for all. Eliminate everyone who might notice Nita's escape.

It wouldn't help with the long-term problem of the online video. You can't escape the internet.

That can be dealt with later. The guards are here now.

Kovit made a decision, snapping his switchblade closed and pocketing it. "I'll find out what they want." He took a step toward the door, and then turned back to Nita. "If it looks like they're not buying it, shoot them."

Nita nodded, but her hands shook.

The first one is always the hardest. Her mother had said that about dissections, but surely it applied equally to murder. Lorenzo and Jorge should be easier, right?

Nita felt like everything was crumbling inside her. All the pieces that made her herself had been shifted, moved out of order, and while she was scrambling to pick them up, life continued, and everything seemed to scramble them up more. This wasn't how it was supposed to go. This was never how it was supposed to be. Nita was supposed to save up enough money to buy herself a new identity and go to college, and leave her mother. She wasn't supposed to become her mother, killing everyone in her way.

Life seemed to have different ideas for her.

Kovit's voice came strong and clear as Nita edged to the door, gun in hand. "Jorge, Renzo. Have you seen Reyes?"

"No," one of them responded. Lorenzo, she thought. It was clear from his voice he wasn't comfortable with something. Kovit? Using English? Nita didn't know. "We looked too. She's not here?"

Nita peered through the door, hoping she could see what was happening. The angle was sideways, so she could make out the profile of Kovit and part of his face, and the backs of the guards.

Kovit shook his head, shoulders loose, creepy smile set across his face like a weapon at the ready. "No. She called me, but wasn't here." His smile widened, and he leaned forward, body language screaming *predator*. "What about you?"

Lorenzo flinched and took one step back, then straightened himself and gave Kovit a challenging look, despite his still shaking hands. Kovit chuckled and leaned back, loose grin crooked like a shattered picture frame.

"Yes. She asked us to pick up the package." Lorenzo turned to Jorge and slipped into Spanish. *"Fuck, Jorge, I can't deal with that monster. You talk to it."*

"No, I can't speak English, remember? Just ask him if he has the package. That's obviously why Reyes called him over."

Lorenzo said, "Give us the package, and we'll go."

Kovit's smile never fell as he shook his head. Slowly. Patiently. Nita had never seen a headshake that menacing. She felt like when he stopped, bad things would happen. Even though she knew he was playing them, she still felt her heart rate spike with each motion he made. "I can't do that without Reyes' approval. I'm not willing to risk her wrath."

"What did he say?"

"He won't give it to us without Reyes' say-so."

"Fuck. The boat is due to arrive any minute. Given how much the customer is paying, I don't think Reyes will want us to keep him waiting."

Lorenzo swallowed, hands twitching, sweat glistening on his forehead. *"What do we do?"*

"Call Reyes." Jorge's voice was firm. *"Get her to tell him to give us the arm."*

"We should just take it."

"I'm not going against that pain-eating psychopath if I don't have to. Are you?"

Arm. They wanted an arm. They assumed Kovit had brought it. Reyes had been going to see Nita at an unscheduled time.

Fuck, had someone bought Nita's arm overnight? Or Mirella's?

Shit shit shit. This was not good. They weren't leaving without an arm.

Wait—how was this person paying for the arm? If it was cash, then maybe Nita could take some of it. After all, the guards would bring it back to Reyes' house, right? But it might be bank transfer.

Either way, if the guards didn't show up with Nita's arm, then there'd be an angry client, who sounded rich enough to have his own guards. Guards who might come up to see what was taking Reyes so long.

Nita needed more time. She needed people to stop sniffing around right now.

They wanted an arm. A woman's arm, presumably—but how would they know who the arm belonged to?

Nita had a bad idea.

But it might work.

"We'll call Reyes." Lorenzo's voice was a little too high, and Nita could hear the beep as he pushed a button on his phone.

Nita peeked through the door and tried to signal Kovit. He didn't see her, his gaze focused on creeping out the second guard. He was doing a good job too, as Lorenzo's whole body was stiff with repressed terror.

Damn it. She needed to get Kovit's attention.

She looked down at her hand. There was one way.

Did she want to do this? It might set a precedent—she didn't want Kovit assuming that this was okay. But when she thought about it, she realized that for the moment, she wasn't too worried about Kovit deciding to hurt her. They needed each other to get out of here.

223

So she switched on her pain circuits in one finger—just one, she couldn't cope with the level of pain she'd have to endure by turning all of them on.

It *hurt*.

Nita clenched her teeth to keep the whimper from escaping her lips and doubled over, pressing her finger against her stomach as every single nociceptor in her pinkie tested to make sure it was still working. It felt like her finger had been dipped in lava, and everything was melting off.

There was a sharp intake of breath in the other room, followed by Kovit's voice. "Good plan. I'll take a look and see if there are any messages on my phone."

Nita backed away from the door as Kovit slipped through. Nita's finger throbbed.

Kovit gave her a tight smile and seemed to suppress a shudder. "I gather you wanted my attention?"

"They came here to get my or Mirella's arm—it's been sold. They won't leave without it, no matter what."

Kovit's hand reached into his pocket for his switchblade. "No other way?"

She grabbed his arm, stopping him. His skin was as sticky with sweat as her own, and she quickly peeled her hand away. Kovit stared at her, one eyebrow raised.

"I'm going to get an arm." Nita opened the shutter on the second-floor window, pushed aside the mosquito netting, and looked down at the ground. She let out a breath. It wasn't too far a jump—she could heal any damage it might cause. Then she turned back to Kovit. "I'll pick up Reyes' phone when I get there. She has your cell number, right? I'll call when I'm back

—you pretend it's Reyes calling and then give them the arm. Stall until then."

Kovit blinked, then frowned. "Where are you going to get an arm?"

Nita just looked at him.

Then it clicked. His eyes widened. "Oh."

A voice from the hall called out. "Kovit? Was there a text?"

Then the door began to open, and Nita dove out the window to go and get Reyes' arm.

TWENTY-FIVE

NITA RACED THROUGH the jungle.

Every time her foot crunched on the branches or the leaves scraped at her hair, she'd wince, half afraid the guards would hear. Which was ridiculous; they were in the house. They couldn't possibly hear her.

Her breathing was hot and shallow, sweat sticking her clothes to her and tickling her mosquito bites in a highly uncomfortable way. As a fly buzzed by and landed on her, then stuck to her sweaty body, unable to get off, Nita determined something: she hated the jungle. When — if — she ever got out of here, she was taking a vow to never go into nature again.

Once she got back to a city, she was going to cling to the concrete buildings and take deep, desperate gulps of the polluted air. She wouldn't ever complain about the crowds again if only she could be back in Lima, with its air conditioning, dry climate, and paved roads.

Nita kept a wary eye out as she ran, trying to make sure she didn't accidentally stray from the path or step on something alive.

She snapped several branches as she stumbled out of the jungle and into the edge of the market. Then she took off, running down the street, Reyes' too-tight shoes pinching her feet in a way that would have been painful if she'd had her pain circuits turned on.

Nita avoided the crowded parts of the market, and she was in front of the concrete prison within a few minutes. Her fingers fumbled as she pulled the key from her pocket and slid it in the lock.

As the door opened, a blast of air conditioning hit Nita. She gasped at the sudden change, then pushed through the shock, toward Reyes' body. She was very grateful for the air con. Without it, given the outside temperature, Reyes' body would already have been stinking and starting to rot.

Nita approached Reyes and then realized she needed tools. She'd seen a few before, in their version of a dissection room. Nita stumbled in her haste to get there, not sure how long Kovit could stall.

Please, just hold them off a few minutes, Kovit. If they decided to turn on Kovit, Nita would be in huge trouble. They'd come for her next.

Nita found a bone saw—not the best option, but something. She didn't have time to go through bone—this wasn't an electric saw, it was manual. She'd need to pop the arm out of its socket and then cut through there, where it would be easier. Not ideal. She would have liked a different tool. An electric one.

She returned to the main hallway, and looked down at Reyes, body partly sprawled on the floor, but her head and a bit of her chest half propped up against the wall.

This was the person Nita had murdered.

The person she was now going to dissect.

When did you cross over into serial killer territory, Nita?

I don't have time for you right now.

A phone rang, tinny and high-pitched. Nita knelt down and pulled out Reyes' cell. It was nice, a brand-new smartphone with a cover and case that clicked against Nita's fingernails. Nita pocketed it, ignoring the ring.

Then she pressed her saw to the body and cut.

She'd told off her conscience better than she thought, because she didn't feel nauseous or guilty while she worked. She just felt sort of sad, a vague, distracted emotion. Like when she looked at someone on her dissection table and saw that they had chronic arthritis. She felt a little bad for them, but it was a distanced feeling, not really empathy, or even sympathy. She didn't know if there was even a word for it. Maybe other people didn't feel that emotion, or maybe they didn't like to admit they felt that emotion and just pretended they had sympathy.

Or perhaps her adrenaline was pumping too high, and her panic was too strong for her to really process anything else. The saw crunch-squish-snapped through flesh and muscle. Nita wedged it in between the shoulder joint and attempted to rip the arm off in full. It tore, flesh rending with a wet, chunky sound.

Nita wiped sweat off her forehead, and replaced it with dark, clotted-blood-black streaks across her skin. But she had the arm. She scooped it up and turned to leave, but stopped.

She couldn't just run through the market holding a human arm.

Or could she? This was Death Market. Hadn't Nita seen worse things peddled on the street?

Tucking the severed arm under her own, Nita pelted from the building and retraced her steps through the market to the jungle and Reyes' house. Her heart beat in time to her steps, and droplets of sweat marked her passing. Her throat was dry, even though the rest of her was soaked.

The branches swatted at her, and a cricket fell down her shirt as she stumbled through the hideous path to Reyes' house. Nita crushed the cricket, angry at the interruption.

When she reached the clearing with the house, Nita pulled out Reyes' phone, only to realize it was locked.

Fuck.

She could receive calls, but she couldn't initiate them. She needed Kovit to call her.

Groaning, she braced herself and turned on her pain circuits in another finger. She fell to her knees, gasping through the pain. She was never going to get used to that.

The phone rang a moment later.

Nita double-checked the caller was Kovit before answering. "I'm sorry I couldn't call. Reyes' phone is locked."

"I got the message."

Clearly. Nita shifted, uncomfortable with the idea of him eating her pain. "I have the arm."

She could hear the whoosh of air leaving him. "All right."

"I'm going to throw it up through the window I left from."

"I see. I'll make a note of it in the files in the study."

Nita paused. The guards were clearly listening in. "So, you want me to throw it through the study window?"

"Yes, that's right."

"Okay." Nita walked around the building to where the study window was. It was right next to the one she'd jumped out of, so it was easy to identify. "I'm throwing it up now."

She swung the arm in an underhand motion. It arced up, hit the side of the house, and then fell down. Nita swore, picked it up, and tried again. This time it went in.

"It's in."

"Great. I'll hand it over now, then. Thanks."

Then there was a click as the line disconnected.

Nita slumped against the side of the house, exhausted. Sweat dripped into her eyes, and stuck her clothes to her body in an unpleasant way. The dried sweat had created a crunchy layer over her body, and the wet sweat piled over it created another layer, until Nita had an entire stratum of sweat on her body.

The front door opened.

Nita froze, realizing she should have hidden while she had the chance. Lorenzo and Jorge were walking away. They hadn't seen Nita, but if they turned around, she'd be right in their line of sight.

Damn it, Nita. If you fuck this up because of such a stupid mistake, you'll never live it down.

No shit, because I'll never live.

"I could just meet you later—" Lorenzo was saying.

"Not a chance." Jorge had the arm in a bag he'd found

somewhere. "I'm not letting you out of my sight. You'll just snort again, and then Reyes really will give you to Kovit. She isn't screwing around, man."

Lorenzo sighed softly and rubbed his temples. "I know, I know. But I just . . . I've been thinking of going back home. You know, now that Italy doesn't have to sign into INHUP because of EU regulations, powdered unicorn bone prices will go back to normal."

"You're leaving?" Jorge sounded hurt.

Nita just wished they'd hurry up and leave so she could move again. The longer they talked, the greater the chance they'd notice her.

Lorenzo shrugged. "I dunno. I thought maybe you could come with me. Italy's nice. You'll like it."

"I don't want to go to Italy, Renzo. I like it here."

Nita's heart slammed in her chest, and her body was as still as a corpse until they left the clearing and entered the trees. Their voices slowly faded, and Nita let the tension fall from her shoulders as she leaned against the side of the house, all her strength stolen by relief.

She was alive.

For now.

TWENTY-SIX

KOVIT LOOKED TIRED. Not hungry tired, just emotionally tired. Nita wasn't even sure how she could tell, just that she could — she thought maybe when he was hungry tired, his movements tended to be sharper, more edged and jerky. When he walked over to her, he was loose limbed, shoulders slightly slumped.

He leaned against the side of the building and looked down at Nita. "While I agree it's definitely time to take a break and just curl on the floor for a while, I vote we do it inside, where there's air conditioning."

Air conditioning. Possibly the only two words that would have gotten Nita up faster would have had something to do with imminent death.

Kovit offered a hand to help her up, but Nita waved it away and rose on her own, and followed him inside. They ascended the stairs and settled themselves in the study, underneath the air conditioner, which Kovit had already turned on.

The cool air did wonders for Nita's mood. She might still be trapped in a market full of people who wanted to murder her and eat her corpse, but at least now she didn't feel like she was having a bath in her own sweat. Somehow that made all the difference.

The two of them rested for a while. Kovit lay on the floor, looking up at the ceiling, and Nita sat against the wall. They were silent, and that was okay—she just wanted to revel in the cold and sort through her thoughts.

Eventually, Kovit rose and brought her a bottle of water.

"Thanks."

He nodded and sat down across from her. Looking at the water bottle, his eyes softened slightly. "I have a friend, and when she was younger, she wanted to scare her brother, so she opened a water bottle and put a plastic snake in. He didn't notice and drank the water, snake and all. Then he had to go to the ER to get it removed."

Nita nearly snorted her water out trying not to laugh.

Kovit grinned. "Every time I open a water bottle, I think of that story."

Wiping her mouth, Nita narrowed her eyes. "Was this friend part of the, uh, Family?"

Kovit frowned for a moment, then his eyes cleared and he shook his head. "Oh, no. Definitely not. She was from an online forum. I think all my friends as a kid were over the internet. I never met any of them."

Nita had never thought of using the internet to meet people. To her, the internet was just where you sold things, where monsters lurked behind glowing screens, claws hovering over scratched keyboards as they funded her mother's murders. She couldn't imagine being friends with anyone there.

She never really thought of the rest of the internet. The non-evil side of it.

"I assume they don't know about you?" she asked.

"Of course not." He looked away, voice soft and sad. "I actually like these people."

His eyes lowered, a stray strand of hair just brushing the tips of his eyelashes. He still looked achingly beautiful from torturing Mirella, and she found it deeply disturbing that hurting people made him look attractive. She found it more disturbing that she noticed.

Nita turned away and took a deep gulp of water. She improved her water absorption as she drank, since there was a danger of dehydration in places like this. Especially given how much running she'd been doing.

When her bottle was empty, Nita set it down on the floor and looked up at Kovit. "So. Now what do we do?"

"That's the million-dollar question, isn't it?"

Nita sighed and scratched at the dried sweat on her scalp. "We're no better off than before we came here."

"No." Kovit tapped a finger on the ground. "Well, I've got my passport back."

"And that helps us get out of here how?"

He shrugged. "It doesn't. But it'll be nice for after we get out."

"I guess." Nita groaned, put her head in her hands, and

clenched it. She'd been trying to focus on the immediate problem of getting out. But afterward . . . "Fuck."

"What?"

"Reyes' video. The one of me she posted online." Nita had been trying not to think about it. But it was persistent. "My face is plastered all over the internet, along with my ability. Every black market dealer in the world will be on the lookout for me once I get out of here."

She felt a sudden surge of rage. Her whole life, fucked up. Even if she got out, she'd have to look over her shoulder forever, wondering if someone was after her. No more anonymity. Always on someone's hit list. Her fist smashed down on the floor.

"You can do things with your body. Can you change your face?" Kovit asked.

Nita shook her head. "No. My ability is to control things — I can only do things my body can do on its own. It's not magic. It's not like I can go change my genes to modify the color of my eyes."

Though, now that she thought about it, she could add or reduce melanin to make them a bit darker or lighter.

"What about, I dunno, making your face rounder with more fat or something?" he asked.

She shook her head. "I could add fat to certain areas. But if I started screwing around with my appearance, I'd be more likely to fuck it up. I mean, what if I tried to get my body to store more fat on my cheeks, but my face wasn't designed for it? So it impeded blood flow or who knows what, and when I fix that, it breaks something else — I'm not saying it's impossible. I mean, I might be able to change other things too, possibly, with an awful lot of research and specialized knowledge, but ... the risk of screwing it up really bad is so high. I've never considered doing anything cosmetic with my ability."

"Huh." Kovit considered. "I suppose all abilities have limitations."

"Unfortunately." Nita picked a splinter out of her finger and stared at the blood that formed around the cut. It was still weird not to feel any pain. "The body is all interconnected. You mess with one thing, it affects others. I try to be careful about larger things."

She sighed, drained. She'd always loved her ability, always loved the insight it gave her into her own and other people's biology. But now she almost wished she were human. Which was ridiculous. Who wants to be normal when they can be special?

Nita, clearly, when she was upset.

Kovit pinched the bridge of his nose. "Now you've got me thinking of the problems awaiting me if I get out."

"Such as?"

"If the Family thinks I killed Reyes and ran off, they might decide to dispose of me. I know a lot of stuff about their organization, where the skeletons are. Enough to bring them down."

Nita thought about that. "What do you think they'd do if they thought you'd run off?"

"Send a picture of me to INHUP, and evidence I was a zannie, for starters." He licked his lips. "Zannies are on the list of dangerous unnaturals. If INHUP put a bulletin out on me, the whole world would see me and shoot to kill."

"Fuck."

What kind of irony was this? Nita was going to be on the run from every bad guy in the world, and Kovit would be on the run from all the good guys.

Of course, if INHUP found Nita's connection to her mother and the black market, she could be on the run from the law too. And Kovit might be hunted by his mafia connections. So really, they were both in trouble with everyone.

Great. Just great.

"To us." Kovit raised his empty water bottle in a toast. "Both well and truly fucked."

Nita tapped her own water bottle against his with a laugh. "To us."

Kovit gave her a cheeky grin. "Now. What are we going to do about all this?"

Nita smiled, not sure how he'd managed to cheer her up so quickly. "This sounds like a problem to deal with when we get out. It's all hypotheticals until then."

"All right." He raised an eyebrow. "So how do we get out?"

Nita scowled. "I don't know. We have no money."

"Yes."

"All right. How do we get it?"

Kovit considered. "This is a market. Can we sell things?"

Nita opened her mouth to ask what they could possibly

sell, when she realized. A grin spread across her face, thin and excited.

Kovit leaned forward, crooked I-have-an-idea-and-it's-so-so-wrong smile on his face. "Are you thinking what I am?"

Nita laughed, lighthearted. "This is a body-parts market."

"And we have a body."

TWENTY-SEVEN

NITA WISHED SHE had her Disney playlist to listen to while she dissected.

Reyes' body lay on the table in the building's dissection room. It was cramped, and the white paint was chipping off, but it was the best Nita had. And she intended to make the most of it.

Her hand shook when she picked up the scalpel—a real, legit scalpel, not one of Kovit's switchblades. It had been hiding in a box of other dissection tools. She didn't shake from fear, but from excitement. She hadn't dissected someone in too long. Oh, sure, she'd ripped off a thumb and an arm. But she'd been in a rush. She hadn't had time to experience the dissection, to dwell and calm her thoughts.

Nita figured everyone in the world had something they did for peace of mind. That crystalline, calm moment when there was no thought, just peace. Some people ran. Others meditated. Nita dissected.

She started by taking a large pair of scissors and cutting

the suit down the center so that it flopped on either side of the body. Then she cut the shoulders of the jacket from neck out to arm, and then the sleeves. Pieces of fabric fell onto the table with a soft flutter, where they blocked the shiny metal from reflecting the light.

Once the body was naked, Nita paused. Should she start with the surface stuff? Or should she dive right in? Kovit had mentioned using the head as a tool to get them out at one point, so she decided to keep that mostly intact.

That meant starting with the body. Nita felt the smile tugging at the corner of her mouth as she pressed the scalpel into the skin and made a long, dark Y incision down the chest. Nita peeled back the skin and cracked open the rib cage, revealing the contents of the body to the open air. Nita sighed, a soft, contented sound, as she ran her finger over each rib, slick and sticky.

Then, carefully, she dipped her hand into the chest cavity. Where should she start? The heart, large and tough, but not tough enough to keep pumping when the skull was smashed. Or perhaps the liver, dense and brown, telling stories of bad habits the body may have had.

The stomach, Nita decided. She reached in for the pouch, wondering what secrets would be contained in the acidic fluids within. She shivered as she pulled it out, her body rippling like she was Kovit getting a hit of pain. It felt so good to be in a dissection room again.

All the little voices in her head had gone away. They knew what Nita needed, and it wasn't their opinion.

Piece after piece went into little glass jars. Fingernails were pried off and dropped into vials with little clinks. Hair was shaved off and tied with a ribbon. The skull was sawed off and the brain scooped out, and portioned into little Tupperware containers like a zombie's lunch. Then Nita stapled the top of the skull back on so they could wave the head around if needed for leverage. It still looked like Reyes.

There was no time while Nita dissected, only motion. So when she finished and checked the clock, she was shocked to find nearly six hours had passed. It was midafternoon.

She stretched her arms above her head, and her back made a satisfying crack. A contented smile crossed her face. She hadn't felt this good, this at peace, since before Fabricio.

Nita's smile fell at the thought of Fabricio. If she hadn't saved him, her mother wouldn't have sold her.

Don't be naive. If it hadn't been Fabricio, it would have been someone else.

She let out a breath. The peace of dissection had been broken by the real world.

Nita took off her gloves and rubbed her eyes. Then she texted Kovit. After the guards had left, he'd taken the phone and unlocked it. The problem with those pattern locks was that if you saw someone open them enough times, you could make a pretty good guess as to their combination.

Nita had been disappointed to find that despite unlocking the phone, there was still no internet. Either Reyes didn't have a data plan (unlikely) or the connection in the middle of nowhere, Amazon jungle, was too shitty (more likely).

Nita's fingers slid across the screen. *All done. Everything's ready for sale.*

His response was quick. *Good. I've told Jorge and Renzo that Reyes wants them to sell some things in the market today.*

And they bought it?

Did you really think they would question me to my face?

No. No one was that stupid.

Nita swiped quickly. *All right. Who are we saying the parts are from?*

"Dolphin Girl."

Nita nearly jumped out of her skin when she heard Kovit's voice behind her. He leaned in the door, mocking grin on his face. He enjoyed startling her, she could tell. Nita just glared.

"Reyes' arms are more white than pink," Nita said, trying to pretend she hadn't been surprised at all.

Kovit clearly didn't buy it, but he didn't comment. "But they look grayish in death, which is sort of close to Dolphin Girl."

"All right," Nita agreed. Kovit was probably right. Easier to pass off these parts as Mirella's than Nita's. "But Reyes was human, right? Won't people be able to tell that they're fake when they don't do anything?"

"Dolphin Girl's body parts didn't do anything either. Or at least, nothing Reyes' tests could detect. But it's fine. Jorge and Renzo have sold lots of useless unnatural parts that way before, as have half the people here. It's a scam, and everyone involved knows it's a scam."

"Why do it? Isn't it easier to just lie about it? Pretend they have some other power?"

"Not really."

"Why?" she asked.

"Because it's easy to test a lot of things. If you say something is zannie blood, all someone has to do is rub it on a paper cut, and they'll know. It's an anesthetic, right? So if the pain goes away, it's real—if it doesn't, it's fake. But if you sell something as 'it's from this type of unnatural, but we don't know what it does,' then people think they can get it cheaper and figure out themselves what it does."

Nita frowned. It sort of made sense. "If it's cheaper, will we make enough for bribes and boat fare?"

"I hope so." Kovit shook his head. "But there's no way to know. This is a barter market. Who knows what we'll get."

Nita sighed and leaned against the metal autopsy slab. "I wish we could sell it ourselves."

"We can't." He wiped a hair from his face. "Jorge and Renzo know I'm not supposed to be outside much. And if they see you in the street, the jig is up. We're lucky you haven't run into them thus far."

Nita grumbled, but didn't complain.

She and Kovit worked to package everything nicely and brought it out to the front of the building. Kovit messaged one of the guards.

"I'm going to tell him to call Reyes to confirm. Can you answer and pretend to be Reyes?"

Could she? Nita, who'd barely spoken to anyone except her parents for the past five years until Fabricio came along? Any plan that relied on Nita's communication skills seemed doomed to fail.

But it wasn't like Kovit could pretend to be Reyes.

Focus on specifics. You have to do this. Don't think, Can you do it? Think, How will you do it?

Nita had heard Reyes speak in Spanish a few times. Her accent was hard to place, mostly because Nita didn't know accents so well. Reyes had used *vos* instead of *tú*, so probably not western South America. But no *sh* sounds instead of *y* like Fabricio had. So, probably not Argentina/Uruguay. Maybe Central America somewhere?

"I can try. I don't know if I can get the accent right." Or even if she was right about what accent it was. For all she knew, there was some part of western South America that used *vos* or some district in Argentina that didn't use *sh*.

"Keep it short, then. Just confirm I speak for Reyes and they're supposed to sell those parts."

Nita nodded and pulled Reyes' phone out of her pocket. There were seven missed calls in the last few hours. Nita, so absorbed in her dissection, hadn't even heard them.

The two of them stood there, tense and waiting, staring at the phone, but they both still jumped when it rang. Nita answered, voice dry. "Reyes."

"*Ah, Señora!*" She thought it was Lorenzo speaking. "I've finally reached you!"

"Clearly." Nita tried to keep her voice level and curt. "What do you want? I'm busy."

"Ah, of course. I'm sorry to bother you. But the zannie has been saying some things—"

"What about them?"

"He says you ordered the dolphin girl's death and her body parts sold."

"I did. And?"

There was a pause. "I just wanted to confirm with you, Señora."

"You've confirmed. Don't waste my time again."

Nita hung up, hands shaking. Had they bought it? Did she make a convincing Reyes?

Kovit winked at her. "Good job. I have no clue what you were saying, but you got that evil deadpan she had down just right."

Nita let out a laugh, more a release of stress than anything else. She almost blushed under Kovit's praise, since she figured he was a great judge of how to do evil voices and threats. If he approved, she'd done well. Though he could just be humoring her.

"Thanks. I hope they bought it." Nita looked down at her phone, turning it over in her hands, thinking about how simple it had been pretending to be Reyes.

"Me too."

A few minutes later, Jorge and Lorenzo swung by to pick up the body parts. They didn't talk with Kovit much. It was clear they were scared of him even though they didn't want to show it. Nita hid around the corner and grinned when Jorge squeaked as Kovit came too close.

The guards took crates of parts and put them up on their shoulders, leaving one arm free to go for their guns. One of them said something curt that Nita couldn't hear, and Kovit laughed his creepy, oh-if-only-you-knew-how-much-I-want-to-hurt-you laugh. Then the guards were gone, nearly stumbling in their effort to get away from Kovit.

Nita wondered how much more scared they'd have been if they knew they were selling pieces of their former boss.

Kovit turned back to Nita after they left, and grinned. Nita returned the smile full force.

All they had to do now was wait.

TWENTY-EIGHT

IT DIDN'T WORK OUT as well as they hoped.

Jorge and Renzo hadn't had a good day selling pieces of Reyes. In fact, they'd sold one eyeball and all her teeth. But nothing else.

And the rest of it was starting to smell. Bad.

Nita had put many of the smaller pieces in formaldehyde —she was no stranger to dealing with bodies. She'd washed the nails, trying to scrape any stray pieces of flesh off. She'd done everything right.

But they still smelled.

It was the jungle. The jungle made everything smell like sweat and rot.

Kovit greeted Renzo and Jorge at the door, and helped them put everything away. Nita hid around the corner again, trying to keep out of sight. The smart thing to do would have been to sit in the cage and pretend to be trapped, but she wasn't getting anywhere near that cage if she didn't have to.

Jorge, Lorenzo, and Kovit didn't talk much as they moved the merchandise.

When all the parts were inside, Kovit turned to the guards. "What did you make off it?"

Lorenzo wiped his sniffling nose, hand shaking from withdrawal, but his voice was firm. "That's for Reyes. I'm not giving it to you."

Kovit smiled one of his smiles. Nita wondered if he stood at a mirror every morning practicing them. This one said, *Oh, an excuse to play with someone! I have such wonderful plans for you.*

Lorenzo flinched, but stood his ground. "Reyes said to never give you money."

Well, that was annoying. Nita hadn't predicted that.

"I guess you'll have to call her and check with her, then." Kovit's eyes danced, excited.

Nita could see Lorenzo second-guessing himself, and then Jorge elbowed him. Both guards stood their ground.

Damn.

"We will."

That was Nita's cue to slip away. She crept to the back of the building, where she couldn't hear them and they couldn't hear her. A few moments later, Reyes' phone rang. Nita picked it up and answered.

"Reyes."

"Señora. It's Lorenzo."

"Yes?"

"The zannie is getting . . . demanding."

"And?"

"You want me to do like we discussed if he became a problem?"

Nita wondered what plans Reyes had for Kovit. Nothing nice, she was sure. "No. What's the problem?"

"Wants your money. Says you said to give it to him."

Nita paused. How to do this so they weren't suspicious? She needed that money.

"How much money?" Nita asked.

"Just over two hundred dollars, a couple hundred soles, and sixty reais."

Nita had been hoping for a lot more than that. There was no way she could book a boat for both of them and bribe the guards with that little.

Nita forced her voice to remain calm, not allowing any of her emotions to show. "Count it. Then give it to him."

"Señora?"

"I want to see how much goes missing in transit with him."

"Oh." A static crackle. "Why?"

"Are you questioning me?" Nita's voice was icy.

"Never, Señora."

"Good." Nita's shoulders were tight. She could do this. She could be a convincing Reyes. "That will be all."

She hung up the phone and waited, thinking. They didn't have enough money for a convincing bribe. Yes, it was possible that Kovit could bring Reyes' head down to the wharf and terrify people into doing what he wanted, but Nita was worried they'd just get shot. A lot of money was really the only thing that felt safe to Nita.

And it wasn't like she could ditch Kovit here—for one thing, she barely had enough money to get passage for herself now. And for another, she just felt . . . bad about the idea of ditching him. They were in this together.

Kovit himself approached her a moment later and showed her the money. "Pathetic."

Nita sighed. "We need more."

"Yes." He shrugged. "Or we take the head and threaten our way onto a boat."

Nita shook her head. "No. I feel like that's riskier."

"So, what's the plan?"

Nita hesitated. "You won't like it."

"Try me."

"How many other big players in this market have secluded houses?"

"A few." Kovit considered. "Reyes took me to Boulder's place once."

"Boulder."

Nita remembered Boulder, with his shiny black shoes and shinier white smile. Mirella's dying cries echoed in Nita's memory. She wondered how many other people who'd stayed in Reyes' cages had lost body parts to that man's hunger.

"You met him. He likes to, ah, sample pieces of unusual unnaturals."

"I remember." Nita's jaw clenched, trying to push away the image of Mirella with white gauze over her eye, blood trickling down like tears. "Tell me about him."

Kovit shrugged. "He's another crime lord here. He's part of a big American organization. Most of the American organizations like to partner with other countries, but this one just sets up their own . . . franchises in various parts of the world."

Nita licked her lips. "Anything unusual about him?"

"He's an unnatural."

"He is?" For some reason, Nita hadn't thought any of the people in power here would be unnaturals. But of course some would be. After all, Nita was an unnatural, as was her mother, and they killed and sold people too. "What kind?"

Kovit clicked his tongue. "He's an aur."

Aurs were essentially bioluminescent people. About the most harmless, useless type of unnatural Nita could think of. Nita had only ever seen one on TV. He thought he was the second coming of Jesus and that God had given him a full-body halo. He'd drowned in Lake Michigan on live TV trying to walk on water when Nita was a kid.

Nita paused, thinking. "But aurs—I mean, I thought they'd fetch a pretty penny on the market. Isn't their blood considered an aphrodisiac?"

"Probably." Kovit grinned. "But who's going to take on someone like Boulder just for that?"

Nita stared at Kovit, a slow smile curving her lips. Half-formed ideas flitted through her mind, nebulous and wild. Nothing Nita could give voice to, not yet. But a plan was building itself in the back of her mind, and she thought she liked where it might be going.

"You said you'd been to his house. Why?"

Kovit scowled. "He asked Reyes to bring me over when he heard she had a zannie in her employ. He'd found a spy. He wanted me to torture information out of the man."

Kovit paused as though waiting for her response, but Nita only raised her eyebrows and said, "I see."

"I warned him that torture isn't great for getting information. It's not reliable." Kovit examined his nails. "He was still angry when no useful information came from it."

"I imagine Reyes was also unhappy?" Nita's fingers slid over Reyes' phone.

"I have no clue. She never said anything."

"Hmm." Nita leaned against the wall. "Did he seem like the type to carry cash?"

Kovit tilted his head to the side. "I dunno. I didn't really think about it then."

"And now?"

"Maybe?" Kovit shrugged. "I know he has things that sold in the market today. I imagine they were paid for in cash. He probably has some somewhere."

Nita nodded, a sharp movement. "We're going to find it."

Kovit paused and gave her a long look. "We are?"

"Yes." Nita met his eyes. "We need bribe money. We're going to go over there and get his money."

"How?"

Mirella's screams bored into Nita's memory. Not the ones elicited from Kovit's torture, but the ones of pure rage as she fought the guards trying to take her away to have her eye gouged out.

Nita raised her chin and met Kovit's eyes. "You're going to give him that torture session he wanted."

TWENTY-NINE

I T WAS CLOSE TO DARK when they made their way to Boulder's house. Much like Reyes', it was set slightly out of the market, in the woods. Kovit had said putting the phone light on would alert Boulder and any guards he might have with him of their approach. Given that they didn't know how many people were at this house, subtlety was the safest bet.

However, walking through a sketchy path in the dark rainforest was not.

Nita had spent ten minutes trying to increase the concentration of rods in her eyes so that she could better absorb light. She'd considered trying to create a tapetum lucidum on her retinas, like predators had to see at night, but it seemed like dangerously detailed work with little room for error. So she went with increasing rods.

When she opened her eyes afterward, despite the dark, the world was much clearer and sharper than it had ever been before, albeit in grayscale. She blinked a few times, adjusting.

They crept through the forest, Kovit holding Nita's hand as she led. It wasn't quite so hot at night, and their skin didn't stick together from sweat anymore. Kovit's hand was warm, and his grip light, almost invisible, as if he were nothing more than a ghost.

Nita held Reyes' gun in her other hand. Just in case.

There would be guards, and she couldn't expect Kovit to take care of all of them. Nita would do whatever she had to in order to get out of here. And if some body-part lord had to die on the way out, well, who cared? No loss to humanity. And the guards that supported him? Enablers.

I'm going to kill him, Mirella's voice whispered in Nita's memory.

Nita's hand was steady on her weapon. Though she was sure it wouldn't be when she fired, because she had terrible aim. When she got out of here, she was going to work on that. Maybe take a shooting class.

They came out of the woods and into a clearing with a small house. This one was far more elaborate than Reyes', and looked more lived in. There were decorations on the side, light shining through the windows, and laughter leaking through the cracks.

Nita nodded to Kovit and they approached.

Kovit paused, tilted his head and whispered, "There's five people in the building."

"How can you tell?"

"Pain. Everyone is always in pain. Whether it's a loose hangnail, a sore joint, a cramped back muscle — something. No human is never not in at least a minute amount of pain."

That was interesting. Nita had never thought about it, but it did make sense that people always had some pain. She wondered if she was invisible to Kovit right now. "You can sense all that?"

"Yes."

Nita nodded. "All right. How do we want to proceed?"

Kovit flicked his switchblade out. "They're separated. Three in one room, two in another. I suggest we go together into the room with three, take them out before they know what's happening, and then when the other two come in, we'll be ready."

"Three against two isn't great odds. What if we make a noise to lure one away?"

He shook his head. "I don't think they're stupid enough to fall for that. They'd leave as a group. Surprise is our best strategy."

One minute you're obsessing about having murdered Reyes, and the next you're planning to "take out" people? How the mighty have fallen.

Oh, do shut up.

"Okay." Nita held her gun up. "You lead."

"Try not to shoot Boulder, or we'll have the same problem we had with Reyes. I'm sure she had cash squirreled away in her house somewhere, but damned if we can find it without her help."

Right. Killing Boulder was bad. Kovit needed to extract money from him.

Once that was done, though, the man was dead. Mirella deserved at least that much.

They circled around to the other side of the house, over to a screened window. Kovit used his switchblade to cut through the mosquito netting, and he crept inside. The room they'd chosen was dark, and Nita was glad she had Kovit here, aware of where everyone in the building was at all times.

She hauled herself through the window and onto a plush carpet. The floorboards squeaked when she put weight on them.

Kovit moved silently, and Nita wished she knew how he did it. She'd have to ask him to teach her. It seemed to be a useful skill.

Kovit moved to the door of the room. She could hear muffled voices beyond, speaking in English. Kovit looked to Nita, pointed to the door, and held up three fingers. Nita raised her gun in response.

He kicked the door open.

There were three men in the next room, sitting at a table with liquor and cards. They all wore sweat-stained white tank tops and camo pants, and had multiple weapons hanging from their belts.

None of them were Boulder.

All of them were surprised, mouths open in little o's. Nita wondered how long it had been since someone had the audacity to try to assassinate Boulder in his own home. Once you were feared enough, the fear itself acted as a deterrent. It had made Boulder cocky. He would regret that soon.

Nita tightened her grip on her gun, aimed at the man reaching for his own weapon, and fired.

And missed.

Kovit, however, didn't. Moving with the speed and grace of a martial arts film stuntman, he was across the room and stabbing within seconds. His knife was everywhere, moving from one man to the next, leaving only blood and fallen bodies in its wake.

Kovit had two down on the ground in moments, but the third raised his gun. Nita pulled the trigger on hers first. Three times, this time, just to be sure.

This time, all three shots hit.

They didn't hit the best places. One in the arm, one in the shoulder, and one in the thigh. But the man crumpled, screaming. Kovit's foot snaked out and kicked the man's fallen weapon away.

Then the door on the other side of the room burst open, as the other two men ran toward the sound of shots. One man was like the other three, in tank top and camo pants. The other wore a white button-up shirt with the sleeves rolled up and slacks. Also, a really big gun. A bazooka? A machine gun?

Of course Boulder had brought a massive gun. Just great.

Nita shot the last guard, and Kovit moved in. Despite all the posturing and the giant gun, Kovit had a knife to Boulder's throat in seconds, before he had enough time to even aim. Boulder's hands clenched on the gun, but with a knife at his throat, all that firepower was useless.

"Drop the weapon, please," Kovit hissed, a crazy smile beginning to quirk the edge of his mouth, his face trying to hold in his barely contained excitement.

On the ground, the guards groaned. All but one were still alive, though all were injured badly. Kovit was shivering with pleasure, making his knife hand shake a little on Boulder's throat. A trickle of blood from a small cut slid down Boulder's neck.

Boulder dropped his weapon on the ground, eyes never leaving Kovit. Nita went around the room and picked up the guns, taking them from weapons belts and the floor. One man made a faint grab for her, but Kovit moved faster and crushed the man's hand beneath his foot.

Kovit sighed in pleasure, and used zip ties they'd taken from Reyes' place to attach Boulder to the chair.

"What do we do with the guards?" Nita asked.

Kovit's whole body spasmed, almost like the precursor to a seizure, and one of the men on the floor died. Nita saw the man's body slump, seeming to shrink as his soul left him.

Kovit let out a breath, a contented smile crossing his face. He looked at the remaining guards and tilted his head. "Leave them. They're going to die soon without some serious medical intervention." He closed his eyes. "I can always tell."

Nita watched him, then shrugged. If they were going to die anyway, why not let Kovit enjoy them for a few minutes?

Kovit had a crazy, fucked-up, *wrong* smile on his face when he sat across from Boulder, twirling his switchblade in one hand.

Boulder glared. "What is this?"

Nita laughed. Boulder turned to stare at her, and Kovit's expression briefly slipped into worry, before the crazy mask went back on.

Nita wasn't sure why she laughed. It wasn't a normal laugh, it was a little high-pitched and hysterical. She was standing in a room full of dying people, asking someone to torture a crime lord so she could steal his money. When had this happened? How had her life ended up like this?

When had she decided this situation was something she was okay with being in?

When he took Mirella's eye. When he didn't even realize who he'd murdered.

This man deserved everything he got.

"Mr. Boulder." Nita grinned at him, and she was sure it was an even crazier expression than Kovit's. "My friend and I are looking for some capital."

"What?"

"Money." The humor drained out of Nita as fear flickered behind Boulder's swamp green eyes and his shiny white smile vanished. "Where's your money?"

His voice was cold, arrogance leaching out of every word. "I'm not giving you a cent. You can't do this to me. You have no idea who you're dealing with."

Nita shrugged, gave one last edged smile to Boulder, and said, "Well then, if you don't want to answer me, you can answer my friend."

Nita turned and left the room, leaving Kovit to do what he did best.

THIRTY

THE SCREAMS DIDN'T last long. Thirty seconds was Nita's guess.

Then Kovit came out and rolled his eyes. "He caved."

"That was fast. You think he's lying?"

"Nah." He shrugged, "This one, he's terrified of being hurt. He'll do anything to avoid torture. Having him break this fast is a good sign he's telling the truth."

"Ah." Such interesting things Nita had been learning since she came here.

"Can you check for the money? Upstairs bedroom, safe under the bed. Combo is 09-04-18."

"Under the bed?"

Kovit just shook his head in amusement. "I know. So sad and cliché. We didn't even need him."

Nita went upstairs, and sure enough, there was a safe right where it was supposed to be. She pulled it out and spun the dial. It clicked open, and Nita hauled on the heavy safe door. Inside were stacks of what must have been thousands of dollars. Nita pulled one stack out and took a bill out of the elastic band holding the roll together. She held it up to the overhead light so she could see the watermark. Looked real.

She sat there for a moment, just letting herself take it in. She'd done it. She had the money.

She could escape.

Hell, she could pay for college with this much money. Her lips stretched in a giddy smile at the thought, and part of her wanted to laugh, but she felt like if she let the sound out, there would be something hysterical about it, so she kept it locked inside.

Nita shook her head, stupid smile still covering her face, and pulled the other contents of the safe out. A folder with pictures of a man she didn't know going into a building. She flipped through the pictures until she saw the man enter a bedroom with someone clearly far too young, and then stopped. Blackmail.

There was a stack of similar folders, all pictures of people she didn't know. There was also a hard drive, which Nita was willing to bet was password protected. More blackmail?

She sat back.

She looked at the pictures spread around her, the money stacked in the safe, and then down at Reyes' phone. She patted her pocket, where she'd tucked the lists of corrupt police officials.

She wondered how much they were worth to the right people.

There were footsteps on the stairs, and Nita stiffened, turning around. She picked up her gun and stood at the ready, but lowered it when Kovit walked into the room.

His eyes widened at the display of money. "Wow."

"Yeah."

Kovit grinned. "I don't think there's a guard in the world we couldn't bribe with this."

Nita looked over at him. "Where's Boulder?"

"Still downstairs. He pissed himself waiting, and it was starting to stink. Also, you were taking a while. So I thought I'd come check on you."

"Sorry." Nita brushed a strand of hair out of her face. On the floor, Reyes' phone began to jingle. Nita glared and wished she could figure out how to change the ringtone to mute.

She briefly considered answering, but didn't really see the point of keeping up the ruse of being Reyes. With any luck, they were going to be on a boat leaving this horrid market in a few hours.

"Anything interesting?"

"Some blackmail. Money."

He laughed. "I see the money. It looks like freedom to me."

Nita had to smile at that, but her fingers lingered on the blackmail photos. Boulder was an unnatural, just like Nita. He could have been sold on the black market at any time, but because of who he was, no one tried. It was like celebrities could get away with murder when ordinary people couldn't. If you were someone important, you were beyond the normal rules of society.

"Nita, what are you thinking?" Kovit asked. He knelt down beside her, face concerned.

Nita examined Kovit. She studied his dark eyes, the coiled

grace with which he crouched. She thought of how quickly Boulder had caved to Kovit's demands. Every dictator and mafia boss worth their salt had a zannie working for them. They were a symbol of power — and power was protection.

She sighed, running her fingers across the money. "Just . . . seeing this made me remember that even if I get out, I'll still be screwed. With the video."

Kovit frowned. "You wouldn't consider living anonymously? Stay out of the limelight, maybe in a small town . . ."

"That doesn't guarantee safety." She sighed. "And I don't want to live my life terrified I could end up in the background of the wrong person's selfie and be exposed."

"Good point."

Nita's fists clenched. "And . . . there's also . . ."

She swallowed, searching for the words.

He tilted his head to the side and rested his chin on his fist, waiting.

Nita looked down. It felt weird to talk about her dreams with anyone. She'd only had her parents before, and her mother had been . . . critical . . . of Nita's goals. Nita didn't think Kovit would be. She didn't have any justification for that, but she thought he'd listen and not mock.

"I always wanted to be a scientist. Go to conferences, publish papers in *Nature*, study various unnatural biology." She paused, trying to gauge his reaction, but she couldn't tell what he was thinking. "I want to be *someone* in my field. Someone recognized. I don't want to have to hide my research, or let other people take the credit. I want to be able to choose my life, not hide it."

Kovit was quiet for a moment before he said, "I think you'd make a great researcher."

Nita's eyes widened, and she ducked her head before he could see the trembling expression that had crossed her face. It was the first time anyone had ever said something nice about her dream.

"Thanks," she whispered.

He half smiled. "You would." His smile fell. "If you could find a way around the video."

She nodded and cleared her throat. "Exactly. I was just wondering if . . . if I had enough power, if I was someone as feared as Boulder, would I be safe?"

Kovit shook his head. "Boulder may not have been targeted because he was an aur. But his power made him a different type of target."

Nita picked up a wad of money. "I suppose you're right. It didn't help him in the end, did it?"

"No, it didn't." A sad smile crossed Kovit's face.

But it might help you, a small voice in the back of Nita's mind whispered, unwilling to let the idea go. *If you were more feared than Boulder, more feared than Reyes, even more feared than Kovit, more feared than anyone else . . .*

Nita opened her mouth, but before she could say anything, she heard a click outside the door. Then a creak of floorboards. She spun around, and Kovit's head snapped up.

Nita's mind raced. If there was someone here, shouldn't Kovit have been able to tell? He said he could sense pain and everyone was in pain. No one should have been able to sneak up on them, right? Unless Kovit was in on it and had betrayed

264

her. A quick glance at him told her that wasn't the case; he looked just as confused and wary as she did.

She reached for her gun on instinct and pulled it up in time to see Lorenzo and Jorge enter the room. Both of them were grinning.

"Sorry to interrupt the heart-to-heart," Lorenzo sneered.

Nita began to squeeze the trigger, but not fast enough.

The sound of the gunshot echoed through Nita's skull. Her gun dropped from her suddenly limp fingers and her body fell backwards, head cracking on the floor.

It took a moment to register what had happened, because she still had her pain circuits off.

Nita had been shot.

THIRTY-ONE

NITA HALF EXPECTED Kovit to leap up and slaughter everyone. He was fast and well-trained, and he had no compunctions about killing. But he wasn't stupid, and there were at least two guns Nita could see trained on him. There was nothing he could do that wouldn't involve him getting shot.

Like Nita.

I can't believe I've been shot.

There was something unreal about the whole experience. Partly because getting shot just seemed like a thing that would never happen to Nita — it happened in movies. To action heroes. Nita was no action hero.

But the lack of pain made everything more surreal, like she was watching a movie where someone was shot. Unreal. Fake.

Nita's eyes were heavy, and she let them drift shut. She couldn't focus on what was going on. She needed to start healing now, before she lost concentration or blood or something and couldn't use her ability. Thank God her pain circuits were off — she'd never have been able to focus on healing herself with that much pain running through her.

The bullet had entered through her shoulder, cracking and shattering bone as it went. It hadn't nicked the artery, so that was good, but it had crushed a lot of blood vessels and torn through muscles. Nita was bleeding. A lot.

Too much.

She needed to stop it. She increased her blood-clotting factor, threw platelets at it, and cut off circulation to the area. She tried to repair veins, just temporarily, quick fixes to keep the blood in until she could get something more done. She needed to focus.

She felt dizzy. Bad sign.

There was pressure on her shoulder. Someone was trying to stem the bleeding. Nita cracked her eyes open and saw Kovit kneeling above her. He'd taken a bedspread and had wrapped it tightly around her shoulder. His face was tense, mouth a tight line.

Nita let her eyes drift closed again, turning her focus inward to her body. This was going to take time, and she didn't know how much she had.

"Get her up." That was Lorenzo's voice.

"Let her lie here for a minute or two to stop the bleeding. She'll be easier to move if she's not dripping everywhere." Kovit's voice was chilly.

Lorenzo laughed. "You really expect me to believe you care? You're just stalling for time."

Kovit's fingers tightened around Nita's shoulder. "Perhaps."

"Pick her up. You can carry her."

There was a long silence, and then Kovit shifted position beside her. She could hear the rustle of his clothes, the creak of his feet on the floorboards. He tucked one arm under her shoulders and the other under her knees. Nita hoped the movement wouldn't make things too much harder to heal. She'd already managed to stem a lot of blood, and she was working double time on putting things back where they were supposed to be so they could heal right.

The world whooshed as Nita was lifted up, and she felt even dizzier than before. She gasped for breath, feeling things she'd just started putting back into place come loose again. Tenuously held together blood vessels broke apart.

Nita opened her eyes, hoping that seeing what was happening would get rid of some of the dizziness.

Kovit was looking at someone else, his face turned away from her. His eyes were tight with worry, and though he held her gently, his grip was tense.

Nita let her eyes rove around the room. Lorenzo was taking stacks of Boulder's money from the safe and shoving it in a bag. Jorge still had his gun trained on Kovit.

Kovit's eyes flicked to the money. "Is Boulder dead, then?"

"Not yet. He's still tied up downstairs." Lorenzo's voice was cool. He blurred in Nita's hazy vision.

"I assume he won't be surviving, since you're stealing his money."

"Nah, you stole his money. We have no idea where you put it," Lorenzo sneered. The pile of money was now gone, and instead there was a garbage bag slung over Lorenzo's shoulder.

Jorge nodded, then turned to Kovit and said in Spanish, "Time to go."

They left the room and descended the steps. Kovit was careful, but each step still ground against Nita's wound, damaging her progress and sending her right back to the beginning. She clenched her teeth, trying to focus. She could do this. She had to do this.

A trickle of sweat ran down her neck. She wondered if it wasn't sweat, but blood.

They made their way outside into the night. Lorenzo and Jorge turned on their cell phone lights and led the way through the woods. Kovit kept his pace deliberately slow, though Nita wasn't sure why. Stalling for time? Trying not to jostle her?

Nita used the time, pushing herself in ways she never had before, trying to repair the damage. She'd started on rebuilding the shattered collarbone, and trying to get the bullet lodged in it to come out.

After a few minutes, Kovit started talking again. "How did you even find us?"

"We got a call." Lorenzo laughed.

"From who?"

"From the guard you left half dead. Didn't think to take his cell phone away, did you?"

Nita groaned, and Kovit shifted his grip. Cell phone. How had they been so stupid?

"But why would he call you?"

"He didn't. He called Reyes, to tell her that her pet zannie had lost it and to come put it down. But he couldn't reach Reyes, so he called me to ask if I could contact Reyes." Lorenzo laughed again, a little higher, and crunched through the branches as they entered the path to the market. "A few questions later, it wasn't hard to figure out the little girl was out of the cage. And suddenly all those suspicious phone conversations today made a lot more sense."

Nita deserved to be shot for how dumb she'd been. She should have just answered the damn phone earlier. Or searched for cell phones. Something. So many mistakes, piled on top of each other.

"I see." Kovit's voice was calm. She wondered what he thought of all this. "I'm curious, though. How did you sneak up on us?"

A branch brushed by Nita's cheek and tangled in her hair. It tugged, pulling her head back. She made a sound, and Kovit paused, untangling her hair.

Lorenzo half giggled. "Unicorn bone."

"Unicorn bone?"

"You think we're stupid?" Lorenzo sneered, then sniffed loudly. Clearly someone had been overusing. "Everyone knows zannies can feel pain. The only way to sneak up on them is to have no pain."

That was smart. Smarter than Nita would ever have given them credit for. There was a lesson for the future, if she survived to see the future. Never underestimate the intelligence of underlings. They had access to Google too.

"I see."

Kovit's voice sent shivers down Nita's spine. It was a voice that promised horrors would soon be visited upon both men.

She hoped Kovit got his chance to inflict each and every one of those horrors on the people who'd shot her.

Jorge was visibly unsettled by the tone of Kovit's voice, even though he couldn't understand the words. Lorenzo elbowed him, and Jorge waved his gun, reminding them who had the power right now.

Footsteps stopped, and then there was a squeak of hinges and a groan as a door opened. Fluorescent lights burned pink into her closed eyes, and air conditioning bombarded her over-heated body.

No.

The soft scuff of shoes on concrete was the only sound as they were led down the hall. Nita opened her eyes to see her cell, glass wall all around, torn pages of the book scattered across the floor.

Lorenzo smiled at the two of them and gestured with his gun. "Back in the cage you go."

THIRTY-TWO

THE CAGE DOOR clicked shut behind Nita, and the guards left, laughing. She was right back where she'd started.

Kovit set her down on the ground and stepped back. "Is there anything you need me to do?"

"The bullet."

He knelt beside her. "What about it?"

She met his eyes, breathing harsh. "Get it out."

He was silent for a long moment. Then he took his switchblade from his pocket and leaned over her.

Nita closed her eyes, not wanting to watch. She heard the *shruuuk* of tearing fabric as he ripped pieces of her shirt off her shoulder. The caked blood and sweat made the material stick to her skin, and it had to be peeled off.

He leaned in close, so close she could faintly feel his breath on her neck as he worked. He used one hand to gently press her chest, just below her collarbone, into the floor and pin her so she couldn't move. His hand was warm, and her skin tingled with the unfamiliar sensation.

She couldn't remember the last time she'd been touched by anyone, aside from being jostled in the crowd. Her mother would sometimes pat her on the head, and her father used to give her hugs. But she hadn't seen him in years.

It was fine; she didn't like being touched anyway. But there was something strange in the realization, something that made her a little sad inside. Maybe it was the fact that the first real contact she'd had in years was with a pain-eating psychopath digging a bullet out of her shoulder. That all her other contact had been her mother patting her on the head like a favored pet. And like a pet that had gotten too rowdy, Nita had been sold.

Nita shoved away the emotions accompanying that thought before they could fully form. She could deal with them when she escaped. Right now, she wanted to focus on healing.

She tried to keep still. She didn't want to move and cause more damage. She let her consciousness sink into her body, following the path of the knife.

The blade did not go in easily. It scraped on bone, and she could feel it, scratching and tickling, moving the flesh inside her around. It was strange to feel something so invasive, yet not be in pain. Normally, the pain would mask all these other sensations.

There was a squelch as pressure shifted and blood globbed out of the wound like pus, thick and sticky. It trickled along her collarbone and pooled against the hand Kovit was using to brace her.

Nita tried to focus on her breathing, on stemming the blood she could, on clearing the passage for the scraping knife. Her teeth clenched every time the knife hit bone, and she almost gasped when it finally hooked onto the bullet lodged in her collarbone. It wasn't pain she felt, but something completely different. Similar to the sensation when she was on a plane and the pressure in her ears changed so they felt tight and strange and not right, and she wanted to shake her head and dislodge whatever was in her way, and then suddenly they popped and everything felt normal again. This felt like an extended *pop* sensation.

She was so happy she couldn't feel pain for this. Kovit would never have been able to keep his hands steady and take the bullet out.

It took more time for him to dig the bullet out from her cracked and crumbling bone, but when he did, it came out with another squirt of blood. Nita couldn't help the squeaky gasp she let out, like a weird hiccup, as air and blood suddenly rushed into the hole where the bullet had been.

Kovit sat back, and Nita opened her eyes. His hands were painted red, as was the front of his shirt, but he held the bullet out in his palm for her to see. It was smashed almost flat, melted and warped and dripping. "Gone."

Her body sagged in relief. At least now she could start healing properly. "Thanks."

"Need anything else?"

"No." Nita let out a breath. "I just need to lie here and heal for a bit."

He nodded, then sat on the other side of the cage, elbows resting on his knees. He began wiping his hands fastidiously on his already gory shirt. It didn't help. He leaned against the wall of the cage and let out a soft sigh.

Nita gave him a bitter smile. "Familiar?"

"It's like déjà vu," he agreed.

"Except this time we're both on the same side of the cage."

Kovit tut-tutted. "We were both on the same side of the cage before. Now we're just both on the *wrong* side of the cage."

Nita snorted, but smiled a little. She appreciated Kovit's efforts to keep the mood light.

Too bad they didn't work.

Nita was in the cage again. And she had no one to blame but herself.

"We should've just killed all the guards." Nita's voice was soft.

"Probably."

She finished clotting over the last of the veins and capillaries damaged by the shot. When that was done, she could start putting bone back together, fusing things into some semblance of a collarbone. Then she could move on to internal tissue damage. She didn't know how far she'd be able to go before she became too exhausted to do any more.

"But." He gave her a cheery grin and moved to the food tray mechanism. He picked up the piece of plastic she'd shoved in there before. "We know how to get out now."

"Assuming they feed us."

He shrugged. "They're not going to leave us here to die. Either they'll feed us, or they'll open the cage to kill us. Either way, we'll get an opportunity."

Nita nodded, then stopped, because that shifted the pieces of her shattered collarbone. "Good idea."

"I can't take all the credit." He winked at her.

She smiled, heart rate spiking for a moment. She quelled it, worried it would worsen her blood loss.

They sat in silence for a long time after that. Nita focused all her energy on trying to repair her body, and Kovit examined the items in the room, eyeing each of them as though considering their potential as a weapon. Some he discarded quickly, like the torn remains of the crappy book. Others he lingered over, like the blanket she'd trapped him with.

Nita wasn't sure how much time had passed when Jorge and Lorenzo returned. Enough that she'd exhausted her healing abilities, taken a short nap, and then started working on her wound again, despite the grumbling of her stomach.

The sound of boots on concrete was distinctive, and Nita turned her head, part of her certain she would see Mirella in the other cage, huddling under her blanket in fear, eyes wide, body quivering.

But there was no one there.

Nita felt as though she were the one covered with a blanket this time, suffocating her with memories.

Kovit crouched beside her, tense. His eyes flicked to hers. "You ready?"

Nita let out a breath. She needed to focus. She didn't have time for memories now.

Jorge and Lorenzo entered first. Lorenzo was glistening with sweat, and his pupils were so dilated they almost encompassed his blue irises, while Jorge had bloodshot eyes and a concerned frown as he watched Lorenzo. Clearly Lorenzo had used Reyes' disappearance to indulge.

Nita was shocked to see Boulder walk in behind them, his

expression a strange cross between a sneer and hair-trigger rage. His white teeth gleamed in the fluorescent lights, except for the black space where he was now missing one. Dark stains on the nearby teeth attested to its recent violent demise.

She wondered if Kovit had done it to get the safe combination.

If so, it was genius. Because it wouldn't just hurt physically, it also hurt psychologically. Nita could tell Boulder had been very fond of his bleached white smile.

Kovit raised his eyebrows. "I didn't think you were working together."

Lorenzo hiccupped. Nita stared at him, the way his whole face seemed to look like someone had painted it with tinsel. *Way* too much unicorn bone. Couldn't you overdose on that?

"Boulder made us a very good deal." His voice was as high as the rest of him, and his eyes were unfocused, as though watching something no one else could see.

Boulder gave him a disgusted look, quickly covered by a smile. "I found myself in need of employees, and they found themselves with a lack of an employer."

Kovit laughed. "How'd he tempt you? I thought you'd be all over that pile of money."

Lorenzo smiled and waved a clear bag of white powder. "What can I say? The perks are great. Better than with Reyes."

Jorge looked away.

"I see." Kovit narrowed his eyes.

Boulder took a step forward. "Speaking of Reyes, what did you do with her?"

"You haven't realized?" Kovit gave them one of his creepy, oh-I-can't-wait-to-tell-you-the-bad-bad-things-I-did smiles.

Lorenzo flinched back from it, and Boulder scowled.

"Surely you saw all the body parts up for sale?" Kovit's voice was silky and smooth, wrapping around them like a boa constrictor. "Jorge and Renzo were peddling them all day."

"But that was the dolphin girl . . ." Lorenzo's voice trailed off. Jorge nudged him, and Lorenzo switched to Spanish and explained. Jorge looked ill.

"Well." Boulder's lips thinned. "Reyes was weak."

Kovit laughed, full and terrifying. "Oh, was she? Because as I recall, you were the one who pissed yourself with terror before I even started working on you."

Boulder stiffened. "You —"

"And such squeaky screams, like a mouse." Kovit's chin lowered, so he was looking up at Boulder from under dark brows, smile the very definition of psychotic. "Gave me everything I asked for within thirty seconds."

Lorenzo started translating for Jorge, and Boulder snapped his arm out, gun in hand and pointed at Lorenzo's head. "One more word, and I'll blow your brains out."

Lorenzo was silent.

Kovit tilted his head to the side, like a predatory bird. "Oh, don't want your men to know how weak you are?"

Rage suffused Boulder's features, turning his face an unhealthy purple, and his gun swung around as though to shoot Kovit.

Nita's heart rate spiked. She knew this was part of the plan, knew they were trying to lure Boulder into doing something stupid like open the cage, but she hadn't imagined he would just shoot Kovit through the glass.

But then he lowered his gun. A slight smile crossed his face.

He turned to Nita.

"What was your name, girl?"

"Nita." She clenched her jaw.

"Nita." He tasted the name. "You were acting very high and mighty earlier."

She didn't respond.

"I recall you referring to this zannie as your 'friend,' no?" Boulder's smile was dangerous, not creepy like Kovit's, but mean. "Ordering me around, telling the zannie to hurt me. But you know, zannies, they're not terribly loyal."

Nita didn't respond, but her eyes flicked to Kovit, wondering what game Boulder was playing.

"I hear you can't feel pain. That must be useful, dealing with this monster. But I think you've forgotten, it *is* a monster." He took a step closer to the cage. "And it will turn on you the moment it thinks it'll gain some benefit from it."

Nita resisted the urge to look over at Kovit.

She wasn't sure Boulder was wrong.

"What's your point?" she finally asked.

Boulder ignored her. He just turned to Kovit. "Zannie."

Kovit's eyes were wary. "Yes?"

"I have a proposition for you."

Kovit didn't respond.

"See, I'm rather displeased by your actions. What I'd like to do is shoot you, and then sell your body for money. But see, having a zannie gives me a bit of a reputation, you know? So

I'm willing to overlook today and let you live your days out in that cage, torturing people I bring to you."

Kovit remained silent, face impassive.

Boulder took a step back. "So. I want to eat that girl in there and gain her immortality. Every day, I'm going to come in here, and ask you to cut off a different body part."

He smiled, and savored the moment, before turning to Kovit and whispering, "Once she's all eaten, I might even trust you enough to let you out, zannie."

Boulder leaned back, cocked his gun, and aimed at the cage. "So, what piece shall we start with?"

THIRTY-THREE

NITA STOPPED BREATHING.

He was going to eat her?

It wasn't like she didn't know he wanted to—he'd eaten Mirella's eye, and the strip of skin Kovit had peeled off for him the first time they met. She recalled the sound of him swallowing her flesh, and his words.

Immortality awaits.

So she knew, without a doubt, that Boulder wasn't bluffing. He wasn't just using scare tactics. He actually wanted to eat her.

Piece.

By.

Piece.

How long would it take for her to die that way? Months? Years?

She thought of Fabricio, screaming in the cage as her mother hacked off his ear. She imagined Kovit holding her down and cutting hers off, and then Boulder, smiling while he popped it in his mouth.

Kovit.

Her head began to turn toward him involuntarily, but she forced it to remain staring straight ahead, at Boulder. She didn't want Boulder to think he was getting to her.

And Kovit . . . He wouldn't do it, right? They were friends.

But . . . were they really? Their arrangement had always been a matter of convenience, built on shared goals. And . . . well, he *was* a zannie. Boulder was right, they weren't loyal to anyone aside from themselves and their creepy pain addiction.

What would Nita do if their places were reversed? If she were told to cut off someone's body part in exchange for her life. Someone alive and breathing.

She thought of Fabricio, and the ear. But she hadn't had a gun to her head at the time. If her mother had been holding a gun, would she have cut off his ear?

She thought she would have.

Could Nita really expect Kovit to choose her over his own life? After all, then they'd both still be alive. For a while, anyway.

Boulder smiled, gun steady. "So, what part shall I start with? An eye?"

Nita's shoulders tensed, thinking of Mirella and her bloody eye patch. She imagined the knife sliding in, scooping her eye out, cutting it at the roots. How Boulder would pop it into his mouth like a boiled egg and swallow it whole.

"No." Boulder paced back and forth. "Only two of those. They're a delicacy. Maybe I should start with something small. To test the waters, see how potent the flesh is. A toe, then." He laughed. "Don't worry, I bet you won't even miss it."

Nita's breath hitched as Boulder turned the gun on Kovit. "Now, bring me that toe, zannie."

Finally, Nita's eyes turned to Kovit.

It was harder than she expected to make herself look at him. Her neck felt stiff, and her whole body resisted, as though scared by what it might find. It was like a horror movie, where you knew something was behind you, but you could never seem to make your body turn quickly.

The gun sat in Boulder's hand, a constant threat in case Kovit disobeyed.

How much was his freedom worth to him?

Her head finally turned, and she found him watching her, head tilted to the side, face unreadable. His mouth was tight, and his brows drawn. His eyes were dark, so dark they seemed to suck out the light in the room.

Her breath hitched, and the sound that came out was like a hiccup murdering a sob in her throat.

"Kovit . . ."

That was all she managed. She didn't have anything else to say. What could she really say?

He approached, stride slow and sure, and then crouched beside her, weight resting on the balls of his feet so he seemed to be perching beside her, like a hawk. He was silent. The knife was loose in his hand.

Behind him, Boulder was smiling.

Nita swallowed, throat choked. This couldn't be happening. Where had she gone so wrong?

Heart thundering in her chest, she tilted her chin to meet his gaze square on. She wasn't going to go down without a fight.

He quirked an eyebrow.

And just like that, all the tension shattered, and she felt like the ass she was.

Her shoulders loosened, and she squeezed her eyes closed and let out a breath. "Don't scare me like that."

"I didn't do anything."

She gave him a half glare.

He grinned and twirled his knife. "All right. I did think about it, for about half a second."

She shoved him gently. He smiled at her, and an answering smile tried to pull the corners of her mouth up.

Then he sat back and turned to Boulder with mocking eyes.

"You think I'm a fool?" Kovit's voice was jeering. "I see how you hate me. I see what you think of me. You despise me. Once I cut that toe off, you're going to shoot me anyway."

Boulder's eyebrows rose. "Aren't you going to do it just in case?"

"No." His eyes were challenging, and a smile played on his face. "If you want that toe, you're going to have to come in here and get it."

Boulder shrugged. "Fine. I will."

He nodded to Lorenzo and Jorge, and the three of them approached the cage. Kovit tensed beside her, and Nita's adrenaline spiked. She gripped the edge of the blanket. She was ready. This was their chance. The cage was opening.

Kovit was very good at taunting people into doing what he wanted.

The cage door buzzed, unlocking it. It opened an inch.

Boulder shot Kovit.

Nita screamed as the bullet barreled into his side, propelling him back. She kicked up the blanket, blocking their view, and tried tackling one of the men, she didn't know which, and scrambled for his weapon.

Someone smashed her injured shoulder with the butt of his gun, and Nita's grip slackened. Furious, she shoved forward, trying to throw herself out of the cage at the very least, but there was a hand around her wrist yanking her back, and somehow she found the ground rushing up and smashing into her.

Before Nita could scramble up, Lorenzo grabbed her arms and yanked them above her head, pinning them. Snarling, Nita reached her head around and sank her teeth into his arm. He swore, but didn't let go until Nita ripped a piece of flesh off. It tasted salty and wet and made her mouth feel tingly, and she wondered if that was the effect of the unicorn bone in his bloodstream.

He cried out, and released her. Nita spat out the piece of flesh and tried to roll over, but someone booted her in the stomach, and she fell backwards. Her head smacked into the ground, and for a moment she couldn't see anything; the force of her fall had temporarily blinded her.

And then her sight was back, but she felt nauseous when she looked at things and her eyes couldn't seem to focus right.

Jorge knelt over her, pressing his bony knee into her stomach and shoving the breath out of her. She gasped for air as he forced his knee up into her diaphragm, and he grabbed one of her legs, knife in hand. Screaming, Nita reached up and grabbed his shirt, yanking him back, but the knife slipped in his hand and the blade dug into the side of her face, carving a deep gash down her cheek and approaching her ear. She could feel the blade scratching against her cheekbone, and it made a sound like chalk on a board, squeaky and ear piercing.

There was blood everywhere.

It got in her eye and blinded her, masking the world in a haze of red and stinging nonpain. She couldn't stop the instinctive blinks as her eye tried to clear itself and failed. Her eyelashes dripped and stuck together.

Someone was screaming above her, and the pressure on her middle released as Jorge moved. But she couldn't see what was happening, so she kicked and flailed blindly, and then tried to crawl toward the door. Jorge was shrieking, and Nita realized with a flutter of relief that Kovit must be alive, must be doing something, because no one else was going to help her.

But Boulder was watching it all, and he raised his gun again.

Nita howled and, half blind, launched herself at him, trying to knock his aim off before he hit Kovit again. She smashed into his legs, toppling him. She heard the crack as his body thundered to the ground, and the snarl that broke from his lips. Roaring, his body jerked, and he kicked at her face.

His boot connected, and her nose snapped with a *crack* and *pop*.

There was more blood, all down the front of her face, mixing with the gouge from her cheek. So much blood.

Hands were grabbing at her legs again, and then more

hands were holding her down and someone removed her shoe and Nita screamed and screamed, but no one paid any mind.

The knife slid across her flesh with a sound like someone was shucking oysters.

Her baby toe came off with barely any pressure.

One moment, she could feel it, every capillary and vein, the cartilage and bone, all of it one piece of her body, all of it under her control. And then there was nothing, absence where once there had been sensation.

They hauled her back into the cage, and she continued thrashing, swinging around to try to hit the person responsible, but he'd already let go, and then she was on the ground in the cage.

There was a click as the door locked.

Blood dripped onto the floor. Nita couldn't look, didn't want to see the place where once her toe had been.

She twisted her head so she could use her clear eye to look out the door. Boulder and the guards stood outside the cage, all of them covered in blood.

Nita snarled at them. Her mouth tasted like iron and the bottom of Boulder's boot.

"Well, that was unnecessarily difficult. Look at your face now. You really should have just cooperated from the start." Boulder smiled.

Nita spat on the ground, a giant glob of clotted blood. One of her teeth came out too. She picked it up and put it back, hoping to repair the damage to the root before it was too late.

"Charming." Boulder shrugged and turned to the guards, slipping into Spanish. "Bring me water and lemon juice."

Jorge ran off.

Nita's eyes went to Kovit, on the floor. His breathing was short and harsh, and there was so much blood, his blood, her blood, guard blood, she didn't even know where his injuries were.

"It's about time he got a taste of his own medicine." Boulder's voice was bitter.

Nita sneered. "Really? I thought he was giving you a taste of yours earlier."

"Cute. I see his poor humor has rubbed off on you. But you have nothing to laugh about, little girl."

Boulder turned away as Jorge returned with two glasses. Boulder popped the toe in the water first, and washed it. Then he dropped it in a glass of lemon juice, and it bobbed on the top, like a cherry on ice cream.

He toasted Nita. "To immortality."

Then he drank it.

He swallowed her toe with an audible gulp and licked his lips after. "I love toes. Small and sweet."

She wondered if he was the one who'd bought Fabricio's toe too.

"Thanks for the entertainment and the snack." His voice was mocking. "I'll be back tomorrow. And maybe then I'll try something different. That eye, perhaps, or even your sarcastic little tongue."

Laughing, he turned away and left, leaving Nita trapped in

a cage, missing a toe, to await her fate of being slowly eaten alive.

On the other side of the room, Kovit slumped on the floor, slowly bleeding out.

THIRTY-FOUR

THERE WAS A sense of finality to the sound of the door slamming behind Boulder. The silence of the room was only broken by Kovit's gasps of pain and Nita snorting out clots of blood.

She wiped her bloody eye and grabbed her nose, pulling it back into alignment so she could work on setting it. Then she started patching the tooth up enough that at least she wouldn't lose it.

It was good to do these things. She could focus on them. What she could do. Not on the fact that she was trapped in the cage. That Boulder was going to let them starve to death. And then eat her. That their escape plan had completely and utterly failed. That Kovit was injured, and she didn't know how badly.

Kovit.

Swallowing, she turned around and crawled over to him. He was lying on his side, his eyes closed and breathing shallow. He made a small whimpering sound when she approached.

"Kovit? Where were you hit?"

His eyelashes fluttered as he opened his eyes and winced. "On my side."

"How bad?"

"I don't know."

She grabbed his shirt and tried to pull it off, but he cried out, and she stopped. She licked her bloody lips, then took the switchblade from his hand. It felt both slippery and sticky at the same time, and slid uncertainly in her palm.

Nita coughed up another clot of blood that had trickled down the back of her throat from her shattered nose. She tried not to think of how deep the gash on her cheek was, or how close it was to her eye. How she could feel the blood rolling into her eye socket, drying and sticking her eyelid closed.

And she especially tried not to think about the empty space where her baby toe used to be.

The blade sawed through Kovit's T-shirt, and she peeled strips of it off his body. Beneath, his skin was so covered in blood she couldn't figure out where the wound was.

She ran her hands gently over the sticky flesh until he winced. Leaning in with her good eye, she saw the bullet hole. It had entered into his side and exited his back. Just above the hip. An inch to the left, and it would have missed him. An inch to the right, and it would have hit his kidney.

She let out a breath. It wasn't fatal.

Assuming she had water to wash the wound.

And soap.

And stitches.

Or something hot to cauterize it.

Or anything, really. But she didn't. She had a switchblade, a torn-up novel, and . . . no, she didn't have a blanket anymore; it was outside the cage now. It must have migrated there during the fight.

She used Kovit's already gore-covered T-shirt to plug the wound and applied pressure, hoping to slow the blood flow.

Her throat closed and she snorted out another glob of dried blood. This was bad. The wound itself wasn't horrific, but she didn't think she could stop the bleeding. And judging by Kovit's tight expression, it hurt a lot.

She leaned forward, throat parched. No water. No medical supplies. She didn't dare waste her moisture on crying.

Kovit groaned and sat up beside her, and she scrambled, trying to keep the soggy T-shirt pressed against the wound. He leaned against the glass, face making a bloody cheek print on the surface.

"We're really fucked, aren't we?"

She nodded, mute.

"Any brilliant ideas how to get out?"

Nita shook her head.

He sighed, and picked up his switchblade from the floor where Nita left it. He rubbed it with one thumb, as though drawing reassurance from it.

"I'm sorry." Nita's voice was quiet.

"For what?"

"For doubting you." Nita let out a breath as her nose snapped into place. "I was wrong."

He shook his head, faint smile on his lips. "No. You don't have to apologize."

"I do. It's my fault we're here. It was my plan to get the money from Boulder."

"And it was my plan to lure them into the cage to get out. And look how well that went."

She snorted, but there was less blood this time. "True, that."

Kovit tapped the glass with his pocketknife, eyes distant. He dug it into one pane and started drawing with it, carving stick figures. Nita was amused. He wasn't a good artist.

"How's the wound?" he asked.

"Which one?"

He laughed. "All of them."

"Fine. It'd be a lot worse if I could feel pain." Nita paused. "How do you feel?"

"Awful." His eyes slid to meet hers briefly, and he gave her a wry grin. "I'm not good with pain."

Nita stared at him, wondering if that was meant to be a joke.

Kovit didn't seem to expect a response, as he turned back to his glass art.

Nita closed her eyes and kept up her healing. Her face wasn't important. She just needed to stem the blood and set her nose. Her face didn't need to be pretty to run away. Her toe, though, that she needed to do something with. She was worried it would screw up her balance with it missing, make it harder to run.

Nita let out a breath. If they were going to escape, they needed to do so quickly and treat Kovit's wounds if he was going to survive. The clock was ticking.

She rolled her injured shoulder. The bones stayed fused. That was good. At least there was something positive.

They sat for another few minutes, the only sound the *scritch-scritch-scritch* of Kovit's blade on the glass.

She eyed Kovit's knife. She hadn't had one of those last time she was in here. "Any way we could use that knife to escape?"

"How?"

"I . . . don't know."

He shook his head. "It's a switchblade. It can't cut through solid glass."

"Right."

They sat for a few more minutes, Kovit idly twirling his knife.

Finally, he asked. "Can't you do something? I mean, you made your eyes have night vision. You just healed a fucking bullet wound. Can you do something with your muscles?"

She sighed. "I tried that before. I can make my muscles stronger, simulate the effects of steroids, push everything to the limit. But, um, I don't know what to do after that. I nearly snapped my wrist last time—I ripped a tendon and shattered some fingers. Not a great time."

Kovit stared at her, then a slow smile spread across his face.

"What?" she asked.

"Nita." He gave her a semicondescending smile. "You're talking to someone who grew up in the mafia. I can teach you how to throw a punch."

"Oh." Of course he could. Then she hesitated, looking at his switchblade. "Can you teach me how to use a knife so it breaks glass?"

He looked down and laughed. "I can do that too."

Nita smiled, cracking the dried blood on her face so it fell in small flakes to the floor. "Then what are we waiting for?"

Elevating various chemicals in the body was step one. Adrenaline, to start with. Then a few others. Densify those arm muscles. Get some testosterone too. She felt like a witch, creating a potion in a pot, but her cauldron was her own body.

Kovit considered. "It might be good to throw first."

"Throw?" Nita sat up, her whole body singing, ready to take on whatever was in store. Her muscles burned with the pressure. This was why messing around with your body was a bad idea—she knew she was going to crash, and it was going to be so awful she wouldn't be able to mediate the aftereffects.

Kovit rose, wincing, blood dripping down his jeans, and demonstrated the right posture. Nita imitated, right foot in front, left behind, so that she'd be using her undamaged arm. Kovit grabbed one leg and moved it to the side. He squared her shoulders and then nodded.

"I don't think throwing will do much."

"I once saw a guy throw a playing card so hard it sliced an inch into a watermelon. It's not necessarily about strength. It's about physics. Velocity, angle of impact. That kind of thing."

Nita's mother had taken her out of school a long time ago. Nita had learned everything from her biology journals. She'd never studied physics.

She wondered if she needed it for college. When she got out of here, she should look that up.

"Good." Kovit seemed satisfied with her stance. "Now, we're going to practice the throwing motion."

Nita blinked. "You just . . . toss, right?"

She demonstrated the motion. Kovit shook his head and tut-tutted. "No, no, it's all in the hips. You need to have twist. That will increase the torque. Whether you're punching or throwing or anything, you need that hip swing."

And so it went. Kovit wouldn't let her practice throwing the actual knife, because he thought she'd break it if she did it wrong. But eventually, he was satisfied with her swing and posture, and gave her the knife.

Nita took a deep breath.

"Loosen your shoulders. They're too tight."

Nita complied, but they tightened right back up again. She ignored them.

Then she threw.

The knife twirled through the air and embedded itself in the glass.

Nita lowered her hands. That was . . . disappointing.

She wasn't sure what she'd expected. For the glass to shatter? For the knife to open a hole big enough to crawl through?

Kovit, however, was delighted. He examined the knife, then fished around in his pockets and around the room, but all he had was his shitty cell phone. He looked at it, shrugged, and held it flat against the knife.

"What are you doing?" Nita asked.

"Like a hammer and a nail. We're going to hammer this knife through, and it's going to crack the glass." He gestured at the cell phone. "You can't hit right against the knife handle. So I'm going to hold this here, and you're going to punch the phone. The force will then flow through the knife and into the glass."

"Okay."

Then they practiced Nita's punches. Kovit seemed most concerned about how she twisted her hips, and when she twisted her arm during the punch. Flow of energy or something.

When they were ready, Kovit held the phone back up, Nita took a breath and steadied herself. Then she punched.

The phone shattered into a million pieces.

The knife shot all the way through the glass window and into the room beyond.

Thousands of massive cracks radiated from the hole.

Kovit grinned. "Punch again. Right on the hole."

Nita did so. Two knuckles broke and her arm fractured from the force.

But the glass broke too, more cracks radiating outward. Small pieces chipped off and fell on the ground of their cage. Nita healed her damaged bones and hit again. And again.

And then she punched right through.

Glass rained down on them. Kovit covered his head and closed his eyes, but the force of her punch took Nita right through the window and out of the cage. She landed on a bed of glass.

She was very glad she had no pain receptors, because there was an awful lot of glass embedded in her body. She kept her eyes squeezed closed and her mouth shut. There was glass everywhere. Blood too—she could feel the tickle as it ran over the small hairs on her arms.

"Nita!" Kovit's voice was close. There was a crunch of glass nearby. "Are you all right?"

Nita nodded, not wanting her mouth to end up full of glass if she opened it. She felt hands close over her wrists and help her up. She stumbled to her feet, and felt something brushing glass out of her hair. It made clinking sounds when it hit the ground.

Kovit's voice was gentle. "You can open your eyes now."

She did so. There was glass and blood all over the room. Pieces large and small, but mostly small. They were also all across her body, soaking her in red.

She looked back at the cage, wall shattered. At the very least, she would never be going into that prison again.

THIRTY-FIVE

K OVIT REALLY WAS weak against pain.

He whimpered when Nita poured disinfectant on his wound, fingers digging into the sides of the table in the dissection room. His hair fell over his forehead in a tousled mess, sticking to his face from all the blood he'd managed to get on there.

Nita wore a set of clean clothes she'd changed into from the other room, because there was too much glass in her old ones, and she was afraid she'd lean over and drop glass into Kovit's wound while she stitched.

He moaned softly as the needle went in for the first time. His skin resisted the small blade, but she pushed through, even as her hands grew bloody again. She'd just washed them in the sink before she started, but it didn't take long for them to become grimy.

"I'm surprised. I always thought zannies would be more resistant to pain," Nita said, trying to start some sort of discussion, anything to distract him.

"How resistant to pain I am is directly proportional to when I last ate pain, and how much."

Nita paused, needle in hand, and stared at him. "Really?"

His eyes were closed, brow pinched. "Yes."

Well, that was interesting.

She kept stitching. "Why is that?"

"I don't know." His breathing was shallow, and there were dark circles under his eyes. "I'm not a scientist." He licked his lips. "But . . ."

"Yes?"

"I think it's related to hunger." He hesitated. "Do you know what happens when a zannie doesn't eat pain?"

The needle slid in her hands. "No."

"Hunger for us . . . it's not like with other people. We start to hurt. Whatever pain we last inflicted on someone, we start to feel ourselves. First faintly. Then stronger and stronger, and if we still don't eat, it becomes all consuming, rising in intensity until something, usually the heart, just gives out from shock and stress to the system."

Nita paused and stared at him, his dark eyebrows pinched in pain, eyelids fluttering so his lashes swept his bloodstained cheeks.

"That's not a nice way to go," Nita finally said.

He shrugged and winced. "That's life."

Nita realized she was just staring at him and immediately resumed stitching. The needle slid in and out, in and out, and the wound began to look less like a gorefest and more like the disturbing smile of a horror movie doll.

"Will eating pain make you heal faster?"

He snorted. "I wish. No more than having a balanced diet."

Too bad.

She tied off the sutures with an expert's precision. Nita had spent her whole life studying bodies, taking them apart and sometimes putting them back together for display or sale. This was the first time she'd ever worked on a living person. She was rather pleased with her handiwork.

She took a swig from the water bottle and then offered it to Kovit. He finished it off and tossed the empty plastic container aside.

Kovit winced as he stood and stumbled to the sink. He splashed some water on his face, and it came back red. Then he looked down at his gore-spattered, cut-up, ruined T-shirt and made his way to the door.

"Let me get a new shirt, and we can go."

Nita followed him into the other room, worried by the way he seemed to shake as he walked.

He leaned over the laundry basket of clothes, and then turned to raise an eyebrow at her and give her a faint, teasing smile. "I didn't watch you change."

She turned away, blushing. "Sorry."

Her eyes roved around the rest of the room. The security camera feed showing the shattered cage, the small table and chair. She frowned. There was a box on the table, large and made of metal. She would have remembered if something like that had been there before. Her legs moved of their own volition, bringing her closer to it. She hesitated. It was unlocked, but closed.

"Kovit, what's this?"

He came over, tugging his new, clean T-shirt down over his wound. "Oh, that's Reyes' storage box. She usually keeps it in the workroom. Jorge and Renzo must have moved it here."

"Why didn't you mention it earlier when we were looking for money?"

He shrugged. "Because last I saw, it was locked. And I know what's in it, and it's not money."

Curious, Nita flipped the lid.

Inside was a variety of items, but no cash. There were a stack of papers, a cell phone, the two UV flashlights the guards had used on Zebra-stripes the vampire, black gloves, and a few other assorted things.

Nita picked up the top paper and glanced at lists of names, dates, and descriptions.

"What are these?"

"Lists of customers and potential customers. Everyone who came through here."

Nita put the papers down and surveyed the rest of the items. "And these?"

"Various things relating to customers and merchandise, I guess. She always kept things she might need in case certain types of customers showed up." He picked up the gloves. "I think these are in case you have a unicorn. So they can't make skin-to-skin contact to steal your soul. Not sure."

Nita hesitated and picked up another piece of paper. "And this?"

Then she stopped.

It was a picture of herself. She stood in front of a sunset, and the sun seemed whole because of the reflection on the water. She remembered the picture — she'd taken it her last day in Vietnam. It had been on her phone.

Her heart rate spiked.

Why would there be a picture from her phone here?

"Ah, that's one of the pictures Reyes used to ID you after she caught you. She printed a few out because they were too small on her phone screen."

But Nita wasn't listening to him. She was flipping through the other photos, all of them from her personal phone. Her breathing was too fast, and her hands were shaking.

"Nita? Are you okay?"

She kept staring at the photos. Had her mother snuck onto her phone and stolen pictures before Nita freed Fabricio? But why? That made no sense. And her mother had better photos of Nita, lots and lots of better ones. Why use these ones?

Hand shaking, Nita pulled out Reyes' phone. Trembling fingers scrolled through the text message history, looking for phone numbers she recognized. Her hand stopped. There.

Nita's phone number.

She clicked on it and pulled up the message history.

Here's the pictures.

And you're sure she can heal?

Definitely.

"Nita?"

Somehow she was crouched on the floor, hyperventilating, and the phone was on the ground beside her. When had that happened? There was a blank space in her memory, as though her brain had been so overloaded it just glitched and shut down for a moment.

Kovit's hands were on her shoulders, and he was leaning in, voice concerned. "Nita, what's wrong?"

"Those pictures . . ."

He frowned. "What about them? They're probably taken from Facebook."

No. Those photos were only in one place—Nita's phone. Which she hadn't had with her.

It was with Fabricio.

"Kovit." Nita's voice was calm, so calm, like there was so much emotion inside her it didn't know how to manifest itself, so it didn't even try.

"Yes?"

"Have you ever heard the name Fabricio Tácunan?"

He frowned, eyes distant. "Not Fabricio . . ."

"But Tácunan?"

"Yes." His head tilted slightly. "Alfredo? Alfonso? Tácunan. Argentinian. He's a lawyer. He's a partner at . . . well, I guess technically it's a legal firm, but in actuality its a business that provides tax havens, money laundering, and stuff for people in the criminal underworld. There's branches all over the world. The Family I worked for was one of his clients, but I don't know many details."

My name's Fabricio. Fabricio Tácunan.

No.

It couldn't be.

"Nita?" Kovit's mouth made the word, but she couldn't seem to hear him, hear anything except the whirring in her head like an overactive computer fan, and the sound of her own heavy gasping breaths.

Fabricio.

Fabricio had betrayed her.

He'd mentioned employees, hadn't he? His father's employees. But Nita's mother had said he was owned by a wealthy collector in Buenos Aires—but her mother lied. What kind of property had a father with employees?

The kind that wasn't property.

Fabricio knew about her ability too—he'd seen Nita injure herself, and her mother demand that she heal it. He knew what she was.

Nita had never seen him get on the bus. He could have easily used her cell phone after she left and called for reinforcements. He knew where the apartment was. He could have called someone to come kidnap her. Hell, he could have even doubled back and followed them himself.

It all fit.

She'd been played.

There was a horrible, light feeling in her chest, like her chest cavity had been filled with helium and it was trying to burst through her skin and pop her body like a balloon, leaving shattered bones and chunks of flesh in its wake.

The one moral decision she'd managed to make in her life turned out to be a lie. Fabricio had betrayed Nita, sold her, and destroyed her life.

Nita pressed her fists against her eyes, as if she could shove her memories right out of her mind.

Stupid, stupid, stupid. Nita wasn't moral. She had no rules or lines—she was just easily playable. That was why her mom never brought live ones home. Because Nita was too stupid to realize when she was being played. Nita had botched everything. She'd misinterpreted every cue.

She'd been blaming her mother this whole time. *Of course* her mother hadn't sold Nita. Her mother loved Nita. Why had she ever doubted it?

Besides, if Nita's mother were going to sell Nita on the black market, why wouldn't she have just done it herself? Why use a middlewoman like Reyes?

The more things clicked together, the more they fell apart, and Nita realized the extent of her folly.

Everything seemed to blur, a muddled mess of memories, changing as she looked at them with different lenses. What other things had Nita misjudged?

She looked up at Kovit, still leaning over her, eyes flicking back and forth across her face as he continued to ask her what was wrong.

She stared back impassively, mind calming as the truth settled around Nita like a scarf. Morals were nothing but things to be manipulated with. They were tools you could use against others, and weapons others could use against you.

She didn't need them.

Didn't want them.

Nita quietly rose, pushing aside Kovit's offer of assistance.

"Nita?"

"We're leaving now." Nita's voice was calm, so calm, like a fire had burned everything else away and there was only the calmness left.

She took a lighter out of the box, where it was wedged between the two flashlights. She flicked it on, and finally, there, she scorched the last of her morals from her soul.

"But we're going to burn this market to the ground before we go."

THIRTY-SIX

O UTSIDE, IT WAS DARK. Not quiet, because the jungle was never quiet. The cicadas' hum seemed to overwhelm all other noise, like having a generator right next to your ear wherever you went. How did normal people sleep here?

Well, there might not be normal people here, so that wasn't really a valid question.

Mirella's voice echoed in her head. *This place isn't a town—I shouldn't call it that. It's a shopping mall. And the only people here are the buyers, the sellers, and the products.*

Nita checked Reyes' phone. Nearly three in the morning. Everyone would be sleeping or whoring or gambling or whatever one did in the black market at night. Guards on the docks would be scarce, since most people weren't stupid enough to try boating in the dark.

She'd considered deleting the conversation with Fabricio or leaving the phone out of sheer rage, but she kept it. She kept it close, like a scar, a reminder of her own fallibility.

Nita still had her night vision, so she could see the world with a clarity most others couldn't. That could be an advantage.

Though she still wasn't sure how well she could actually steer in the dark. Or do anything boating related. She hoped Kovit knew how to do that kind of thing.

"How do you want to do this?" Kovit asked. He had his hands in his pockets, faux casual.

Nita flicked the lighter and thought. "We split up. On my signal, we set fire to everything around us. This whole place is made of wood—it should light up pretty easily. Once the fire is good and roaring, we run for the docks."

Kovit shook his head. "We can't split up. How will I contact you? How will you signal me?"

Right. Kovit's phone had been sacrificed in their escape effort. Nita swallowed, then looked up at him. There were other ways she could signal him.

Why was she even considering this? She didn't want to give him ideas, did she?

When she thought about it, though, she realized she wasn't scared of Kovit hurting her anymore. Not now, not in the future. She wasn't sure when the fear had fully disappeared, but it had.

And she wanted this place to burn. A funeral pyre for everything stolen from people like her.

Two big fires in different parts were better than one. One fire might be caught early by someone. Two fires, that was less likely at this time of night.

"I'll signal you." Her voice was quiet, decision made. "You'll feel it."

His eyes widened in understanding. "You're too far for me to feel a finger."

"I know." She clenched her hand to stop the shaking. "I'll make sure you feel it."

Nita turned away before she could see his expression. She didn't want to know if he did one of those creepy smiles.

Then she asked, "Is there any fuel here? Something to really set the fire going?"

"Yes." His footsteps crunched as he moved away. "There should be a couple of propane tanks behind the building for the generator. I'll get them."

Nita crossed her arms while she waited, and Kovit returned momentarily, dragging two propane tanks, each about as tall as his knee. He winced as he tugged on them, and Nita trotted over and took one from him, dragging it across the rocky ground. She'd almost forgotten about his wound.

"These are both full. And big," Kovit said. "When they go, it will be . . . explosive."

Nita considered. "How long from opening them and setting a fire will we have?"

"I don't know." He frowned. "I imagine it depends on how close the fire is to the open tank."

She pressed her lips together. "Okay. So on my signal, we set the fire and then run like hell toward the docks."

Kovit thought a moment, and then nodded. "All right. First one there tries to get a boat."

"Agreed."

Well, there were the guards to deal with too. But hopefully the fire would distract them.

They each took a propane tank. Nita went to one side

of the market, and Kovit the other. It wasn't that large, so that really only meant each of them walked six or seven blocks.

Nita dragged her propane tank along the darkened roads. She picked it up after a while, sick of the thunk as it went over a bump or dip. Her feet occasionally fell in potholes — was it okay to call them potholes when there was no pavement? There was often water at the bottom, and it soaked into her shoes so they squelched with each step she took.

She stumbled often. Her balance was off, body subconsciously relying on a baby toe that was no longer present.

She tried not to think about it.

Sometimes she could hear music from within buildings, roars and laughs and screams. Occasionally a thud as something hit a wall, or the scrape of a chair across the wooden floor. The sounds of life.

Nita made sure to avoid any area with noise like that when looking for a place to start her fire. If they were awake, they might notice the smoke and try to stop her.

She found a good spot and set the propane tank up against the side of a large, two-story wooden building with mosquito nets hanging over the windows instead of mesh. She kept the cap on the tank — she'd open that at the last minute before she ran.

She took a deep breath and stepped back from the propane tank. She hesitated, then detached her vocal cords. She didn't want her scream to wake people up or draw attention. That would ruin the whole thing, and she'd end up in that cage again before she could blink.

Okay. She was ready. Well, not ready, never ready, but she had to do this at some point. So. As ready as she'd ever be.

Then she turned all her pain circuits back on.

Her whole body was on fire. She was melting in lava, burning alive, as every single cell in her body checked to make sure its pain function was still working. A thousand needles poked her eyes, digging deep into the membrane and scooping pieces out. Hot chili pepper had been shoved into all her tenderest places, scalding and searing and stinging.

Her back arched and her mouth opened to scream, but no sound came out. She crumpled to the ground, sobbing from agony, gasping for breath.

Then it was over.

Nita trembled. When she'd turned her pain circuits off and on as a child, she remembered it hurting, but she didn't remember it hurting *that* much. She revised the memory accordingly.

After that, the lingering pain from the healing bullet wound, the remaining cuts from the glass, and her shattered nose were nothing.

She stumbled to her feet. Her legs shook a little, but a few long breaths, and they stopped. She needed to set her fire. Kovit had his signal now; she needed to get a fire going near this tank and make for the docks.

Nita moved away from the propane tank. She found a likely building nearby to start with — it looked like the type of building to burn. The wood felt dry when she touched it, and slightly brittle.

She used the lighter, first to get some twigs on the ground burning. Then she tucked the flaming twigs in the woven reed, wood, and leaf thatching and let it smolder. There was some laundry hanging on a line nearby, and Nita lit that on fire too. She made sure it was good and fiery, and tossed it against the side of another structure.

The buildings began to burn.

Nita dragged the propane tank a little closer—not too close; she didn't want it to explode early.

Her fingers trembled when she unscrewed the cap on the propane tank. Not from memory of pain, just nerves. Her eyes were burning, like dozens of mosquito bites were on her irises. She scrubbed them, annoyed at herself. Then she sat back. There. The cap was off. It was done. There was no going back.

The buildings were burning at a steady clip now, and the fire had caught and jumped to another building.

It was time for Nita to go.

She ran. Down the street, tripping on the uneven road, trying to look in front of herself rather than down to avoid running into buildings. She passed through the main square, which seemed much bigger at night, without all the stands and peddlers that were out during the day. Then finally down the path to the harbor, trying not to slip on the slope and end up rolling down to meet Kovit.

On the other side of the market, a bright orange glow seemed to be gaining steam. It wasn't neon lights—there were few of those due to generator demands, most likely, but they gave off a much different type of light. Whiter. Brighter. The glow on the other side of the market was dim and deep, and it was orange, the color of insanity.

She picked up her pace.

A hand reached out and snagged her from behind. She opened her mouth, but before she could scream or turn around and fight, Kovit's voice whispered, "It's me."

She stilled and turned to look at him, but his face was so cast in shadow she couldn't even see the outline of his features.

"We have to wait for the fire to start and distract the guards. There're too many."

Nita's heart thumped in her chest, remembering the last time she'd tried to distract the guards. And how well that had gone for Mirella.

But she nodded. "How long before the—"

She never finished her sentence, because one of the propane tanks blew.

Nita and Kovit both fell to the ground and covered their heads when they heard the sound, and Nita's ears rang with a horrid echo that didn't seem to end even when the explosion did. Beside her, blood soaked through Kovit's shirt as his stitches tore.

Fire soared into the air like a volcano spout, a strange, almost bluish fire that lit up the whole market for a brief moment. Sparks rained down, catching on other buildings and on the surrounding woods. Large pieces of burning wood arced through the air above Nita's head and set the pier on fire.

Only one more explosion to go, she thought. Then she paused, realizing her mistake. There were probably other propane tanks in the market, with other generators. In fact, almost every building was liable to have one.

Kovit grabbed her hand and dragged her onto the dock.

314

The guards were ahead of them, already fleeing the market and leaping into boats.

A burning piece of wood had flown onto the pier and set a small part of it on fire. Kovit kicked the piece of wood into the water, but the embers lingered. It wouldn't be long before the fire began consuming the pier in earnest.

Behind Nita, the market had begun to scream. She could hear voices over the roaring of the flames. Shouts, voices raised high in anger, panic, fear. The thunder of footsteps as people began running for the river and the boats. Sometimes she thought she could make out individual words, but mostly it just sounded like noise.

Then there was another explosion.

The dock shook, the support beams shuddering with the earth, and the pier rippled. Kovit cried out, more in startlement than fear, as he tripped, overbalancing and tumbling into the water below with a splash.

Nita screamed, calling his name, but she couldn't hear her own voice over the roaring in her ears and the echo of the latest explosion. Had she even remembered to turn her voice back on? She must have—she'd talked to Kovit earlier. But no matter how she shouted, she couldn't seem to hear herself.

After a moment, Kovit's head surfaced, followed by his torso as he stood at the shallow riverbank. He gave her a thumbs-up and pointed to one of the rowboats, the kind that were old and slow but didn't require keys, which neither of them had.

The steps down were farther along the dock. Nita stumbled toward them, trying to beat the hordes of people already running from the market, swarming to the pier and the offer of escape the water promised.

Another explosion. Nita tripped.

And fell over the side of the pier.

The water slammed into her like a brick wall, and she gasped as it shoved itself up her nose. Everything around her was wet, not shower wet, but kind of gooey wet, like something oily might have been added to the water. She hoped a boat wasn't leaking fuel. Something tangled around her ankle, maybe a plant or vine. She hoped not an anaconda.

Where was up? Everything was confusing and it was weird to be hurting again and the world swirled.

Then her head was above the water and she was snorting out bits of river. Gasping, she shoved her wet hair out of her eyes to get a view of what was going on. Above her, the pier was on fire, and people were running through it anyway, trying to get to their boats. There was screaming, but it was hard to hear over the ringing. One man—she thought it was a man, but she couldn't really tell because of the flames—ignored the pier and ran straight into the river. Bubbles rose where he went in, and steam too.

Nita turned her attention to the market, and her jaw dropped open. All she could see was fire.

True, her angle was bad in the water, she couldn't see the whole thing. Just one corner, but it seemed a wall of light and flames. It glowed, lit up even the sky and blocked out the stars like there was an entire city's worth of light pollution concentrated in this single fire.

The trees and surrounding jungle had caught fire too, and the screams and cries of animals punctuated the darkness. A whoop, a howl, a caw. The sky was full of fleeing birds, their forms arcing like shadows in the night, lit from the fire below.

"Nita, come on!"

She turned to find Kovit had already untied the boat and was waiting for her. He was doubled over, and she thought it was in pain at first before she saw him shudder, back arching, eyes half lidded. Then she realized he was in pain — just not his own.

Nita half swam, half walked through the shallow river edge to the boat. She grabbed the side and heaved herself over the top. The boat tipped from her weight, rocking back and forth, and Nita dripped water all over the bottom. There was already a carpet of water, though, so it was fine.

Or there was a leak. It would be her luck to end up in the one leaky boat.

She glanced at Kovit, but he lay at the bottom of the boat, completely oblivious to the outside world. His body rocked with pleasure, his eyes half closed, mouth twisted into the most brilliant smile she'd seen on him. His fingers twitched, as though playing a piano only he could see, and he moaned softly, indiscernible words to a song only he could hear.

Nita tried calling his name, but he didn't respond. Too high on pain.

Grunting, Nita grabbed an oar from the boat and stuck it in the water. She pressed against the bottom of the river, trying to lever the boat so it would move away from shore. Her arms were surprisingly tired after a couple of these shoves, and her bullet wound ached, but she ignored that. They weren't safe this close to the flames.

A motorboat zoomed past her, nearly capsizing her vessel. Water sloshed over the side, and Nita grabbed the edges, heart slamming in her chest. A panicked woman in pajamas shot away down the river on a water scooter. Another boat followed.

Once Nita felt she was far enough into the river to be safe, she looked back at the market.

There was nothing but fire. Even the pier was gone, and based on the boats in the water, she suspected fewer than a dozen people had gotten out before it became impossible.

There was the occasional boom as something else blasted within the inferno, but other than that, all Nita heard was the roar of a nearby engine, her still-ringing ears, and the panicked caws of birds above her.

She sat down on the bench.

She had done this.

She thought of the screams she'd heard during the burning. She almost thought she could hear them now, even though there was no way that was true. Everyone in there was surely dead by now.

Not all of the people burning in there deserved to be. Some were victims, just like Nita had been. "Products," as Mirella had put it. And now Nita was responsible for their deaths.

But . . . whatever life they had there, it couldn't have been good. Like Nita and Mirella, their days were already numbered. And this way, there wouldn't be more victims. This was the last batch that would ever see the shores of Mercado de la Muerte.

While Nita believed that justification, it didn't stop her from curling herself into a ball at the bottom of the boat. The water soaked through her already drenched clothes and made her shoes squelch and squeak.

There, cold and wet, her mind replayed the screams while Kovit rolled on the floor, gasping in ecstasy from their pain.

THIRTY-SEVEN

NITA ENDED UP floating on the boat in the middle of the Amazon until Kovit regained his senses. Mostly because she didn't actually know which way to start rowing.

She was worried about him at first. Even though all the pain was clearly gone, he kept twitching and moaning, and didn't seem to be quite conscious. She wasn't sure if that was normal or not, or if there'd been so much pain he'd blown through the mechanism in his body that let him absorb it, like a computer overload. Could that even happen?

She wondered if he was sick. She wondered if there was anyone in the world who could fix him if he was. She wondered if anyone would care enough to help him.

No. She was sure some crazy dictatorial psychopath must have funded some sort of medical research at some point. After all, zannies were rare and highly paid in certain circles. Those circles had to care if they died. Right?

He turned over, and his face shone with . . . not sweat, that wasn't right. Oil? Something else? His lips were parted slightly, and his breathing rapid.

Nita squeezed some of the cool river water out of her shirt and onto his face, hoping that would either help or at the least get him to regain his senses long enough to point her in the right direction.

He made a small sound, almost like a kitten's mew when the water hit him. His eyes cracked open, and he looked up at her.

"Kovit. Which way to Brazil?"

He stared at her, eyes squinting, and she wasn't sure he understood her until he whispered, "Left. Left from the harbor for Tabatinga."

Nita let out a breath. "Okay. Thanks."

Nita picked up the oars. Kovit's eyes drifted closed again, and he shuddered his way into what she thought might be sleep, or maybe some sort of pain coma. Something not conducive to helping her row the damn boat.

Nita started rowing by the light of the fire, which still raged, pumping smoke into the sky and spreading farther into the forest. By the time she passed the fire, the sun was rising, and that provided more light. Her arms became sore quickly, but Nita removed the stresses, pumped her strength, built her muscles faster than she should have. It wasn't too much effort —she still had all that muscle built to get out of the cage. But all this modifying her body was beginning to take its toll. It became harder to focus, harder to use her power, harder to do anything except methodically row and be glad the current was helping her.

As she went, she noticed some of the other boats that had left the market went the same way she did. Some went the other way, west into Peru. Most of the boats going her way were motorboats, and they zoomed past her, heading for Tabatinga.

Nita wasn't sure what to make of it when she saw the first capsized motorboat. There was no sign of the people who'd been on it.

A few minutes later, she encountered another one, a ghost ship on the water, floating there with no one in it.

Nita began to get nervous.

She continued rowing, her eyes alert, watching for rocks or other things that might catch on a boat. She couldn't see anything.

Across from her, another set of rowboats slid through the water. Other people from the market who hadn't been able to get on motorboats and had taken whatever was available.

There was a splash, and one of them capsized.

Nita stiffened and stopped rowing. She heard the voice of a man, coughing and gurgling as he cursed the river. He thrashed by the side of the tipped boat, his arms flailing in the water, fingers scrabbling for purchase on the side of the water-slicked hull.

Nita frowned, trying to find what had tipped him over. Was it something in the water? Rocks?

Then he screamed.

Nita stiffened. Was he being attacked by piranhas? Nita had heard that was a myth, and that piranhas were actually fairly harmless when left alone.

What else could be in the water?

A pink-gray fin crested the surface, like a shark in a horror movie, and the man was dragged under, still screaming.

A dolphin. A pink Amazonian dolphin.

Like the ones in the legend Mirella was based on.

Nita's heart rate shot up. Dolphins didn't attack people, did they? But Mirella, Mirella would. Did Mirella have more connection to the dolphin legends than she'd been willing to admit?

Nita remembered Mirella tumbling off the dock and into the river in one final act of defiance. But what if it hadn't been defiance? What if it had been escape?

But she'd been shot. Nita didn't think Mirella could survive without medical treatment. That was stretching credibility.

The rowboat nearest Nita began to speed up, the men in it paddling faster and faster, trying to distance themselves from the previous accident. As they came closer, Nita recognized them.

Boulder. Jorge. Lorenzo.

Nita felt a wave of fury. Almost as if the dolphin felt it too, the boat began to tip, as though something underneath the water was knocking on it.

Somethings, Nita realized, catching the flash of at least three different dorsal fins, pink as the water wrung out of a bloody shirt.

Boulder raised his oar and began jabbing at the water, and Lorenzo did the same. Jorge pulled out his gun and started shooting wildly into the river, eyes searching for movement.

It was in vain.

The boat gave a slosh, and Jorge tumbled over the side with a yelp. He surfaced, gasping, and grabbed the side of the boat to haul himself back in. It tipped from his weight, and Boulder snarled, smashing the paddle into Jorge's head.

Jorge went limp, grip slackening as he slipped back into the water, and the boat righted itself.

Lorenzo screamed, dropping to the bottom of the boat and reaching over the side for Jorge. But the dolphins got there first, and his hand flinched back when a pink fin rose from the water.

Screaming, he turned and launched himself at Boulder. The two of them overbalanced and tumbled over the side, howling and punching and clawing each other the whole way. The splash when they landed rocked the boat to near capsizing.

Lorenzo surfaced, gasping, but Boulder was swimming away.

Toward Nita's boat.

Nita's eyes widened, and she quickly raised her oars and began rowing away.

Boulder was a much faster swimmer than Nita was a rower, and he closed in quickly. Nita gave up on rowing and instead stood in the boat, gripping one oar and waving it at him as he approached, hoping she looked threatening.

He ignored her and grabbed for the side of her boat, tipping it dangerously. Nita shrieked, smashing the oar down on his fingers.

He howled and released the boat, but then used his other hand to try to pull himself back up. Nita's oar came down, but he shifted his hand at the last minute, gripping a different place. And Nita swung, like she was playing a demented game of Whac-A-Mole.

Gasping, Nita leaned forward, and used her oar like a fishing spear, aiming for the head bobbing in the water. Boulder saw it coming and dove underwater with a slosh. Nita swore, her eyes flicking over the surface of the river, trying to figure out where he'd come up.

But Boulder didn't come up.

Bubbles rose from where he'd disappeared — first many, then fewer, until the river was still again.

Nita's breathing was fast and harsh, and her fingers gripped the oar so tightly she thought she might snap it in two.

A pink fin crested the water and then went back under, back toward Boulder's boat, where its podmates circled.

Lorenzo had managed to scramble back into his boat and regain an oar. He'd started paddling toward shore, his eyes fixed on land as if it were his savior.

The boat flipped before he'd made more than three strokes with the paddle. He tumbled into the water with a scream that was abruptly cut off. More bubbles rose.

Nita decided she should take a page from Lorenzo's book and head for land. Right now.

Her paddling was frenetic, but she knew she'd never make it to land before the dolphins turned their attention to her.

She was right.

The boat rocked, and Nita dropped her oars. Shit. What to do?

She swallowed and leaned over the side, looking into the

325

darkness of the water, eyes searching for a shape. "Mirella? Do you guys know Mirella? She's a friend of mine."

The boat stopped rocking. Nita took that as a hopeful sign.

"I got out, see? I was a prisoner too." She swallowed and resisted the urge to look at Kovit, unconscious in the boat. If this was Mirella's doing, Kovit would never survive discovery. Neither would Nita, if she were being honest. Mirella would never forgive Nita for befriending the man who had tortured her.

Nita certainly wouldn't have forgiven Mirella if their positions were reversed.

The water was still. Sweat slithered down her back.

"Is it you, Mirella?"

Still no response.

Nita sat, leaning over the edge, waiting.

Her eyes bulged as the water rippled. A gray hand reached up like a zombie from its grave, and grasped the edge of the boat. Nita jerked back, and another hand followed. Then a small face surfaced, long pink hair swirling on the surface of the river like seaweed.

Mirella.

She wore no cover on her eye, which was a mess. It looked like it had been sewn closed and then gotten infected. The skin was swollen and almost melted. But her other eye was clear and the same pink-gray it always was.

"You're alive." Nita couldn't stop staring.

"Yes." Mirella shivered, and her skin *rippled*. "I don't have much time. Water makes me shift. It's hard to stay like this."

"Oh."

"I'm sorry I left you behind." Mirella's voice was soft.

"It's okay." Nita shifted, uncomfortable for reasons she didn't fully understand. Her heart twisted in her chest, and she resisted the urge to glance guiltily at Kovit on the floor of the boat. "I got away, didn't I? I even took the market down with me."

Mirella laughed, and then gave Nita a bright smile. "You did. Thank you."

Mirella gasped, and her eyes crossed as the muscles beneath her face moved like ocean waves.

"I have to go," she whispered. "But I promise, I'll make sure no one escapes." Her voice became throaty and raw. "And that they'll never rebuild the market here again."

Before Nita could respond, Mirella had released the boat and sunk beneath the surface.

There was a soft splash and a single pink-gray fin rose out of the water, as though waving goodbye, before disappearing.

THIRTY-EIGHT

KOVIT WOKE SOME TIME LATER. He sat up with a sleepy, slightly contented expression.

He swallowed, and looked around before croaking, "Water?"

Nita shook her head, mute, and continued to row as the sun beat down on her and sweat trickled down her face. She could feel her scalp burning but didn't have the energy to do anything about it.

Kovit looked down at the river, considering. The water rippled gently as they passed. Close up, it looked clearer than it had from a distance, more drinkable. He licked his lips.

Then he sighed and turned away from the water and settled himself in the boat. Nita had eyed the river too. But she wasn't that desperate yet. She knew she could fight off all the microbes in there, but . . . she wasn't sure she could do it right now. And it would be a real hassle to do it later.

She wondered when they'd get desperate enough to drink the water, regardless of the danger.

Kovit held out his hands and Nita passed him the oars,

grateful for the respite. He began rowing, clumsily at first, and then slowly improving. The boat shook a little as he found his rhythm, and the water sloshed on the bottom.

Nita leaned back, letting herself lie down across two benches, and closed her eyes. There was a gap between the benches, and her back sank in between, but it wasn't too uncomfortable.

God, she was tired. Not just in body, but in mind. She couldn't remember the last time she'd slept. Or eaten. Or not had terror-based adrenaline pumping through her system. It would be nice if she could have a meal, maybe some fast food — McDonald's, KFC, oh, or some of that wonderful street food in Lima, maybe some *picarones* and *causa*. She also wanted a big drink of water and a soft mattress. Mmm. Heaven.

But she was also excited, too excited to actually doze. It was almost over. She was almost out. Almost safe.

"Nita?" Kovit's voice was still hoarse.

She opened her eyes and rolled over to look at him and get a different part of her face crisped. "Yeah?"

"Did the market . . ."

"It's gone." Nita's voice was firm. Almost hard.

"Did anyone escape?" Kovit rowed a little faster.

Nita thought about the overturned boats on the river, and the pink fin sliding through the water, silent and deadly.

"No." A bitter smile crossed Nita's face.

Kovit watched her. "We killed a lot of people."

"Yes." Nita looked away.

"Mmm." Kovit's gaze was heavy lidded. "Nita, can I ask you something?"

"Yeah."

"Do you have rules?"

"Rules?"

"Lines you won't cross. Things you won't do."

She closed her eyes. "I thought I did. But I don't."

No, things like morals just got in the way. They let her be manipulated by people like Fabricio. They made everything she needed to do to escape harder. She didn't want them.

"Ah." He stopped rowing and knelt beside her. "Look at me."

She looked up.

His eyes were dark and searching, and he sighed. "I never told you about why I turned my mother in, did I?"

She shook her head, wondering where he was going with this.

"My mother . . ." Kovit's expression morphed, shifted into something both sweet and sad. "I loved my mother very much. When I was growing up, she was my idol. She'd fled Myanmar when she was a teenager. Her parents had been involved in some shady things for the government—the kind of things that get you on human rights watch lists. But my mother, she wanted no part of it, and she fled to Thailand.

"She used to take me around town to try to find places where bad things happened. And we'd try to find some pain to eat."

Nita hesitated. "She didn't hurt people?"

Kovit laughed. "Oh, she did. We had a basement. There was always someone there. Mom made me join her when I was young—I don't recall how young, but certainly before I was five. She said it was important for me to know where my food came from. There was a zannie we knew, and his family kept everything from him, and when he realized he'd been eating people's pain, he committed suicide."

Kovit paused, maybe expecting Nita to react. But she was silent, listening.

"Well, at any rate, my mother didn't want that to happen to me. So we started young. It was all good fun. I didn't know anyone there, nothing seemed, well, real." He hesitated. "But things . . . changed. Slowly. I mean, I didn't notice at first."

He didn't seem to know how to continue. Finally, he let out a breath, and the words came out in a rush. "You know that children's pain is stronger? It hurts more, they feel more, I don't know. But it's stronger."

Nita didn't like where this was going.

"I brought a friend over one day, and . . . I thought she went home. There was a lot of pain that night. I mean, Mom always had someone in the basement, and I . . ." He huffed a breath. "When I found . . . found her, I freaked. I tried to stop my mom, and she decided to punish me . . ."

He stopped, arms falling limp at his sides. He stared at the floor, all his muscles clenched.

Nita stared at him in growing horror. "She hurt you."

He nodded. "The mother I knew . . . the mother I grew up with wouldn't have done that. She ran away so she could avoid participating in government interrogations. She loved me. She loved my sister. She never would have hurt us.

"But she changed. It was slow, over time. And by the time I noticed, it was too late."

Kovit was silent for a long time. Nita swallowed and put a tentative hand on his shoulder. "What happened?"

"I got away. Obviously. And I called INHUP." He sighed. "But . . . after that, I started paying attention to other zannies. Talking to people who knew them. Meeting others.

"I guess I wanted to know what happened. What caused this. And I found patterns, lots of patterns. Zannies, all the ones I met, they were . . . Well, let's just say you would never, ever want to meet them. Already souls so black there was nothing left of anything human, just an addict's desire to harm others."

He met Nita's eyes. "I won't ever say I'm a good person. I don't want to be. I *like* who I am—and I don't want to lose that. I don't want to lose me. Because it felt like that's what happened to all of them. They'd lost themselves to their monsters."

"What did you do?" Nita's fingers clenched against her side.

"I made rules. I drew lines. I looked at the things that seemed to make the others fall, and I refused to do them. I won't hurt my friends or my family. Or their friends. I won't eat the pain of anyone under fifteen. Even if I'm not the one hurting them. I won't eat it. I won't eat any pain that's sexual in nature." He grimaced. "You asked why I never went out in the market? It was full of *children in brothels*. It was a nightmare. I couldn't go out there."

Nita looked at the floor. That was sick. She hadn't even thought of the brothels in the market more than to notice they existed.

A thought struck Nita. "There's a rule about hurting people

who can't feel pain, isn't there? That's why you didn't cut my fingers off when Reyes ordered it. Or Boulder, later."

He blinked and nodded. "Something like that."

"Do you have rules about killing?" she asked.

"No. Nor do I have rules on a lot of other things you probably think I should." He shrugged and gave a self-deprecating smile. "But I also have lots of rules that make very little sense. Including one about teddy bears. I was twelve when I started making my rules, and I'm too scared to ever change them. If I let myself cross one line because I tell myself 'I was twelve, I didn't understand,' then I set a precedent. I won't allow that."

Kovit leaned forward, only inches from Nita's face. "But you know what? They've worked. I'm still me." He gave her a cheeky grin. "Crazy monster I may be. But still *me*. So far."

Nita looked into his dark eyes. "You think I need rules."

"I think in the past few days, you've discarded a lot. I think the girl who came here a week ago would never have asked me to torture someone, or shot people, or burned the entire market down to the ground."

He was right about that.

"I'm not saying it's wrong. I'm not here to preach morality." He gave her a wicked grin. "But the problem with losing your morality is that sometimes it takes other things with it. You don't realize the things that are important to you, in order to be the person you want to be, until you've already damaged them beyond repair."

He sighed. "I just want to make you think about the lines you thought you had before. I'd hate to see you lose yourself."

Lose herself? Had Nita lost herself?

She'd murdered people. She'd asked Kovit to torture someone. She'd dissected someone she'd killed.

She closed her eyes and decided Kovit was right: she didn't like it. Because when she looked at her actions, they were too close to what her mother might have done. And Nita never, ever, wanted to become her mother.

She didn't realize she was crying until Kovit put a hand on her uninjured shoulder.

Wiping the tears off, she looked up at Kovit. "I'm sorry."

"For what?"

"For asking you to kill people. For assuming you would."

His eyes curled like upside down smiles. "You have nothing to be sorry for."

"Thank you."

He leaned back, a faint smile on his face. "You're welcome."

Nita took a deep breath and started making rules for herself. She would never cross a line she didn't want to again. Not because of something as transient as a conscience, but because of something more concrete. Resolve.

THIRTY-NINE

THE HOURS BLENDED together as Nita and Kovit took turns rowing the boat under the blistering heat. What would have been four hours in a high-speed motorboat took significantly longer in a shitty old rowboat.

Sometimes they talked. Mostly, they were silent, trying to conserve water.

At one point, when Nita's sunburn started to throb and she didn't have the energy to heal it, Kovit dragged a bloody hand over her shoulder and the pain instantly numbed. Zannie blood was a famous analgesic, excellent for lessening pain, but it was Nita's first time experiencing it. She could see why it was so high in demand on the black market.

Later, when it was Kovit's turn to row again, he suddenly burst into laughter and nearly dropped the oars into the river.

Nita blinked and stared at him, his hair with its shampoo commercial glow, and his skin looking like it had been Photoshopped. She wondered if the heat and his still-oozing bullet wound had finally gotten to him.

"Is something funny?"

He smiled, relaxed, and returned to rowing at normal speed. "The Family. I just realized. They'll assume I'm dead."

She let a smile cross her face. No INHUP on the hunt for him, no face posted on the Dangerous Unnaturals List. She was glad. "Looks like we both escaped."

Kovit laughed. He knew she wasn't just talking about the market. She liked that about him — he understood. She never needed to explain.

"Have you thought about what you're going to do now?" he asked her, after a few minutes.

She hesitated, almost afraid to say the words out loud. "I'm going to INHUP."

"INHUP?" He raised his eyebrows. "Is your new plan to be their scientist so they can protect you?"

"Not a chance in hell." Nita's response was fast. "I would never join INHUP."

His eyes were laughing. "Oh? Why?"

"Where to start?" she snorted. "They wouldn't approve of my past — I'm sure they'd be more than eager to put me in jail if they ever got a whiff of my family's activities." She met his eyes. "Or if they found out I was associated with you. INHUP would put you to death."

Kovit's smile fell, and he looked at her with sad eyes. "They would."

Nita leaned in close, so she was only a few inches from his face. A strand of hair fell in front of his eyes, and she resisted the urge to reach out and brush it aside. "I would never let that happen."

She knew it was true the moment she said it. She'd always

believed the Dangerous Unnaturals List was one of the best things about INHUP. She still did. Just not when it came to people she knew.

Kovit looked lost, uncertain how to respond. His brows pinched, and his eyes examined her face, flicking back and forth, as though looking for the lie.

But there was no lie to be found.

She turned away, suddenly aware how close they'd been.

He swallowed and looked away as she pulled back. His voice was slightly unsteady. "Why, then? Why go to INHUP?"

Nita pulled the list of corrupt INHUP agents from her pocket. It was a soggy mess, and the ink had run something terrible. She spread the list out and hoped it would dry. A few names were still legible. Sort of. Maybe.

"Plane ticket." She swallowed, trying to moisten her dry throat. She never could have imagined a day she would willingly go to INHUP, yet here it was. How times had changed. "I have no money. I don't know what's happened to my parents. INHUP will at least get me out of here."

Her mother had to know what had happened to Nita. She would have seen the video, would have known exactly where Nita was.

And she hadn't come.

Initially, Nita had assumed this was because her mother was the one who sold her. But now she wondered if something hadn't happened to her.

"I see." Kovit's voice was soft. He licked his lips, and then looked down at her. "I . . . well, I mean, you have another option."

"What?"

He stopped rowing, and folded the oars on his lap. Nita sat up on her elbows, wondering why he had paused.

Finally, he raised his eyes to hers. "You could come with me."

She stared, unsure how to respond.

She was tempted, more than she'd thought she would be.

But she didn't want to go underground. She didn't want to spend her whole life hiding, fearing the black market kidnapping her in the night.

In a way, she was still trapped in a cage. Except this one was the size of the planet, and the only way to escape would be to somehow scrub her face from the internet. Which was impossible.

If she ever wanted to be truly free, she couldn't spend her life living in fear.

She imagined life on the run with a zannie. She imagined the screaming, a million voices echoing through her life as she went deeper and deeper into hiding. The constant fear of being captured, by INHUP, by rivals, by whoever.

"Do you even have money for that?" she asked, avoiding an answer.

"Some. Not much," he admitted. "If we get to somewhere with internet, I can access my account. I can check. Maybe a thousand dollars."

Enough for one ticket back to North America. If that. Not enough for Nita to come too.

"Thank you for the offer, Kovit. It means a lot."

"But you want to go with INHUP." He swallowed and

bowed his head so his hair obscured his face for a moment before he put the oars back in the water and started paddling again.

"I want their plane ticket." Nita was blunt. "You don't have enough to take us both back to the States. And I want to see my father again."

Nita was worried he might be offended by her decision, but he just grinned and winked at her.

"The offer is open-ended, Nita. There's no expiration date."

For some reason, that made her feel tight in her chest. It kind of hurt.

A short while later, the boat thunked against something, and Nita lifted her head to find they were at a dock. They were at the far end of a large port. Dozens of docks were scattered down the coast, anchoring riverboats, ferries, small motor-boats, and other rowboats. The water had clearly swamped the dock many times over the years and stained the wood darker, giving it a permanently wet look.

Around the dock, there was a combination of small *tiendas*, restaurants with large, brightly colored umbrellas, and larger port-related buildings. Motor taxis buzzed down the streets like motorized rickshaws, small and nimble as they bumped their way over the pavement and wove in between cars. The green and yellow flag of Brazil was painted on a wooden build-ing nearby.

"We're here." Kovit dropped the oars and leaned back.

Nita drank the sight in. The people walking around in shorts and flip-flops, the hawkers in the distance trying to drum up customers for their boat, or their store, or who knew what. Signs around were mostly in Portuguese, though she saw some Spanish too. The riverboats disgorged people and products, like miniature cruise ships.

Finally she turned back to Kovit, reluctant to say goodbye. "What will you do now?"

He stretched his arms high above his head, and something popped in his back. Then he swore and clutched his side. His fingers were bloody. He gave her a warped grin. "Go to the hospital, I think."

Nita leaned forward to look at the wound, cursing herself for forgetting about it, but he shifted away.

"It's silly, but I almost forgot it was there." He shook his head. "I haven't felt pain since we left the market."

Right. Because his pain was proportional to his feeding. She hoped he didn't have blood poisoning from falling in the river with an open wound. "That's probably not a good thing."

He waved her concern away. "I'll be fine. We're here, after all."

Nita was more worried than she cared to admit. But she kept her tone light, trying to make the feeling go away. "And where to after the hospital?"

"I don't know." He grinned and shaded his eyes against the sun. "You know, I've spent most of my life in the mafia. I don't really know who I am outside it. But"—he met her eyes—"I want to find out. I want to try something different. See if I can. See who I am in a different life."

Nita huffed a small laugh and looked down. She found something amusing about the fact that a zannie wanted to get out of the criminal underworld. It was just so contrary to expectations. She wondered what kind of alternative life he was thinking of. Would he still torture people? Was that something that mattered to him? Nita didn't know.

There was a lot she didn't know about Kovit.

"I'll go somewhere I can speak the language, to start." He considered. "Somewhere it's not hot."

"I second that."

"I'd like to find my sister too." His smile was sad. "I haven't seen her since INHUP took her ten years ago."

"Oh." Nita blinked. "How will you find her?"

He shrugged. "I don't know yet. I'll figure it out as I go, I guess."

They were silent for a few minutes before Kovit rose. He stepped onto the dock with a wince and pulled the boat in closer, looping a nearby rope around it.

Nita approached, hesitant. He stood up, rope tied, and Nita realized she'd misjudged the distance and they were barely an inch apart now.

Kovit looked at her pocket, and she could feel his breath tickling her skin. "Do you have Reyes' phone?"

"It's probably dead. I jumped into the water with it."

"Ah. Well, then." He leaned forward, so close she thought he was going to kiss her. Her heartbeat skyrocketed, and she couldn't seem to move. Then he leaned past her face, cheek almost brushing hers before he whispered an email address in her ear. The hairs on the back of her neck rose. "If you want to get in touch with me."

Heart slamming in her chest, Nita nodded, voice catching in her throat. "Thanks."

He took a step back and grinned. She wondered if he was playing with her the mocking way he played with other people. Or if this was something else entirely.

She looked up, and their eyes met. His were dark, thickly lashed, and sad. It was strange to see them sad. She'd always thought of them as happy, dancing with the screams of the people he tortured.

"Good luck, Nita." His voice was soft.

She nodded, heart still pounding, chest still tight. "You too."

He extended his hand to help her out of the boat. She took it, and with one step, suddenly they were both on the pier.

She gave him one last smile and then turned away before she could change her mind. As she walked, she tried to recall Mirella's screams as Kovit tortured her, because she couldn't let herself get sentimental about a monster. But the only screams she could pull up were the people in the market, as Nita burned them alive.

FORTY

NITA RESTED HER head against the window of the car. Bogotá whipped by her, districts she'd never heard of. Rebar stuck out from the tops of houses in some places, roofs unfinished. Signs for *tiendas* or *bodegas* intermingled with boarded-up houses that seemed to be collapsing in on themselves.

Then they crossed some invisible line, and it looked like she was somewhere in Florida, with drooping palm trees, clean plazas with elaborate fountains or monuments in them, and wide, well-paved streets. Nita didn't understand the logic. The rich districts next to the poverty-stricken ones. But then again, American cities were just as divided.

The car stopped in front of a ten-story modern glass building beside a group of other modern glass buildings. Nita had a moment of heart-stopping terror. This was INHUP. It was to Nita what the boogeyman was to other kids. She'd always expected that if ever she went into INHUP, it would be in handcuffs.

But really, she could never have predicted any of the past week.

A tall woman in a suit gestured for Nita to enter. Letting out a breath of tension, she did.

Nita had showed up at the office in Tabatinga, dripping wet, with not a cent or piece of ID to her name. Normally, a place as small as Tabatinga would never have had such a well-staffed INHUP office, but so many unnatural body-parts bootleggers frequented the town it was a great place to nab them before they crossed the border. Hence, office.

Nita had squelched into the lobby and said, "Mercado de la Muerte has been burned down. I escaped. I was a prisoner there. Help me."

She was quietly led to a room, given a bottle of water, and told to wait.

She used the time to sleep.

She was woken several hours later and told she was being taken to the continental INHUP headquarters in Bogotá, Colombia. Nita would have thought Rio for headquarters, or maybe Buenos Aires, but what did she know?

A helicopter was sent, and Nita was flown to a larger airport, where she was transferred to a plane that took her to Bogotá.

She spent the plane ride watching the Amazon River twist below her like an uncoiled rope. Around it, treetops covered the ground like a forest of broccoli heads. As they were taking off, she thought she saw a macaw.

And now Nita was taking her very first steps into a

place she never thought she'd be. INHUP headquarters, Bogotá.

Her fingers twitched for her scalpel.

She was led to a small white room. Her first thought was that it would have made a great dissection room. It didn't have one-way mirrors, but it did have a blinking security camera in the top left corner. Nita watched the security camera watching her.

The INHUP agent sat down. "Nita."

Nita looked up, startled at first that the woman knew her name, and then remembered that she'd asked ages ago. What was the agent's name? She had buzzcut black hair, a square face, and medium-brown skin. Her suit was sharply pressed, and the white shirt beneath it pristine.

She looked a lot like Nita's father, enough that they could have been mistaken for siblings. Nita's heart tightened at the thought, and she swallowed. Soon. She'd be home soon.

"Nita," the INHUP agent repeated, and the name finally dredged itself up from the back of her mind. Agent Quispe. Quispe was a Quechua name; the language of the Incans.

Nita blinked and focused her wandering mind.

"Nita, can we talk a bit? I promise, you can go have a shower in a few minutes, but I want to ask you some questions first." She spoke slowly, as though uncertain of Nita's Spanish comprehension.

Nita nodded, then licked her lips. "All right."

Agent Quispe leaned in. "Firstly, is there anyone you want us to contact for you? Family? Your parents, perhaps?"

Nita nodded, then hesitated. Her father's phone was in police custody. He might have been arrested for his crimes selling unnatural body parts.

But the more she thought about it, the stranger it seemed that it was in the Chicago PD's custody and not in INHUP's. There was something she was missing there.

Well, there was no point thinking about it. She'd come here for a plane ticket and a way home, and she wasn't going to get it without telling them who she was.

"My father's name is Enrique Leonardo Sánchez Roca." Nita looked around for a pen, but there was nothing in the room. "If you give me a pen and paper, I can write down his phone number and address and such."

Agent Quispe went to the door and called something into the hall. A moment later, pen and paper were brought. Nita wrote down the details, and then the paper was whisked away to someone outside, who was presumably going to track her father down.

"Now, Nita." Agent Quispe sat down and pulled a phone out of her pocket. "Is this you?"

She played a video. Nita stood, frightened, at the back of the cage as Kovit advanced and skinned part of her arm. His ecstatic shudder cut off abruptly as the video stopped, then focused in on Nita, ignoring Kovit. Nita closed her eyes. It felt like so long ago that the video had been made, when she was a different person.

"Yes. That's me." Nita watched as, on screen, her wound started healing.

Agent Quispe took the phone away. "I'm sorry you had to relive that."

"It's fine." And it was. Nita didn't really feel anything about the video. She'd got cut, she'd been scared. But so much had happened since then that the fear at that moment lost all power over the girl in the present, sitting in this room.

"Can you tell me what happened?"

"In the video? You just watched it."

"No." Agent Quispe frowned at Nita's evasion. "From the beginning. How did you get to be there?"

Nita looked down at her hands, folded on the table. "I was kidnapped. Someone injected me with something, and I passed out. And then I woke up in that cage."

"Were you alone when you were taken?"

Nita made a quick calculation. She was seventeen, and the likelihood she was living alone in a foreign country was close to zero. Then they'd start asking questions, dig into her parents. And that could cause problems—especially given her mother. So Nita decided to nip it in the bud, just in case.

"No." Nita clenched her hands. "My mother was there. I didn't see what happened to her. But later on, Reyes—my captor—implied she was dead."

Agent Quispe leaned forward, brows knitted with sympathy. "Continue."

Nita shrugged, uncomfortable. She wasn't going to admit to multiple homicides in front of a police officer. Reyes. Boulder's guards. Nita couldn't even remember what they looked like. That's how insignificant her mind had classified them. And she'd snuffed them out.

It was scary that a life could be so unimportant.

And she'd killed a whole market full of people with fire.

She felt surprisingly numb about it all now — maybe the panic attack would happen later? Maybe it was all a delayed reaction? Or maybe she'd had all the reaction she was going to, and she'd emotioned herself out.

Whatever the reason, her numbness made it easier to lie. "I stayed in the cage. Sometimes Reyes brought potential customers to see me. One of her customers bought me last night. When he led me out of the cage, we saw the fire starting. I ran away, down to the harbor, got in a rowboat, and made my way to Tabatinga."

The end. Nita would make a master storyteller.

"How did you get away?"

"I shoved him."

"You weren't chained?"

"No."

"And did you see anyone else escape?"

"No." Nita's voice was cold. "They all burned. They're dead."

Agent Quispe watched Nita with a cool intensity, and Nita returned her gaze with a tired, are-you-really-going-to-interrogate-me-after-all-I've-been-through look.

"Can I have a shower?" Nita asked, plucking at her sweat- and bloodstained T-shirt. She had no idea what her face looked like. Her dunk in the river had probably washed some of the blood off, but she hadn't healed the vicious gash across her cheek, and she knew there must be blood pooling under her eyes from her broken nose.

Agent Quispe gave her another long look and then a tight nod. "Of course."

Nita was led to a small private bathroom with a glass shower. Someone had placed a folded towel, a pair of baggy gray sweats, and a white shirt next to it. Nita itched. Her skin was flaking from all the dried sweat and blood.

Agent Quispe gestured to the shower. "Here. We can continue to talk afterward."

The door closed, and Nita slumped against the wall. She lay there, finally letting herself relax.

It's okay to cry now, if you want, she told herself. *You're finally safe. You can cry from relief, or grief, or whatever you want.*

But the tears wouldn't come. She just leaned against the wall, breathing hard, willing herself to get her meltdown over with. She always felt better after letting her emotions out.

But nothing happened, so she stripped and had a shower. The water felt good against her skin — warm, almost hot — but she had to scrub to peel the layers of blood and sweat off. Afterward, she slid on the oversized clothing they'd provided, reveling in how clean she felt.

She was led back to the white room — really, to be fair, it was an interrogation room — and Agent Quispe sat down opposite her again. She slid a photo across the table to Nita.

"Have you ever seen this man before?"

Nita expected it to be a picture of Kovit, but it wasn't. It was Zebra-stripes the vampire, wearing a trench coat and hat like a '30s-style gangster.

Nita pushed the picture back. "He was one of the potential customers Reyes brought in."

"Was he?" Agent Quispe's voice went dangerous. "Did he say anything? Do anything out of the ordinary?"

Do anything out of the ordinary? Like start asking Nita questions about finding her mother? That kind of out of the ordinary?

"No," Nita lied. She definitely did not want to go down the line of questioning where her mother got involved. Too dangerous. Nita couldn't let her own involvement in dissecting and dismembering unnaturals be known. She'd never get out of prison, and that was not Nita's intention. "No, he didn't speak. He watched them cut me, watched me heal, and then he left."

Agent Quispe was silent for a long time.

Nita felt uncomfortable. Something was wrong. "Who is that man?"

"Not a man. A vampire." Agent Quispe sighed. "He's a fixer for certain mafia groups."

A fixer? As in someone who fixed problems, usually with death or blackmail?

What the hell was someone like that doing looking into Nita's mom?

Mom, what did you do?

Agent Quispe was still talking. "He was spotted in your hometown recently."

Wait. What?

Nita got a horrible, terrible feeling in her stomach. "Why was he there?"

Agent Quispe was silent for a long time, folding and refolding her hands. "Nita, I'm so sorry to tell you this. Your father was murdered just over a week ago."

Nita sat there, rigid in shock. Then, finally, she broke and began to cry.

FORTY-ONE

S HE SPENT THE next three days curled up in bed sleeping, trying to recover from the crippling migraines that had been plaguing her since she'd abused her powers so thoroughly. When she felt well, she wandered the parts of the facility she was allowed into and sat in the park behind the building, crying into the flower bushes.

She tried mentally going through dissections, but she couldn't focus. Each piece of the image would crack and break, fading into memory, until there was only Nita standing with a scalpel in the dark.

At first, nothing had seemed real, everything just a blur of pain and horror. After the grief calmed down a bit, Nita paused to wonder: How had Zebra-stripes found her father? He was clearly tracking her mother, and knew of both her mother's and her own abilities.

The fact that Nita's kidnapping and her father's murder were so close together was also suspicious. Could Fabricio have heard Nita mention her father? No. And even if he had, there was no way he knew enough details to find him.

So, on a surface level, her father's murder seemed unconnected to Nita's kidnapping. But Nita couldn't shake the feeling something was wrong.

And why was Zebra-stripes hunting her mother in the first place?

Nita shook her head. Too many questions, not enough answers.

Nita sat in a small lounge, staring aimlessly at a large portrait of Nadezhda Novikova, the founder of INHUP. Nita had heard she was still technically its president to this day, though she was more of a figurehead at this point than anything else. The picture had been taken sometime near the founding of INHUP in the 1960s, and Nadezhda looked young in it, Nita's age.

Supposedly, Nadezhda had established her reputation as an unnatural hunter when she was only sixteen, by killing one of the most notorious vampires of the age, Bessanov. Nita had always wondered if INHUP had started out as an organization for hunting unnaturals and then gradually changed into protecting them, or if both ideals had always been there from the start.

"Nita."

She turned to find Agent Quispe on the other side of the room.

"Yes?" Nita's voice was soft.

Agent Quispe stretched out her hand, and there was Reyes' phone. Nita reached out and took it.

"We submerged it in rice for the past three days," Agent Quispe said. "It turns on, but you have a passcode, so I can't check whether it still works."

Nita nodded. "Thanks."

She tucked it in her pocket. Later, when there were no INHUP agents hovering over her shoulders, she'd see if there were messages from her mother. She'd email Kovit and ask him how his wound was.

Now that her father was gone and her mother was in trouble, possibly dead too, she felt frighteningly alone in the world. Kovit's anonymity plan didn't seem so bad at the moment.

She thought of him on the pier, whispering that email address in her ear, and she shivered with something intangible.

"Also," Agent Quispe continued, "we've booked a flight for you to our North American office. Representatives will pick you up in Toronto."

"Okay."

"Oh, and we have another refugee from the black market. There was an issue in the Quito office, so he's come here. You'll be seeing him around. It'll do you both good to talk to someone who's been through the same thing."

Nita stiffened. Quito office. In Ecuador.

Agent Quispe turned around at the sound of footsteps. "Ah, this will be him now."

A young man with dark brown hair and blue-gray eyes walked into the lounge. Nita felt her heart stutter in recognition.

It was the boy whose life Nita had saved. The boy who had sold her. The instigator of this entire, horrid mess.

Her betrayer.

"Nita, meet Fabricio."

ACKNOWLEDGMENTS

This is not the first novel I've ever written, but this is the first one that's made the journey all the way to publication. I could never have gotten here without the help of a lot of amazing people.

Firstly, my wonderful agent, Suzie Townsend, who loved this book and found it the perfect home in record time. My editor, Sarah Landis, who saw the potential of my dark little monster book and helped me take it to the next level. Nicole Sclama, who helped guide me through the entire publication process.

Brenda Drake, for creating the wonderful Pitch Wars contest, which gave me the opportunity of a lifetime. My amazing mentors, Rebecca Sky and Stacey Trombley, who picked me out of a slush pile of talented people, helped me edit, and supported me through this journey. You guys are incredible, and I'm so lucky I met you both.

My early readers, the Dark Forces of Narnia, who looked at a rough first act and helped reorganize it.

The Storybook Dreamers for helping me polish that first act so it gleamed for submission. Thanks to Allison Latzko and Michaël Wertenberg, who read the first, truly appalling draft of this novel.

J. S. Dewes, who read the second, much better draft, and went above and beyond answering questions and loving the story and the characters. Aurora Nibley and Julia Kantic, who read a whole bunch of the book just because they liked it, and gave me wonderful comments to make it even better. Lynn Miller, Rebecca Carter, and any other beta readers whose names I have forgotten from that mad editing summer in my life.

Xiran Jay, who read it twice with a critical eye and is basically the reason the science makes sense in the novel. And who listened to me rant and rave, and helped me cook up vengeance schemes whenever bad things happened and celebrated when good things did.

Special thanks go to my sensitivity readers, especially Yamile Saied Méndez. The book is so much better because of the time you spent. Any errors in the book are entirely my fault. I apologize for any mistakes.

Thanks to Koech, the company I worked for in Peru. Without the opportunity to live and work in Lima, this book would likely be radically different. *Gracias por todo.*

I also have to thank Marie De Zetter and Sam Markham for reading my last God-knows-how-many novels and providing critical, honest, and invaluable feedback, which made me grow and learn and rewrite. I wouldn't be the writer I am without either of them.

Publishing is a crazy wild stressful business, and I definitely need to thank the entire EaF group for being so amazing and supportive, especially Kester Grant, who pulled me into the group and out of a bad time. You guys are the best, and I love all of you.

Thanks also to my publishing house sister Alexa Donne, who helped me with my website; to Jerry Quinn, who let me crash on his couch when I pitched the book at the NYC pitch contest one time; and to all my fabulous friends and fellow writers whom I've met along the journey to publication. I'm constantly blown away by how supportive the writing community is, and I'm so grateful I've been able to be a part of it.

I also want to thank my parents, for supporting me in this journey from a young age. Thanks to my mom, for typing out my handwritten novel back in grade seven, and for letting me crash at her place for several months to write this book. And thanks to my father, who read and edited all that trash I wrote in high school and university even though he didn't like fantasy. I couldn't have asked for a better or more supportive family.

And finally, thanks to all the readers who make this possible. Thanks for loving my little monsters and joining them on their journey. I promise many adventures ahead.

TURN THE PAGE FOR A SNEAK PEEK
OF THE RIVETING SEQUEL!

VENGEANCE IS A VICIOUS VICE

ONLY ASHES
REMAIN

REBECCA SCHAEFFER

ONE

"NITA, MEET FABRICIO."

The fluorescent lights of the INHUP refugee center made the white walls glow like a hospital, and Nita wondered for a brief moment if she was in some sort of hallucination. After all, the set of circumstances that had brought her to the International Non-Human Police had the quality of a nightmare—complete with kidnapping, torture, and Nita burning all her enemies alive at the end.

All but one.

He stood in front of her now. A few inches taller than her, his pale face was framed by slightly mussed dark brown hair, and his huge blue-gray eyes stared at her with shock she knew was mirrored in her own gaze.

Fabricio. The boy she'd saved.

The boy who'd betrayed her. Who'd thanked her for helping him escape, taken the money and bus ticket she'd offered him, then turned around and used the phone she'd given him to sell her to the black market. Who'd left her to be kidnapped, cut up, and sold piece by piece.

Rage boiled in Nita's veins, heating her body from the inside out. Her jaw clenched tighter and tighter, until she forced it to loosen to avoid breaking a tooth.

"Nita?" Agent Quispe, the INHUP agent in charge of Nita's case, stepped forward, the lines of her buzzcut black hair sharp in the bright light. Her Spanish was slow and calm, with a distinct flavor that reminded Nita of her time living in Peru. "Are you all right?"

Nita blinked and forced herself to nod. "Of course. Sorry, I must have spaced out. What were you saying?"

Quispe frowned slightly and squinted, an expression Nita had come to associate with the agent trying to parse Nita's Spanish. Her father was Chilean, but she'd lived in Madrid until she was six, and the blend of accents was often hard for people to understand.

"I was saying that I've noticed you keeping to yourself a lot. And since we just received another refugee your age, I thought you two might want to meet."

Quispe waved Fabricio forward. His eyebrows pulled together before smoothing out. A tentative smile crossed his face.

Nita glared. What the hell was he smiling about?

Then she realized: he didn't know she'd discovered he was the one who sold her to the black market. Fabricio was still playing a part, resuming the role of the scared victim.

Nita stepped forward, fist clenched, wanting nothing more than to smash his skull into the floor and dissect him while he lay dying, the way she should have done when her mother caught him the first time.

She took a deep breath. She was in the middle of the INHUP headquarters in Bogotá. There was an agent standing right beside her. This was not the time to commit murder.

No matter how much she wanted to.

Nita swallowed and forced a grimace onto her face. She needed to play it cool for now, and not give any indication they'd met before. And hope Fabricio didn't give her away.

If INHUP found out how they knew each other, Nita's connection to her murderous mother would be exposed, and Nita's crimes would be laid bare. And she had a lot of crimes under her belt. You didn't grow up with parents in the business of dissecting unnaturals and selling their body parts online without committing a few felonies.

Nita couldn't force herself to extend her hand to him. In a clipped voice, she said, "It's nice to meet you."

He blinked and hesitated, then smiled softly, his voice gentle and whispery. "You too."

Quispe looked between them, as if she could sense the tension. "Fabricio will be staying here for the next little while. I thought you two would have a lot to talk about, since you've both spent time in the black market."

Nita could almost hear her unspoken comparison. Both of them had body parts hacked off. Both of them had those parts sold and eaten.

Nita shifted her foot, trying not to think about the gaping absence where her toe had once been, and she kept her eyes firmly away from Fabricio's missing ear. It wasn't too hard, since the evidence was covered by hair.

Nita turned to Quispe. "Yes. It was a good thought. Thank you. I'd like to get to know my new floormate."

Nita swallowed after the words came out of her mouth. Stilted. Fake. Why couldn't she be better at this kind of thing?

But if Quispe noticed Nita's failing communication skills, she didn't comment. "Of course."

She turned and left them alone. After she was gone, the silence was overpowering. Fabricio opened and closed his mouth like he wanted to say something. Nita pursed her lips and looked around.

She didn't like being inside an INHUP building. INHUP was a means to an end for her, and she didn't trust them. Supposedly they both prosecuted and protected unnaturals—or "non-humans." Honestly, Nita thought calling people like her "non-human" was just as offensive as calling her "unnatural." It probably traced back to INHUP's monster-hunting roots, before they started advocating for unnatural rights as well as policing them.

Nita was using INHUP for their protection, but she knew corruption had burrowed into the soul of the organization. She was concerned about building surveillance, and the conversation she wanted to have was not one that should be overheard. By INHUP or whoever INHUP might be selling the information to.

"There's a garden outside," Nita announced. "Let's talk down there."

Fabricio nodded once, slowly, and followed her.

They made their way through the office. Pristine white walls and white tiled floors caged them in, like a futuristic prison. Other unnatural refugees wandered the halls of the protective housing. Some Nita could've passed on the street and never known they were different.

Others were part octopus. Nita's eyes examined a tired-looking man in a hall, her eyes sliding down to the eight purple tentacles he had instead of legs. *Ningyo.* Japanese mermaid. She would have bet money on it.

People said that if you ate their flesh, you'd gain immortality.

People said the same thing about eating Nita.

She tried to pull her mind away from the thought. The memory of Boulder cutting off her toe, popping it in his mouth, and swallowing it whole. His promise to come back the next day and the next, each day taking a different part of her and consuming it until there was nothing left of Nita but bones and teeth.

It didn't happen. You escaped. He's dead. It's over, a soft voice whispered in her head.

But it didn't feel over. Not when she was hiding in INHUP. Not with Fabricio walking next to her. Not with her face and her ability circling the black market forums. People were willing to pay a lot for a girl who could manipulate her own body —they thought eating her would grant them the same power. Who knew, maybe it would.

Nita didn't intend to find out.

Her hand twitched at her side, reaching for a scalpel that didn't exist. What she wouldn't give to be in her dissection room right now, all her problems vanishing in the simple, clear peace of a dissection. Taking a body apart piece by piece, the world reduced to the organs in her hand and in the jar on her desk.

But the image was spoiled by the memory of Fabricio, trapped and screaming in a cage, disturbing the perfect solitude of the room.

As they turned a corner, Nita tilted her head to get a look at the side of Fabricio's face, but his hair hid the bandages well. She could hardly believe it had been less than two weeks since she'd first seen him in that cage.

He caught her staring and flinched. Then he looked away, his hand hovering protectively over where his ear had been. He swallowed and lowered his hand.

"It's better," he replied, answering her unspoken question as they walked. His accent softened the edges of his words, *y* sounds whispering into *sh* sounds. "I'm getting the stitches out tomorrow."

Nita didn't respond.

She wished her mother had killed him. She wished she'd dissected him. None of this would have happened then. Nita wouldn't be missing a toe — even though she'd used her ability to meld the skin over where it once was, there was an absence, as though her nerves hadn't quite realized they ended in a new place now and still reached out, expecting a toe to be there.

She also wouldn't have spent the past week watching people die in the black market. Wouldn't have had to murder them herself.

She could still remember the moment she read the text exchange on her captor's phone and realized that the person who'd sold her to the black market was Fabricio all along. The moment of sheer disbelief, followed by the sudden rush of rage, hot and vicious.

Now her anger simmered, a steady glow in the pit of her stomach. If she let it loose, she'd only end up with more problems. She wasn't sure she cared. She wanted to let it all out, no matter what the repercussions.

Be rational, Nita. You can't murder him with all these surveillance cameras around.

Nita hated when her brain made sense.

On the first floor, near the back of the building, thick metal double doors opened into a small garden. A high brick wall surrounded it, covered in vines and ivy, and several people sat on benches and under trees. The sun was steady and hot, and sweat quickly dripped down Nita's back.

Nita led Fabricio to a secluded part of the garden, near a floripondio tree. The bell-shaped flowers hung from the branches like unlit pink lanterns, beautiful and gentle. Also, one of the most poisonous plants in the world. Nita plucked one of the flowers and twirled it in her hand. So deadly. Hidden in such a pretty shell that no one ever guessed until it was too late.

Finally, Nita turned to face Fabricio. He shifted awkwardly under her gaze. He wore blue jeans and a plain gray T-shirt, a twin to Nita's own INHUP-issued clothes.

"I'm glad you decided to run away," he finally said.

Nita opened her mouth to tell him he very well knew that she didn't run away. But she stopped. She could accuse him all she wanted, but he'd just deny it. Even if he admitted it, what point was there in tipping him off that she knew what he'd done? She couldn't kill him in front of all these people, and if he knew she knew, he'd be on his guard.

And he should be. Because there was no way Nita was going to let him get away with what he'd done to her.

So instead, she said quietly, pretending she believed his ignorance, "I didn't run away. I was sold on the market."

He winced, and his face twisted in sympathy. "I'm so sorry. I know how awful that can be."

He ran a hand through his hair, exposing the hint of stitches creeping down one side of his head. Nita turned away and tried not to remember his screams as her mother tortured him while Nita stood by and watched. And did nothing.

Maybe that was why he sold her. Because she did nothing until the last possible moment.

"Was it your mother?" he asked, voice soft. "Was it punishment for helping me?"

He seemed so genuine in his concern, and Nita felt a sliver of doubt creep in. Could those messages have been sent by someone else? But then she remembered how easily he'd played her before, stared at her with huge eyes, manipulated her into thinking he was completely innocent so she'd free him. Her eyes narrowed. She wasn't going to be played again.

"No."

His hands hovered, then lowered. "I'm sorry. I didn't mean to pry. If it's all too fresh."

He gave her a gentle smile, and Nita wanted to punch it off his face. Manipulative little sneak.

He hesitated, then asked, "Your captor . . . she didn't hurt you, did she?"

"Well, she was working with a zannie, so why don't you take a guess?"

His face went gray. "A zannie?"

Zannies ate people's pain, which made them expert torturers. Nita could see Fabricio's imagination filling in all the blanks of her time in the market with all the horrific things zannies did.

"Yes." Nita's voice was cold. "Sometimes, when I close my eyes, I can still hear the screaming."

Fabricio flinched as though she'd hit him. His eyes widened, and something passed across his face, something that looked like it might be guilt or regret. But it was gone in a blink.

Nita carefully didn't mention she'd ended up making an ally of the zannie in her escape. She wanted Fabricio to feel as shitty about what he'd done as possible.

Also, she wasn't sure what the fact that she'd befriended a monster like Kovit said about her. Nothing good, likely.

"God, I'm so, so sorry," Fabricio whispered, and the horror on his face seemed so genuine, if Nita didn't have evidence against him she'd really think he meant it. "I can't believe she hired a zannie."

Nita opened her mouth to make another caustic remark, but stopped. Fabricio had specifically said "she" when referring to Nita's captor. Multiple times.

Nita hadn't mentioned her captor was female.

Nita played back the conversation, checking to see if she'd

used any feminine descriptors, pronouns, any cue in her Spanish that could have indicated gender. Nothing.

More proof. As if she needed it. She already had the messages between him and her captor, Reyes, hammering out the details of the deal.

But perhaps some small part of her had wondered if someone had stolen the phone from him, or if maybe a corrupt INHUP agent had confiscated it or . . . something.

Nita crushed the flower in her hand. All doubts were extinguished.

"We'll have to be cautious where we talk," he said, eyeing a passing agent. His eyes roved around at the walled-off garden, lingering on all the security cameras and INHUP agents. "You might get in trouble if they knew who your mother was."

Ah. There it was. The veiled threat. The reminder that he knew exactly who she was, and if he wanted to, he could destroy her chances of getting a plane ticket home from INHUP.

Well, two could play at that game.

"Yes." Nita loosened her grip and twirled the crushed flower. "And we'll have to be careful about mentioning your father too."

He stiffened, whole body going rigid, eyes widening. Like a poorly oiled puppet, his head jerked to face her, and he whispered, "Pardon?"

"Your father." Nita tilted her head to one side as her fingers played along the petals. "Quite the bigwig, I hear. Knows all the monsters."

Fabricio swallowed and replied carefully, "Where did you hear about my father?"

"The market I was sold in, of course." Nita spoke in the mild tone of someone innocently commenting on the weather. "I hear he runs one of the biggest law firms in the world. They specialize in shell corporations, tax evasion, and all sorts of other things for rich people. Especially rich black market people."

His hands clenched. "And? You of all people should know better than to judge someone based on their parents."

Nita flinched as if he'd slapped her. She looked away.

"Tell me, Nita, if we're judging people by the sins of their parents, who is in more trouble?" Fabricio's voice was tight. "Me? My father helps monsters save their money. Or you? Your mother kidnaps, murders, dissects, and sells innocent people."

"I'm not my mother." But after the events in the market, she wasn't quite sure anymore. She'd killed a lot of people to escape, guilty and innocent alike. "I helped you."

"You did." His shoulders slumped. "And I'm not my father."

No, you're much worse.

Nita didn't reply, just looked at the flower. Fabricio was the same. Beautiful and gentle on the outside, hiding a toxic inside.

Fabricio's jaw was tight and his gaze angry. "Is this why you've been so cold to me? You think I'm just another money-grubbing asshole like my father?"

She shrugged, playing it nonchalant. "I don't know. I don't know you."

"I'm not. I'm nothing like him." His voice was bitter. "And I never want to be. I don't want anything to do with him or his business. All it's ever brought me is pain."

"And money. I hear someone of your standing lives quite well."

"I'd rather have my ear back."

Nita raised an eyebrow. "What does your ear have to do with your father?"

"You didn't really think your mother kidnapped the child of one of the most notorious men on the black market to sell his body on the internet, did you?"

Nita's stomach dropped. "What?"

His lips pressed together into a thin line. "Your mother was sending me back to my father, piece by piece, every time he refused a demand."

Nita swallowed. Fabricio could be lying, but it made sense in a way. Why would her mother kidnap the child of someone so important just to make a few bucks online? No, blackmail was far more her mother's style.

"Are you even an unnatural?"

He sighed. "I'm exactly what she said I was. Pieces of me would make money."

Nita nodded slowly. "But?"

"But . . ." He looked away. "I'm more afraid of *who* I am than *what* I am. No one would go to all the trouble she did to kidnap me just to sell me. But to blackmail my father? The sky is the limit."

Uneasiness coiled in Nita's stomach. She'd wanted power

to protect herself—to make Fabricio's reality hers. Everyone wanted her for *what* she was, and in order to avoid looking over her shoulder her whole life, she wanted to make them afraid of *who* she was.

Now she wondered if that was such a great idea.

"Why?"

He blinked. "Why what?"

"Why was my mother blackmailing your father in the first place? I mean, there are far easier targets if it was simply about money."

He shook his head. "I don't know."

No, this didn't make sense anymore. Something in this picture wasn't right.

"One good thing that's come out of all this." A half smile flitted across his face. "Now I can be a nameless refugee that INHUP will protect. I gave them a fake last name. No one needs to know who I am. I can start over." He looked at her. "I suppose I should thank you and your mother for that. If no one here knows who I am, no one can leak that information or try and use me for my father's connections."

Nita gave him an incredulous look. He was one of those every-cloud-has-a-silver-lining people. She supposed if he were in her shoes, he'd say that her experience in Mercado de la Muerte—"Death Market"—had given her much-needed industry perspective.

Ugh. She hated people like that.

A warm wind slunk through the garden, and Nita realized her nose had started to burn under the hot noon sun, and she healed it before it could progress. She'd been so distracted she hadn't noticed. She wiped her forehead and jerked her head to Fabricio.

"Let's go back inside."

He smiled tentatively. "It's hot out here. They need air-conditioning for outside."

Nita didn't smile back.

As they approached the building, Nita stopped and turned to Fabricio. "Let me make one thing clear."

He paused, smile falling. "Yes?"

"If you in any way reveal who my mother is, or our connection, I will tell INHUP about your father. You'll be sent home, and your little escape plan will be ruined."

His eyes narrowed, flint and steel, and Nita finally caught her first glimpse of the real person beneath the friendly facade. "If you say anything to compromise my protection and put me in danger, I'll tell them about your mother. And your complicity."

Nita pursed her lips. "Then we'll both have to stay quiet, won't we?"

They held each other's gaze for a long moment and then, as one, turned and reentered the building in silence.

Nita shoved the floripondio flower in her pocket as she went, a poisonous promise to herself.